"Ms. Miesel has taken a theme well-known to s-f writers and readers but she has had the skill to give it a fresh twist for a very entertaining story. One enjoys along with the heroine the visits to the charming otter people. I appreciate the chance to read this and hope that many other readers in the future will have the same experience."

—Andre Norton

". . . Sandra Miesel is working with powerful images and responses out of both our waking and our dreaming states; and those images and responses ring true to us, authenticated by the actions and responses we know from our own living to be actual and true."

—Gordon R. Dickson
*from the Introduction*

# DREAMRIDER

Other fantasy titles available from *Ace Science Fiction and Fantasy*:

- Daughter of the Bright Moon, *Lynn Abbey*
- The Face in the Frost, *John Bellairs*
- Peregrine: Primus, *Avram Davidson*
- The Borribles, *Michael de Larrabeiti*
- Idylls of the Queen, *Phyllis Ann Karr*
- Journey to Aprilioth, *Eileen Kernaghan*
- 900 Grandmothers, *R. A. Lafferty*
- Swords and Deviltry, *Fritz Leiber*
- The Seekers of Shar-Nuhn, *Ardath Mayhar*
- The Door in the Hedge, *Robin McKinley*
- Silverlock, *John Myers Myers*
- Witchworld, *Andre Norton*
- Tomoe Gozen, *Jessica Amanda Salmonson*
- The Warlock Unlocked, *Christopher Stasheff*
- Bard, *Keith Taylor*
- The Devil in a Forest, *Gene Wolfe*
- Shadow Magic, *Patricia C. Wrede*
- Changeling, *Roger Zelazny*

and much more!

# DREAMRIDER

## SANDRA MIESEL

Fantasy

## ace books
**A Division of Charter Communications Inc.**
**A GROSSET & DUNLAP COMPANY**
51 Madison Avenue
New York, New York 10010

**DREAMRIDER**

copyright © 1982 by Sandra Miesel

Introduction by Gordon R. Dickson
© 1982 by Gordon R. Dickson

All characters in this book are fictitious. Any resemblance to actual persons, living or dead, is purely coincidental.
An ACE Book

First Ace printing: July 1982
Published Simultaneously in Canada

2 4 6 8 0 9 7 5 3 1
Manufactured in the United States of America

# INTRODUCTION:

## Concerning Sandra Miesel

### by Gordon R. Dickson

If you are like many experienced readers, particularly those who read a great many books, the chances are you have turned to this Introduction not before, but after, you have read the book—DREAMRIDER, by Sandra Miesel; and the reason you will have turned to it will be because the book itself has whetted your interest in its author. That interest is not misplaced.

When I, myself, was a young writer visiting New York in the 1950's, I was taken along to an early evening cocktail and canapes sort of gathering at which the two guests of special note were writers whom I'd certainly never met or expected to meet, but whose names I recognized at once; though I'm ashamed to say I've since forgotten them.

But at that time, I remember, they were important names,

and important people on the literary horizon. Moreover, they were reputedly well paid, something that interested me in them, at my then rate of literary income, almost as much as their work itself. I had hoped for a chance to speak to one or even both of them; but I faced the fact in my own mind that they, as a couple of old and successful professional, would probably want to spend most of their time talking to each other, someone like myself would not be very likely to be included in that conversation.

As it turned out, I did not, indeed, manage to talk to them. This was not because they were fraternizing, however; but because I discovered when I got there that each of them was surrounded by an insulating layer of people who appeared to have known them most of their respective lifetimes (though, this, as I found later, was another misconception born of innocence on my part); and penetration through the massed ranks appeared impossible.

But I was surprised to discover that, far from talking to each other, they took up stations at opposite ends of the room and seemed determined to ignore each other completely. In fact, this attitude was such a positive one on the part of both of them that it effectively polarized the rest of the people present. Puzzled by this, on the way back from the party, I asked the person who had brought me if there had been some important falling-out between them to make them appear to be the equivalent of blood enemies.

No, I was told, they hardly knew each other.

Then why . . . ??? I wanted to know, with at least three question marks.

"But they have the same publisher," my guide said. "After all, they're in competition."

It was my introduction to the idea that published writers, instead of considering themselves brothers and sisters in an elite guild by virtue of the blood, sweat and tears that all had experienced in the making of manuscripts, should consider themselves in competition.

I later discovered that among many in publishing at that time, this was not only an accepted, but a tightly-held theory; which—it was said in some of the publishers' back rooms—not only spurred authors on to do their best at all times, but also kept them from the pernicious occupation of comparing notes on how their publisher was severally treating them; a practice which, in the cases of such high-strung and unstable characters as writers were known to be, could tempt them into delusions that they were being unequally or unfairly treated.

But of course, the notion was nonsense.

It was nonsense because artists in general and writers in particular are of value to the world in general, and to publishers in particular, in direct ratio to the proportion in which they do not compete with each other. In short, their value lies in their individual uniqueness as artists.

The reader knows this without being told. This is why the reader will search a rack in a bookstore holding fifty books of the same general type that reader is momentarily hungry to read, and walk out empty-handed because there is nothing there by any of the authors for whom the reader was in search.

It is also why a reader, having found a writer whose books please, will eagerly devour anything to be found by that author; and feel personally deprived when the realization comes that for reasons of death, retirement or the fact that it can take a year or more to write a book the reader can read in a matter of hours or less, there is no more to be found written by that individual.

The works of Shakespeare and the works of Edgar Rice Burroughs, to pick two writers well spread apart in time and literary attitude, have been derived from the only two possible sources; to wit—one William Shakespeare and one Edgar Rice Burroughs, neither of whom can be looked for as a source of more of the same in the future. Depending upon your taste, a ton of the words of one can fail to satisfy like an ounce of the words of the other. Edgar Rice Burroughs would not have been able to write additional Shakespearian plays or sonnets which would have fully satisfied the hunger of those addicted to Shakespeare's original works. Nor, had Shakespeare been alive to do so and so inclined, could Shakespeare have written in the manner of Burroughs and pleased his readers as Burroughs had.

It is one of the laws of the literature that pastiches, however excellent, can never rise above the quality of being spurious coin; and as a result they do not spend like the real coinage in those special pleasure centers of our mind that we have dedicated to the authors who have won our affections.

Writers are valuable, therefore, not only because they do not and cannot compete—for Shakespeare did things Burroughs could not; and equally, Burroughs did things Shakespeare, for all his talent and skill, could not—but in direct relationship to the proportion in which competition with each of them is impossible.

It is the unique strengths of the individual writer that makes him or her irreplaceably valuable; and it is one of the interesting facts about writers, that those of the greatest promise almost invariably reveal a good share of such strengths early in their published work.

Sandra Miesel is one of those who has shown her uniqueness early. DREAMRIDER is a first novel, but it does not read like one; and there are reasons for this. At root is the fact that she has been a published essayist and writer of non-fiction for ten years; and the discipline required for that work has bred a comparable control that unifies and orders this novel in a way that few first novels are held. Her Bachelor of Science degree is in chemistry and her two Master's degrees are in chemistry and history. If you look closely at all her work, fiction and non-fiction alike, you see the scientific attitude and the historic eye working hand in hand. But even this only begins to explain the unusual qualities of this first novel of hers.

The fact is, that to control a piece of fiction in this manner, aside from the labor of making sure every word is the right word and in the right place to interact with its neighbors to the desired end, is a discipline attractive only to an unusual creative temperament; and it is out of such a temperament, unique in itself, that there grow the type of literary strengths to be seen in DREAMRIDER.

The foremost of these is the fact that Sandra Miesel is—and I use the word in its sense that describes one who is in love with knowledge—a scholar.

True scholars are rare among us. A true scholar does not care how deeply the truth of a matter may be buried. All that matters is that it be found, and put to use in its proper place, whatever the labor of doing so. Guessing, or detouring around the work required to make sure of any fact, is anathema to a scholar; and Sandra Miesel is a scholar.

What this means to her work is important. It is not merely to hear themselves talk that experienced writers, editors, teachers, and everyone else at all informed about writing join in urging the beginning writer to write from his or her own experience. The reason is that when a writer uses settings and human reactions she or he knows from personal experience, use is made of elements the reader also knows and recognizes as real; and because of that recognition, the characters and incidents in the story acquire a reality that is unobtainable in fiction otherwise.

In short, the writer who has been there—wherever *there* is—can take us there also.

But there is a level of art in fiction even beyond this. Given, as in DREAMRIDER, the realities of place and event, drawn from personal experience, the scholarly writer from her warehouse of excavated knowledge can add, even to these, echoes of meaning, so that the scenes, the actions, and the characters concerned are made three dimensional and memorable. The dream interludes in DREAMRIDER, for those readers who already have the special knowledges needed to identify the facts used, are put together with a scrupulous regard for what is known to be true in areas ranging from history to psychology and beyond.

There is, of course, a danger in the writer falling too deeply in love with the facts behind the fiction he or she is writing. Sandra Miesel avoids this trap because she is able to bring into the story balancing elements of action and character illuminated by the same special temperament that brought the eye and the hand of a scholar to the work.

Such elements grow from the purely artistic side of her creative character as a writer. She has an instinct for artistic forms and the story shows it. There is an instinct for form here that matches the shapes of imprisonment with the shapes of freedom—the grim political oppression of Ria's time with the galloping freedom of her studies in shamanism, across time and all the barriers between the alternate worlds; the tragic deaths of the macotters at the teeth of the macrats, with the bubbling joy and aliveness of the macotter community at the festival.

But even this instinct for artistic form requires something more; and happily Sandra Miesel's unique strengths carry her into these areas as well.

To make a story strongly and memorably alive for the reader, in the final essential it must be rendered, not told. The reader must be given the materials to see scene in shapes and hues that will not be forgotten; and for this it is necessary to go beyond craft and training and once more back into an innate area of the writer herself.

One of the oldest of artistic laws is that the reader, the viewer, or listener to a story, a painting, or a musical composition, can get from it only what its maker has put into it. In story-telling terms this becomes a requirement that the writer have a palette of emotional experience containing a sufficient number and variety of colors to evoke the full spectrum which life itself eventually shows to all mature and perceptive human beings.

Dark and light, sorrow and joy, coarse and delicate, sweet

and bitter—all these and as many more qualities as can be imagined—must be evoked for the readers to make an effective, fully realized work of fiction.

The writer has no way to make these shades and hues available unless she has them within her to start with. No good work of fiction is put together without a strong capability in this area. At the same time, there is a vast difference between the unconscious use of such a personal warehouse and a conscious use—which usually only comes with a great deal of experience.

Conscious use of an emotional palette like Sandra Miesel brings to her story in this book, is usually developed by the writer over time in the attempt to duplicate something that is very difficult to do, the experience we have all had, in actual living, of life as a multi-layered reality; a reality in which different and even conflicting things can be happening to an individual at the same time but on different levels of awareness. The contrasting hues of the palette are used to distinguish and identify the different levels on which the story is in process.

Everyone is familiar with the fact that it is possible to be exhausted, hungry, in love, and fearful of the future—all these and more—in the same instant. Only one of these can properly occupy our conscious mind at any moment, just as only one can be effectively conveyed to the reader in bald words at any one moment. But the others can be present in our awareness, and we can be made conscious of their presence in the story, hiding behind the expressed thought and the enunciated word.

The problem for the writer has always been to convey such levels of awareness effectively but unobtrusively; and a means has been found in a controlling of the quality of the literary character's experience—that which the character sees and physically feels at any given instant—so that the reader is led to infer the emotions that would cause the character to notice and respond to those particular things.

For example, a character busy doing his income tax return, while trying to ignore a deep inner feeling of loneliness because an emotional partner is absent, might have a conscious mind full of figures; but at the same time he might equally be unusually aware of the silence of the house around him, the darkness of the night outside his window, and the emptiness of a stomach which had missed the pattern of an accustomed dinner hour shared with a welcome other.

All these physical sensations, properly presented, can evoke the emotion of loneliness for the reader without the author having to spell it out in words. This is a much more powerful way of presenting emotion—and a much more effective way of letting the reader feel the full experience of the story.

It is this many-layered effort that makes DREAMRIDER so quietly effective on the level of action; and developments of similar controls make it effective also on the much deeper levels of belief and instinct. Down deep in these latter levels, the tools are myth and legend; not the specific myths and legends we are familiar with, but the raw material out of which they were originally made—the human dreams and fears that caused the familiar stories to be created in the first place.

All through DREAMRIDER, in fact, Sandra Miesel is working with powerful images and responses out of both our waking and our dreaming states; and those images and responses ring true to us, authenticated by the actions and responses we know from our own living to be true and actual.

This is the strength of consciously symbolic writing. Symbolism in fiction has been in many cases sadly misunderstood. I remember a discussion at a professional writers conference more than twenty years ago in which I happened to refer to symbolism in writing; and was gratified at the response of the rest of those there to the mere mention of it.

That gratification, however, turned to dismay as the conversation went happily on and it developed that those there, children of the Age of Psychology in spite of the fact they were all also experienced writers, had taken the word "symbolism" to have only one use and meaning—and that was in reference to the use of Freudian symbols in writing. I made an attempt to open up the discussion with possibilities beyond this, pointing out that a character's being brought to noticing a sharp knife and having a strong emotional response to it, could be used equally to infer a fear of death (knife in the hand of a possible attacker) and a hope of life (knife in the hand of an emergency operating room surgeon); but I found myself talking to deaf ears. Any object, in the opinion of those around me, had and could have, according to the scriptures of psychology, only one possible symbolic meaning; and only that meaning could be evoked in the reader by it's appearance in the narrative. A knife could equate only with the male sex organ; gently rounded hills could only give rise to the image of women's breasts . . . and so forth.

Of course this, like the notion that authors could be in competition, was nonsense.

The image of anything called up by the author in the course of the story always had been able to be used, like the real object itself in ordinary life, to evoke any one of countless emotional reactions in the reader—depending upon the circumstances under which it appeared, or under which the character's eye was directed to it.

In short, the word used symbolically has always been simply a literary tool. Like any tool in real life its choice needs to be determined by the use to which it is to be put; but the effect of its actual use finally depends upon the purpose and the skill of the one who is using it.

It is the skill of Sandra Miesel in using this and other literary tools in a first novel like DREAMRIDER, that particularly needs to be commented upon. The central image with which she works is the World Ash—the Yggdrasill of Norse mythology which is the axis of the cosmos. She uses the symbol here in the form of an actual botanical tree in which the variant time lines that create alternate universes are as twigs on the tree. The horse, a general symbol of freedom and power with xenosexual overtones for young women in particular, has a symbolic meaning in shamanism. It is the vehicle for the human soul—in this case, of course, Ria's soul. Beyond these meanings, however, Sandra Miesel has put it to specific symbolic use throughout the book in a variety of forms, such as a real horse, as a toy rocking horse, an image on a Tibetan prayer flag . . . and so forth, as the means by which Ria moves between the time lines in her shamanic studies.

Flight as another general symbol associated with the horse and by itself, functions in a number of ways to put psychic distance between Ria and her original world, and bridge the gap to the larger cosmos of the World Ash. This symbol put to use again and again to the momentary purposes of the story, as when the sister of the macotter, Lute (who is Ria's guide in her shamanic studies, and almost literally her good angel), on meeting Ria gives Ria the acronymic, macotter name of Rides-In-Air, or when the flight across the mountains of Ria's first shamanic dream becomes, at the end of the book, another dream of flight that develops out of a real flight, by plane, across mountains.

Beyond these are the understood symbols of fire and water, developed in their shamanic meanings and running through the story in diverse and purposeful forms. Fire, over which Ria's grandmother had shamanic control, and which she will come to control herself in the course of the story, develops in forms reaching from her near-electrocution in the beginning of the story, to her use of her power over it near the end to destroy the macrat that otherwise would kill her macotter friend Lute.

Water, literally and symbolically, is in constant attendance upon the story line, for purposeful reasons. Importantly so. It is the general symbol of mutability; and as such, it is through imagined or real water that Ria always passes into the world of her shamanic trances. The quote at the front of the book of the passage from the Bible dealing with the Pool of Bethesda directs us to the many symbolic uses of water within the story, in its position at the center of things, from the inner pool of the house of Kara, Ria's shamanic teacher on another time line, to the lake about which has grown the macotter village Ria visits at the time of festival.

It is noteworthy that the lakes mentioned are real lakes; the statues, statues that the reader may go and see in the place described in the book; and it is by the way in which she links these realities though the levers of mythic symbology to the imaginative story line of the book, making all these parts work effectively together, that Sandra Miesel achieves the unique and effective literary product that is hers, alone.

In the final essential, by this means, she creates a number of personal, artistic tools that will not be used by anyone else; and by using them here, consciously, artistically and to great effect, she creates a social background with the technological bleakness of a novel like *1984;* and peoples it successfully with, among many other things, moments of human and macotter warmth, humor and sensitivity, that in another's hands would run a heavy danger of appearing to be jarringly at odds with the world in which she causes them to occur.

But, because of her strengths as a writer, instead of these dissimilarities pulling apart the credibility of her story, they work together to reinforce each other; and to give her novel the feeling of those layers of concurrent experience which we all know from our own lives, and which we respond to so strongly when we find them faithfully echoed in fiction.

And, luckily for us all, this is not to be our only experience with Sandra Miesel's unusual and sculptured vision. As far as her fiction is concerned, she has just come on stage. We can look forward to what only she can give us for some years to come.

to
Gordy who inspired
and
John who endured
the writing of this book

# Dreamrider

*"For an angel went down at a certain season into the pool and troubled the water: whosoever then first after the troubling of the water stepped in was made whole of whatever disease he had."*

—John 5:4

# I

The child stepped up to the rocking horse. She threw her right leg over its sleek maple body and pulled herself up on the contoured seat. She bent down to whisper in her mount's ear. Her long black hair hung down along its neck like a mane. She gripped its sides more tightly with her chubby calves and set it rocking. The rhythmic motion soothed her. She closed her eyes and pressed her fingers against the lids to make the spots of brightness flash.

The rocking horse neighed. Living eyes appeared in its blank wooden head. It sprang from the rockers and clattered across the playroom on stiff legs that now numbered eight. The walls dissolved and the horse bore its rider over a prairie of clouds.

Suddenly, a chain of mountains pierced the quiltlike plain. The girl urged the horse forward but the higher they climbed, the higher the mountain barrier grew. They rose until the air grew too thin for her to breathe. The girl shivered in the searing cold. Tears of rage froze on her cheeks. . . .

Ria Legarde awoke chilled and frustrated. The Dream—she invariably thought of it in capital letters—always affected her that way. There was no more reason to feel cold beneath layers of undisturbed blankets than there was to keep dreaming the same childhood fantasy. She couldn't remember a time when she didn't have The Dream. She used to make it come by dozing astride her daycare center's rocking horse. But the teachers disapproved of her attachment to the toy. One day it was removed for repairs and never returned. The Dream, however, had returned at regular intervals for the next sixteen years.

Ria lurched towards the bathroom, picking her way between stacks of papers and soiled laundry. Once there, she automatically snapped the lock to the adjoining apartment. Since her bathmate worked different hours, she had successfully avoided all contact with him in her three months of residence. Unless he complained about her aloofness to the House Committee, her privacy was secure.

The shower failed to clear her head. She had one of those headaches again. It would probably last for hours. A weather front must be coming through. Ria flicked on her display to check the forecast.

"RAIN ENDING TONIGHT. PROJECTED TOTAL PRECIPITATION, .5 CM. HIGH TODAY WILL BE 7°, OVERNIGHT LOW −5° UNDER CLEARING SKIES. KILLING FROST TONIGHT WILL END THE GROWING SEASON IN EASTERN PRAIRIE."

By punching codes for private and University announcements she discovered that a mid-morning staff meeting—"sharing session" as the Director preferred to call them—was scheduled for her section of Information Services. Her headache ought to make that even more of an ordeal than usual.

Ria turned the news updates on audio while she dressed. Her interest in world affairs was minimal—had anything happened since 1600?—but this was a voice of sorts to keep her company. Her own topic search program would be storing anything of personal importance for later examination. The latest disaster unrolled while she was putting on her underwear.

"Yesterday's devastating tidal wave in Sumatra is believed to have claimed. . . ."

She was thankful to live far inland, away from mountainous shores. Nothing like that to worry about here, nothing except the New Madrid fault. Wasn't any place on earth safe?

"At a Sydney news conference following the tragedy, North American Science Minister Jon Detmold again urged increased funding for seismic research. Detmold called for. . . ."

But Ria was far more interested in getting into her uniform than in heeding a bureaucrat's call. She noticed a small rip in the jacket's left seam. She'd better remember to mend it tonight before the whole side gave way. She counted herself lucky to wear the University's blue-and-orange livery although its colors dulled her olive skin and pale gray eyes. The pantsuit thickened her figure, too. She must have chosen the least flattering style among the options available. Back in the bathroom, she pinned up her hair, creamed her hands, and dabbed the excess lotion on her cheeks. She grimaced at the straight-nosed, heavy-boned reflection in the mirror before her.

There was no time for a proper breakfast in the cafeteria downstairs. She'd have to settle for a square of concentrate. But where was the canister? She found it hidden behind a file of microfilm cartridges containing the collected works of twentieth century mythologist Mircea Eliade. She stuffed the printout of his *Rites and Symbols of Initiation* into her briefcase to read on lunch hour. She held a food cake in her teeth while she slipped on her coat and boots.

The commuter bus disgorged its load of University workers at the corner of Wright and Green where they mingled with streams of students. The wet, clean-scented wind struck

Ria's face. She squinted through raindrops at Laredo Taft's heroic bronze *Alma Mater*. There stood Mama Psi as she had for nearly a century, growing ever greener with the years. She stretched out brawny arms towards her children, eager to crush them against the UI monogram blazoned on her bodice. Behind the Mater and oblivious to her hungers, proletarian Labor gripped the hand of olympian Learning.

Little meaningful learning or labor on campus these days, yet the University endured. It had outlived the old State of Illinois by one generation and its namesake Illini Indians by how many? Ten? She ought to look that up when she got to work. The data might prove useful in case of imminent extermination.

Stolidly ignoring other pedestrians, Ria veered right to avoid construction barriers around the new student union. It had to be an improvement over the former building, burnt down last March by a noncomp celebrating Federation Day. Passing the Romanesque bulk of Altgeld Hall, she strode down the quadrangle, irrationally glad the western sidewalk was the quicker path to work. She did not have to pass close by the gaping archway marking the entrance of Noyes or the toothy grillwork covering Foley Center. Someone, anyone might be lurking there on a gloomy morning like this. The crowd with its tramping, purposeful feet ought to be protective insulation. She shortened her strides to match the others'.

She turned her thoughts to the huge locust trees lining the quad. They had grown noticably even in the few years since her parents started taking her to summer band concerts here on the lawn. Now the wet grass was littered with yellowed leaves and long brown seed pods. Tomorrow the grounds keepers would be out to sweep the area bare.

Ria hunched her shoulders against a sharp gust of wind and nearly tripped the woman behind her. Mumbling apologies, she turned left at the end of the quad toward the main door of

Information Services. She went down the steps to the familiar round portal rather too fast and almost slipped on the rain-slicked marble. Mother liked to say she could trip on a mote of dust. But she wouldn't be saying it anymore. The fresh scar reopened. Why had she made such a public mess of it? If Ria had reported her to PSI when the depression set in, she might still be alive. Only there were some things worse than dying.

After a quick detour to the locker room, Ria reached her office just before nine o'clock. As usual, Carey Efroymson and Ali Newton were already there conferring on the day's assignments. Carey, a wiry young man only a few years her senior, always gave the impression of straining at an invisible leash. He tugged at his shaggy mustache and shifted weight from foot to foot while Ali briefed him. Although Ria never saw him after working hours, she assumed he twitched more away from the older woman's calming influence. Ali's looks were as mild as her temperament. Her skin and hair were a uniform tan, the color of weak tea with cream. Few signs of middle age had yet marked her broad face or short, plump body.

Ria took indecent pleasure in the absence of Hannah Wix, the fourth member of the history research unit. Perhaps she would be late again and finally earn a reprimand from Ali. Small chance of that. Ali could no more judge another harshly than Ria could judge another generously.

"Morning, Ria," greeted Ali while Carey made a quick nod in her direction. "Nasty weather, isn't it?"

"I think ice skates may be the footgear of choice by tonight."

"Repair promised to send someone over to look at your terminal today. Maybe it'll oblige us by malfunctioning while they're here. Meanwhile, could you transmit this Lisbon Earthquake bibliography to Professor Clyde for me? He had me work over the weekend to finish it and expects to have the printout in his hand first thing this morning."

Ria's face clouded at the mention of Professor Gunnar Clyde.

"I know he's difficult," Ali remarked, "but we are still responsible for serving him regardless."

"Well, I've never found him the least bit difficult." It was Hannah Wix. She had slipped into the room unnoticed by the others. "He's such a . . . distinguished scholar," she continued with a slight reverential catch in her throaty voice.

"That's easy enough for you to say, Hannah. You've cleverly avoided working for him." But before Carey could relate any pertinent anecdotes, Hannah had glided away to her own console and was examining papers with admirable zeal.

Ria mentally awarded the point to the petite blonde. Her headache was getting worse. She forced herself to pay attention to what Ali was saying.

"I do wish you'd mentioned the problem with your console as soon as you noticed it. Every bit of downtime hurts our productivity."

"I didn't think it was important at first."

"Let me be the judge of that in the future, Ria. I've had many more years to learn the quirks and crotchets of our system."

A gentle reproof was still a reproof. Ria felt like a child who'd been careless with an expensive plaything. She walked over to her terminal and switched on the display. It failed to light up. Was the device plugged in firmly? Ria got down on her hands and knees to check, an operation made awkward by her height. She fumbled for the plug. It seemed in order. As she put her hand on the chassis to lever herself up, numbing current surged through her body before she had time to scream.

# II

Ria awoke on a hard mattress under a blue and white coverlet. An otter was leaning over the bed. She closed her eyes and held her breath for a count of three. But when she opened them, the otter was still there, a sleek russet-furred presence. Its huge brown eyes were level with her own and she could smell its warm, fishy breath. The otter patted her hand. Hand and paw were the same size. It was not her hand.

The nails were flat and broken, the palm calloused. It was a young man's hand. Ria pulled it under the covers, frantically searching for breasts that were no longer there. She was too horrified to utter a sound. The otter apparently suffered no such impediment for it began to speak in a shrill but understandable voice.

"She's here! Kara, she's here! Told you she'd come. Said it was certain this time." Its speech disintegrated into trilling chirrups. It bobbed up and down, jingling the silver bells on the leather harness it wore.

"Calm yourself, Lute. If you frighten her away, she may never return to us."

As the second speaker approached Ria, the otter retreated, still murmurring cheerily. The person it had addressed as "Kara" was a short, stocky woman of great age and even greater dignity. She had moved out of the shadows and into a patch of sunlight at the foot of the bed so Ria could see her clearly at last.

Her costume was remarkable in itself. She wore a kind of white woolen poncho adorned with silver ornaments, some shaped like stars, others like bones. This garment was fringed with strips of snakeskin and fur. A filigreed metal cap rested on thick white braids coiled around her head. In her right hand she held a wooden wand and in her left, a disk-like object which Ria somehow recognized as a drum. A long skirt and soft, high boots—both white—completed the outfit.

These details punched themselves into Ria's memory but it was the woman herself, not the exotic garb, that held her attention. Kara's dominant impression was squareness—in the shape of her face, the set of her jaw, the breadth of her unbowed shoulders. Although her skin was weathered and spotted with age, every feature was still crisply defined. Fearless competence shone in her dark blue eyes.

"By sunlight, starlight, firelight, be welcome here forever, Victoria Legarde." Kara raised her staff like a septre in ritual greeting. "I am Kara ni Prizing, once Wise Woman of the Chamba. This is my companion, Lute Twin Stars of the Rolling Shores."

The otter sprang forward and bowed with such exaggerated courtliness, Ria could not help but smile at it—no, at *him,* she corrected herself. She struggled to sit up in bed but Lute hastily motioned her back down.

"Lie still, dear lady. You aren't used to Julo's body. Best to stay as you are for now and let us talk together."

"What's going on?" Ria had found her voice at last. "Who are you and how do you know who I am?"

8

"You are here this time to answer questions, not to ask them," replied Kara. "For the present it is enough to say we know you very well and are eager to know you better. Tell me, Ria, do you want to see the other side of the mountains?"

"Which mountains?"

"The ones in your Dream."

"You know about that, too?"

"Of course! Seeing as how I designed that Dream specially for you." Lute was anxious to join in but Kara silenced him with a glance. He sat back on his haunches once more and gripped his harness straps with his paws.

"I never really believed it was a natural dream." Ria's bewilderment was giving way to indignation. "What right have you to interfere with my mind?"

"Ask again when you are wiser, child. I repeat: those lofty mountains can be crossed. Do you wish to try?"

"What if I say 'no'?"

"The choice is yours. But are you truly satisfied with your present manner of life? Could a change be made for the better?"

"Or worse." Ria never relished change. Her natural caution was not about to desert her even under these preposterous circumstances. "Suppose I agree. What happens to me then?"

"You will be given opportunities to learn and grow in ways few have ever known."

The desire for knowledge was Ria's one great passion. She wavered towards consent.

"Please trust us," begged the otter with unexpected earnestness.

Should she? Would she? It went against her instincts yet she could not imagine this creature causing her harm. "All right." The words nearly choked her. "I'll try to accept whatever it is you're offering. But I expect a happy ending to my Dream."

"The ending of your Dream, like your life, is yours to

shape. Remember us, Ria, remember our home.''

As if on signal, Ria's eyes swept the small, neat room recording its whitewashed walls brightened with woven hangings, the rag rugs on its plank floors, the bands of carved birds flying across the blue-stained wooden chest and bedstead, even the forsythia boughs in a tall black vase standing in one corner.

"Come back to us when you are ready, child.''

Kara smiled. Lute hugged himself for joy. The scene dissolved into spiraling darkness. . . .

The next time Ria opened her eyes, it was in a blandly ordinary hospital room. Her own hands rested on her own bosom. The brown face staring into hers belonged not to a giant otter but to a slender Pakistani physician.

"Ah, you are back among us again. But unconsciousness is only to be expected after an accident of that sort. I am Dr. Abdullah Zair. Now that you are awake, may I inquire how you are feeling?''

"I've felt better.''

"You are most fortunate to be able to feel anything.''

"What happened? You said something about an accident?''

"You suffered a severe electrical shock at your place of work this morning.''

"I can remember touching my data retrieval console but nothing afterwards.'' Ria strained to recall more.

"You must have only laid the palm of your hand against the device. If you had been gripping it, you would have certainly perished before anyone even noticed you were in peril. But I cannot understand how you escaped being burned. Most strange.''

"I'll tell you something even stranger, doctor.''

"What is that?''

"I don't recall ever being burned in my whole life.''

10

"Surely you exaggerate? Everyone has small mishaps, no matter how carefully the safety procedures are followed."

"I've had my share of those small mishaps but none of them were burns."

The doctors did not reply but a knowing smile spread over his thin face.

"I'm not joking," snapped Ria. "But don't let me bother you with facts."

Dr. Zair's smile faded. He finished his examination in aggrieved silence, then offered his prognosis:

"Your condition is satisfactory. If no counterindications develop, you can be released tomorrow morning. However, I am going to order another dose of muscle relaxant for you. This may make you drowsy. Attempt to sleep or at least rest quietly." He stressed the last word and scurried out.

Ria had not meant to react so tartly but Dr. Zair was as irritating as an unctuous rat. She could almost picture a rat's whiskers sprouting beneath his sharp nose. She shouldn't have allowed him to annoy her. She ought to concentrate on pleasanter matters like being alive and free of that headache.

Although the prescribed medication did not put her to sleep, it blunted the edge of her boredom and helped her endure the Infirmary routine. The effect wore off by dinner time. Then Ali appeared during the evening visitors' hours. She brought Ria tender solicitude and clean clothes to wear home. Ria wished she had also thought to include a book.

In the absence of congenial reading matter, she had time to reflect on her curious dream about the old woman and the otter. It was so much more vivid than her everyday reality. Yet if it was a drug reaction or a hallucination, why hadn't additional medication produced a similar effect? Ria was sure she had never seen a costume like the old woman's before, even in a fantasy film, yet it looked tantalizingly familiar. A man-sized intelligent otter was a novel concept but, she had to admit, a delightful one. She didn't think she could have imagined the amiable creature all by herself.

Too much rest during the day made it difficult for her to sleep that night. She poured herself a glass of water from the supply left on her night table. The steel tray holding the carafe glittered in the moonlight like a small, still pond. Suddenly, the mirrored surface trembled as if stirred by an unseen hand. Ria felt herself drawn down through silvery waves into the depths of thoughts not hers. . . .

How much longer was it going to take? Twelve hours—no, eleven hours, forty-three minutes by her watch—on this wretched beach with no release in sight. And if that thunderstorm brewing out at sea sweeps in, we may all be back here tomorrow running through the farce all over again, she thought numbly.

"Go down there and get the texture of the place," said her editor, "catch those colorful little details the wire services will miss." She had gotten the texture all right—every gritty, sweaty, prickly bit of it. Color was in short supply, though, unless you counted the green of the palmetto swamps. The editor seemed to think he was doing her a tremendous favor with this assignment. Actually, she was only a last minute substitute, pressed into service after Ed had broken his ankle shooting baskets with his kids and Diane had picked up a case of food poisoning. Either one of them would have loved being here. Maybe she would have, too, under better conditions—less heat and more action. At the moment, she'd gladly trade her glory for a deep bath and a cool motel room.

But some reporter had to be right on the spot. Local pride demanded it, what with the Mission Commander being a hometown boy. She felt that her interview with Colonel Zebrowski's wife was a creditable piece of work but she'd gotten it over the phone and called it in by phone. The whole thing could have been handled from the comfort of her own office. Moreover, the interview itself was no weightier than the ones she used to do with clubwomen or visiting celebrities before her recent promotion. This time last year she'd been quizzing hog breeders and expert quiltmakers at the Grant County Fair. Maybe that was the best analogy: a Mars shot was a county fair without the manure.

Once more she walked past the bleachers where the major media people had seats and work tables. Few of these were in use at the moment as their tenants surged aimlessly up and down the aisles or scattered across the beach. She limped slightly. Earlier in the day the heel of her right sandal had broken off. The cuff of her good yellow slacks dragged in the dirty sand picking up cockleburrs. She wished she'd had the sense to wear rugged clothes and a sun hat.

It was dark now—a small blessing—but no cooler. The air was thick enough to swim through. The skin on her face and arms stung from extravagant use of sunscreen lotion yet she knew she'd lost her battle with the Florida sun. An unwelcome crop of freckles was sure to appear in the morning. The insect repellent was still holding its own against the mosquitos and sand fleas but they'd doubtless find some breach in her defenses before the night was over.

She was passing the television networks' prefab headquarters. She repressed an urge to play the hick tourist and stare through the windows at the famous commentators. The box of fried chicken she'd brought along for lunch was a distant, greasy memory. She'd tried one sodden horror of a sandwich from the canteen trailer and vowed not to repeat the experience. But a root beer ought to keep her from fainting. She joined the slow-moving line for refreshments and finally secured her drink.

Then she turned back down the beach away from the stands. Photographers had established their gear in a battle line across the entire press site. A battery of cameras poised on tripods stood ready to shoot the Event—on the off chance the Great Event managed to occur. She found her chosen vantage point in front of the camera lines and sat down in a patch of dead grass close to the water's edge.

She'd studied every item in her press kit four times. Her notebook and pocket recorder were filled with impressions. Hazy ones. She couldn't quite grasp what was happening. The crash briefing she'd gotten at home hadn't prepared her for the Cape. She wished she'd been able to get a prelaunch press tour but those had all been filled before she arrived. There'd been nothing for her to do but wait since countdown had stopped at 10:28 this morning.

Everyone else seemed so relaxed and knowledgeable. They were taking the hold with much better grace than she. Only a few meters away, a dozen or so people were laughing and chatting as they passed binoculars around or took turns looking through the eyepiece of an astonishingly elaborate camera belonging to one of them. She tried not to eavesdrop on their conversations.

The preponderence of gray or balding heads suggested that these were old verterans of space reportage. Maybe they'd even covered the Apollo missions of a generation before. She wondered what papers they represented. They certainly were a jolly bunch. One elderly man with a pronounced cowlick in his shining white hair was sketching a dark and haughty middle-aged woman by lamplight. Many of the others were drinking from cans carefully muffled in paper napkins. She was sure these didn't contain pop.

Perhaps she ought to go over and introduce herself. The longer she sat alone, the more their cheerfulness would irritate her. She watched a trio of tall old men on the edge of the cluster. The fine-boned one spoke directly into his bespectacled colleagues' ears. The rangy one grinned at the one with the crisp moustache. Then they began to sing in low tones, keeping time by clashing their beverage cans together. She didn't know the tune, something about three kings on horseback. So intently was she staring, she accidentally locked eyes with the slender one. He smiled and saluted her with a gallant wave. She turned away embarrassed by her own rudeness.

Best to save long stares for the vehicle yonder. The Orbiter stood only five kilometers away across a stretch of water. With its stubby wings and strap-on fuel tanks, it made a less romantic image than the pictures of earlier rockets she'd seen. After all, it was only a ferry, a means of getting the astronauts up to their obiting Marscraft. Yet it sparkled every bit as brightly in the glare of interlaced spotlight beams and cast as splendid a reflection on the inlet's surface.

She felt guilty for not responding to the wonder of the scene. A pair of ducks bobbling placidly out on the still water mocked her turmoil. They did not care whether men flew to Mars or nested at home so long as there was clean water for ducks to swim in. Plenty of birds around here—that huge fellow she'd seen on the bus trip out to the Center must have been an eagle.

Suddenly the loudspeaker blared: "Countdown resumed." The message was echoed and re-echoed in a babble of newscasters' voices on scores of personal television sets all over the site. The crowd applauded wildly and swept down to the very edge of the beach, anxious to be as close to the coming event as possible. Photographers yelled at the invaders to leave their lines of sight clear and were good-naturedly obeyed.

Tension wound tighter as the last minutes of countdown unreeled. They were all longing for fulfillment "more than watchmen for the dawn" as her pastor would say. Despite her weariness, she found herself captured by the surging current of anticipation. Her pulse quickened and her hands became very cold. She rose to a kneeling position, leaning forward to catch the moment of ignition. The Orbiter rose abruptly on waves of fiery cloud and was soon lost to their sight in the overcast sky.

A tag from Isaiah rose unbidden in her mind: "By the shores of the sea, the people who sat in the darkness have seen a great light. Upon them My salvation rests." She was on her feet now, cheering as madly as everyone else.

The tide of celebrating people carried her towards the parking lot right into the path of the man who'd smiled at her earlier. She threw her arms around him in a short, fierce hug. Then she turned to fight her way back to the buses with soaring heart.

"We're on our way," she murmured. "We're really on our way."

# III

By the time the hospital released Ria early Tuesday afternoon, the accident had dwindled in significance. As far as she was concerned, it had been no more serious than a slip on a loose rug. Electrocution indeed! Why must people be so melodramatic? Did they crave excitement that much?

The dreams were uppermost in her mind now. She chose to walk rather than ride a bus home in order to be alone with her thoughts. Along the way she walled herself off from the crisp bright air and scuffed unseeing through heaps of gold and scarlet fallen leaves. Her inner eye was still fixed on the low broad skies of last night's dream, not on the clear vault above her head.

But arrival at her aparment snapped that reverie. A single day's absence had somehow altered her perspective: she felt like a stranger entering the place for the first time. How had she managed to exist in this midden heap? Drifts of clutter were threatening to engulf the flimsy plastic furnishings that came with the unit. Tell-like mounds of unfiled papers and

17

half-read books rose on every flat surface. Ria could not remember the last time she had cleaned or even straightened up. Her clothing shuttled to and from the laundry room with never a detour through cabinet or closet. Wastebaskets overflowed and the few clear pathways between the rubbish were gritty underfoot. She did not intend to tolerate it an instant longer.

Three hours later, her fury was spent and her apartment shone. She returned the cleaning tools to Supply and made herself a cup of tea in the kitchenette. As she sat down to drink it, she casually brushed the cockleburrs off the seat of her pants. She sprang up again in keen alarm. Burrs? Why had she expected burrs on her clothes? She stared at her hands, looking for pricks and scratches that were not there. Somehow, she was feeling curiously insecure about her body since the accident, as thought it, too, were a dwelling she had left for a while and found unfamiliar on return. Her hands were strong and square as ever; the same white scar still ringed her left thumb. Yet she could not entirely banish the images of two quite different pairs of hands flickering like ghosts above her own.

Perhaps she could cure the delusion with a dose of reality. Nobody had gone to Mars yet—wouldn't for another three or four years. Her tea grew cold while she tapped out queries on her personal data console. There was no record of an astronaut named Zebrowski in the past and none was among the crew now training for the upcoming Unity mission to Mars.

So there. Her dream of the space shot was merely a fantasy, something her imagination had concocted out of old news tapes. But since when were dreams equipped with cockleburrs and cardboard sandwiches? She remembered the details of that launch as well as those from any other real experience. Nothing had faded on awakening. No harm in making a thorough check. She entered a request for pictures and descriptions of Kennedy Space Center's press site in the late twentieth century. She washed the cup and teapot while awaiting results.

When Ria scrutinized the copies of photographs and drawings her console had printed, she found that they corresponded to her dream in every respect. A reporter in that era would've seen exactly what she saw. Furthermore, contemporary articles in obscure publications mentioned the same physical discomforts she'd felt there. The coincidence defied explanation. She couldn't possibly have known any of this. A final question to the data bank revealed that an American Mars program employing the Space Shuttle had been contemplated for the 1990's before worsening economic conditions had forced its cancellation.

So the launch she'd witnessed was plausible, if not actual. Could her dream have been a vision of an alternate reality, one in which history had taken a different course? She'd played the ''what if'' game often enough herself in school. Then did the old woman and the otter belong to another world of might-have-been? Did time itself have branches like some mighty tree? She thought of the University orchard's apple trees she'd climbed as a child. Did every gnarly branch stand for a path in time? Every blossom, fruit, and leaf a world? But why had she viewed those alternate worlds through eyes that were not her own? It would be simpler to assume she was merely losing her mind. People did that every day. The attractiveness of her delusions was an ominous symptom.

Ria stared out of her window at the gathering dusk for a long time. Then she realized she was getting hungry and decided to eat in the apartment complex cafeteria rather than cook for herself.

Tonight the earnest cheeriness of the place failed to depress her. It wasn't important enough to merit attention. Other residents bustled about smiling carefully at one another but she ate alone. Not even the sight of Hannah surrounded by an adoring coterie stirred the usual resentment—let the whole choral dance corps moon over her if they wished. Ria's thoughts were of darkness and dreams.

After returning upstairs, Ria wandered about her tiny apartment trying to think of ways to occupy herself until bedtime. There were no music or videotapes in her collection that she wanted to play at the moment. She considered ordering a reference work on space exploration printed out but facts about space were not at issue. She made herself read a bit of Eliade's *Myth and Reality*. His study of initiation myths was still in her briefcase at work but she'd get it back tomorrow. Then she took a sinfully slow shower, washed and dried her long hair, and climbed into bed.

"*Lente, lente, currite noctis equi,*" she muttered. She wanted the stallions of the night to course slowly but her reasons were quite unlike those of Doctor Faustus. The longer the night, the longer the dream. What would happen if she imagined those silvery waves again, if she tried to call for a dream?

It came. . . .

"No sign of the Rebels this morning, sir. Would the Colonel care to look for himself?" He lowered the field glasses and handed them to his superior who took them.

Then he made his way through the troops to deliver the Colonel's orders about dispatching skirmishers. The men were rousing themselves after a night spent in the open. Some were already gathering wood behind the lines for cooking fires. Others cleaned their rifles and cursed the ravages of dampness.

As he walked, he reflected on Colonel Sully's brisk manner: the Regulars still had the edge there. The Colonel had even contrived to restore a degree of military smartness to his appearance by brushing away the mud of yesterday's engagement. He was just like the Old Man in that respect. Would that he had some of their Commander-in-Chief's famous tact as well. He himself was struggling to develop discretion under the Colonel's harsh tutelage but he despaired of ever achieving the polish befitting an officer. Yet clay-smeared or not, at least he was alive and sound of limb. He had discharged his duties correctly under fire—no cause for shame on that score.

Messages relayed, he returned to his position at the Colonel's side.

"Is there any word on the Lieutenant Colonel's condition, sir?"

"He died during the night."

"So dressing in a private's uniform was no protection from their sharpshooters after all."

"Damnfool cleverness always fails, Major. Let his unhappy fate serve as a lesson to you. You would never see our esteemed Commander stooping to such ruses. And consider what a prime target he makes on that fine horse of his."

The Colonel's orderly handed each of them a mug of scalding coffee. Burly Corporal Haleswood, a former lumberjack, had demonstrated his resourcefulness every step of the way up the Peninsula. He even carried his crushed coffee beans already mixed with sugar in a little cotton sack so the Colonel's beverage could be swiftly prepared anytime conditions permitted a pot to be boiled. By some miracle, it was even drinkable coffee.

The skirmishers had just assembled and were moving north past a dilapidated frame building called the Courtney House. Not long afterwards, squads from the two regiments stationed on their immediate left began searching west of the battle line, making enough commotion in the process to frighten any Reb stragglers away. The three units were drawn up in an arc about 400 yards across what had been fields of wheat and clover. They confronted thick woods which had provided cover for yesterday's Confederate assault. A narrow dirt lane flanked by more trees ran 150 yards behind them.

Maples, pines, and several different varieties of oak grew

among the closely packed trees before them. Honeysuckle vines, some as thick as cable, wove through shell-gouged branches while dense underbrush hid the marshy interior of the woods from view. A few wild rose bushes still bloomed along the edge of the trees. Roses must come out earlier here than at home, he thought. But whatever fragrance they spread on the air was utterly lost in the odors of smoky fires, dung, filthy bodies, and death. Especially death. There could not be enough roses in all Virginia to mask the stench of death. Given the heat and dampness, it would only grow worse as the day wore on. The winds bore faint sounds of church bells ringing in the city ten miles distant summoning the faithful to Sunday services.

A fly buzzed past his ear and tried to land on his face. He batted it away, then realized with a twinge of horror where it must have rested last. He lowered his gaze to the ground in front of the trees. This clearing was strewn with the rags and rubbish of war—gray, white, and red. Surely he ought to feel more revulsion? His present indifference surprised him.

His sensibilities had been otherwise back in St. Paul on the first leg of his regiment's journey to the front. All the way downriver he had brooded about his capacity to face the carnage of battle: how would Tom McCauley measure up? Yet while actually in combat, he had found himself too busy for fear or nausea to master him. During pauses in the firing a curious lassitude had crept over him as though he were about to awaken from a dream. Nothing had seemed real enough to be truly horrible. The half-dozen mangled bodies before him held no terrors. They were merely awkward shapes in rough gray uniforms.

Enough of these morbid reflections. It was time he was getting back to the Colonel.

"Any reports yet, sir?"

"None."

"But the silence must be reassuring?"

"It bodes well enough," said the Colonel, "but messages

from our superiors would be even more welcome. Our failure to detect the enemy is no warrant of his absence.''

"Nothing even from Brigade? How unlike General Gorman to neglect us here in his old regiment.''

"Are you in a position to judge our Brigadier?''

"I meant no criticism, sir.''

The Colonel stared intently at something in the woods. It was only a bird, not a Reb. Then he resumed speaking: "I was favorably impressed with your performance in yesterday's engagement, Major McCauley. You did well for your first time under heavy fire. I have commended you in my official report.''

"Thank you, sir.'' Troops like these would make any officer look good, he thought. "Everything seemed simple enough once we got over Grapevine Bridge alive.''

"I do not fancy corduroy myself, even at the best of times.''

"Who would have thought the Chickahominy could rise so fast? It was only fifteen feet wide on Friday.'' His stomach tightened at the memory of the bucking, swaying makeshift bridge which three corps of infantry had crossed with flood waters swirling over their knees.

"In my opinion, Major, General Sumner saved the battle with that one move. Our other two corps could never have held the Rebels alone. He did well to overrule the young engineer who claimed the bridge was unsafe: 'Impossible, sir? I tell you I can cross! I am ordered!' ''

The Colonel rendered Bull Sumner's bellow to perfection. He appreciated the quality of the mimicry inasmuch as he had been standing right at the General's elbow when the incident took place. But he did not see fit to remind his superior of this.

The Colonel continued: "It was as risky a gamble in its way as our Commander-in-Chief's decision to divide his forces in order to lure the enemy out.''

"But surely both gambles have been justified by their

results, sir. The Old Man seems to know just when to break the copybook rules and still win. Why, if he had been in charge at Bull Run, the war would have ended right there.''

"Need I remind you, Major, Bull Run is precisely why he is in charge now. I believe. . . ."

At that point the first skirmishers returned with the news that the woods were clear of Rebels. They proudly displayed captured enemy muskets and a handful of wounded prisoners, some of whom had been fished out of swamp ponds halfway drowned. He supervised the delivery of the prisoners to an improvised field hospital at the Adams House nearly a mile distant. There they joined scores of their comrades already under treatment alongside Federal casualties. A fresh party of skirmishers assembled to glean abandoned arms and other war materiel along the deserted battlefront.

With the threat of further attack eased, the regiment's most pressing concern was to bury its dead. The climate made it imperative that the fourteen bodies now resting beneath a 'paulin be gotten under the earth as quickly as possible. Volunteers dug shallow graves in the sticky red clay and marked them with crude wooden crosses carved with the names of the fallen. Afterwards, the Colonel himself read the burial service.

He requested the same courtesy for the Confederate dead but the Colonel would have none of it.

"My men turn sods for no damned Rebels."

The brusqueness of his superior's refusal shocked him but he recalled that the Colonel's own brother-in-law was Secesh. Perhaps that shame was what made his Unionist ardor so grim. The Colonel did, however, permit enemy corpses to be gathered into a neat row pending collection by burial details from the other side.

By now, it was late morning. Most of the men had withdrawn to the shade of a peach orchard beside the Courtney House to escape the heat. Some wanted to pry off its clapboards to feed their cooking fires but he passed the word to remind them that standing orders protecting civilian property forbade this. The woods yielded more damp fuel instead. But if the fires smoked, they still served well enough. The men boiled coffee and roasted squares of salt pork on twigs. A few of them crumbled their hardtack and fried it in pork fat rather than eat it dry.

He had just begun gnawing on a piece of toasted hardtack when the long-awaited courier arrived from headquarters. The whole regiment crowded silently around the Colonel to hear the message.

"A glorious victory is ours. The enemy is retreating westward in disorder. We march in ten minutes."

He cheered the news as loudly as the humblest private among them. Could this battle have been the Big Thing that would end the war? Jubilant soldiers drained the last of their coffee, poured the dregs over the fires, and stomped them out. They packed their blanket rolls, shouldered their rifles, and began forming a column of twos. He made his way through the milling ranks to reach his horse, already saddled for him by the Colonel's orderly. He was glad the roan mare had come through the fight unscathed. He would have been hard put to replace a soft-mouthed beauty like her. Two of the artillery horses had been killed but Parrott guns were light enough to be moved by teams of three even over these atrocious muddy roads.

The regiment was now assembled. He mounted and took his place at the Colonel's side immediately after the color-bearer. They fell into line behind the adjacent New Yorkers and Pennsylvanians and tramped across sodden farm fields until they reached the battle-scarred rail depot at Fair Oaks Station. After crossing the tracks, they moved out along Nine Mile Road and were about to turn right onto the Williamsburg Post when their Commander-in-Chief and his entire staff rode into view.

His mounted position at the head of the column was a fine vantage point. There was Sumner. The elderly Corps Commander was bareheaded as usual, letting his long white hair and beard wave freely while clutching his battered slouch hat in one hand. But no one remarked this quaint sight today. All eyes were turned on the Old Man himself. Although younger than Sumner, he was equally whitehaired but there the resemblence ended for his uniform was as splendid as the other's was shabby. Admiring his Chief's erect bearing and sleek gray horse, he deemed him the very image of Leadership. He added his voice to the rousing cheers that followed him all along the line of march, greetings acknowledged with smart salutes as the Commander and his party swept forward.

Now the army's spirit was as high as the noonday sun above. He drank in the universal excitement and felt the splendor of victory burning like liquor in his veins. Even the Colonel's rigid countenance seemed transfigured in his eyes. The strains of *John Brown's Body* flowed down the line of march. One of the German regiments, he would wager, had struck up the song. Could it be the old Abolitionist's soul was in truth marching beside them this day?

*Glory, glory hallelujah!*

And the blue-clad legions of Robert E. Lee took Richmond by sundown.

# IV

The server deftly smothered the last of the flames and carried the platters of *saganaki* back to the corner table where Ria and Carey sat. The sparseness of the early evening crowd permitted them the luxury of prompt attention.

"I wish they still flamed it right in front of you," said Ria. She helped herself to the bubbling cheese. "But I suppose safety must prevail at all costs." She frowned at the candle-shaped electric lamp decorating their table.

"It must've made a better show up close," said Carey.

"It did. That's the only way to serve it hot enough to suit me."

"I don't think I could stand this any hotter." Carey took his first cautious nibble and winced. "Don't get me wrong, Ria, Xenia's is a great place." He ran appreciative fingers over the colorful paper mat beneath his dish. "And being treated to dinner here—"

"Makes it taste even better doesn't it? Relax, Carey, or you won't last the evening. This is the least I can do after your

27

first aid saved my life Monday." She raised her wineglass to him.

Carey ducked his head as if avoiding a blow. He scratched at a rash on his neck. "Everybody has to know resuscitation techniques. Ali or Hannah could've gotten you breathing again just as easily."

"But they didn't."

The arrival of their salads spared Carey further embarrassment.

"Did you hear that Repair is still buzzing about your terminal, Ria? They called while you were on break this afternoon. Even in the shop, they can't find anything wrong with it. They insist there's no way that equipment could've shocked you. The service rep was fairly whimpering at the prospect of all the extra forms she'll have to fill out."

"So why don't they just reinstall it? I've no objection to using the terminal if it's working properly again."

"You don't?" Carey looked up sharply.

Her own boldness surprised her but she continued: "I refuse to let that machine frighten me."

"Well, it's frightened the service rep. She has to come up with an explanation or lose performance points. No allowance for mysteries. So she has this theory—" he leaned forward for a piece of bread—"that the accident was the work of a noncomp."

"That's absurd! Noncomps run amok. They haven't the wits or the patience to plant booby traps, much less traps that leave no trace afterwards."

"Maybe there's a new, incredibly devious breed of noncomps hatching, a mutant breed that skulks in dark corners to plot mischief." He glanced around the dim restaurant melodramatically and finished in a whisper: "Or maybe it would be to someone's advantage to say so."

"Another excuse to watch and pry. Someday Security'll wire the whole world for monitoring. It doesn't bear thinking about. But look!" she excaimed. "Here's our chicken."

Other tables filled, the noise level rose, the honest smells of garlic and cinnamon, lemon and olive oil thickened in the air. Their server pointedly kept returning to check their progress but Ria would not let her hurry their meal. Finally, over coffee and baklava, she dared to raise her question.

"Carey, you're the Americana expert. Tell me something: what would've happened if Lee had fought for the Union in the Civil War? For instance," she added without thinking, "how would he have fared on the Peninsular Campaign?" She knew nothing about the campaign except that it took place on the Virginia peninsula.

"He would've won it, of course. No question about that. Marched right up, taken Richmond in the spring of 1862, brought the war to a quick and merciful end."

"Surely that would've been all to the good?"

"You'd think so. But life is never that tidy. Suppose the rest of the South refused to admit defeat after their capital had fallen? Suppose they waged guerrilla war for a whole generation? Might have been worse than what actually happened." He took another sip of coffee. "Why do you ask? I didn't know you were interested in the American Civil War."

"Oh, I was just playing a sort of mental game, making a list of historical what-ifs." The intentness of his stare was making her uncomfortable. "Haven't you ever wondered: what if Mohammed had died in his cradle? What if the Spanish Armada had conquered England?"

"There used to be a whole genre of speculative fiction based on premises like that. They called it 'alternate history.' "

"You sound as if you've read some."

It was his turn to be defensive. "Anything wrong with a historian enjoying old-fashioned literature?"

"Nothing. We're supposed to like the past, aren't we? I must confess, the past looks better and better every day. Sometimes I think I must have been born in the wrong century."

"I know the feeling." He stopped shredding his napkin and looked directly into her eyes. They grinned in mutual discovery.

Ria returned to her apartment well pleased with herself. Getting to know Carey better had more than repaid the evening's cost in money and alcohol allowance. He was a person now instead of a co-worker. In time, perhaps a friend? Since she felt hopelessly young for her twenty years, making friends was so painful she had convinced herself she really preferred being alone. Where did this sudden hunger for companionship come from?

On Saturday she and Carey were going to the new art exhibit at Krannert. Right now she was eager to follow up some of the suggestions he'd made on Civil War references. She threw her coat on the nearest chair and set to work on her console.

A topic search yielded summaries of the Peninsular Campaign. Ria tracked her data like a huntress. Only in the pursuit of knowledge did she feel wholly alive. By correlating events and proper names, she tentatively identified the action in her dream as the aftermath of the Battle of Fair Oaks, May 31, 1862—an event she was certain she'd never heard of before. European history was her specialty, not American. Could her subconscious have invented so many vivid details without memories to draw on? But which parts were fact and which fancy?

She began checking the identities of all the officers mentioned. There was no Major Thomas McCauley in the First Minnesota Volunteer Infantry or in any other detachment present at that battle although Union Army rolls did list a Private Thomas McCauley of Minnesota serving on the far Western frontier. However, General Edwin "Bull" Sumner was real enough. Her printer even disgorged a full-length portrait of that worthy gentleman looking unnaturally neat. She recognized him at once despite the old engraving's stiffness. Sumner had indeed saved the day at Fair Oaks. One authority compared his crossing of Chickahominy Creek to the fortunate arrival of Blücher at Waterloo. Without his bold decision—

There was a knock at the door. The unwelcome caller was Hannah.

"What can I do for you?" asked Ria.

"Aren't you going to invite me in?"

"I'm sorry but you've caught me at a bad moment."

"It's a matter of some importance." Hannah was not used to refusals.

"So is the work you're interrupting."

"As a member of the House Committee I could demand entrance. If I cared to exert my rightful authority. . . ." She tried to peer into the apartment past Ria's body.

"You wouldn't do anything that direct." Ria became pleasantly aware of her own superior size. She lounged against the doorframe and folded her arms.

"The purpose of the House Committee is to facilitate cooperative living among the residents and thus enhance their proper mental, physical, and emotional functioning." Hannah recited the quotation in her mellowest tones.

"That's word for word from the Guidebook, isn't it? Are you here to charge me with some infraction of the rules?"

"You make me sound like a Security Officer!"

Ria shrugged. She wanted to say "you have all the right instincts," but thought the better of it.

"It's just that people—several people—have remarked that you keep to yourself all the time." Her pale brows wrinkled with an approximation of concern.

"I don't have the time to mingle because I'm working so hard at being a productive member of society."

"Unmutual behavior is not permitted."

"Laziness isn't permitted either—at least in theory. I'm sure there's a point in this conversation somewhere, Hannah. Once you state it I can get back to my desk. My keyboard's getting cold." Ria began tapping her fingers on her arm.

"You simply must make some gesture of mutuality."

"No doubt you have a specific one in mind."

"I'm going to offer you the chance to make a healthy show of community spirit." The hint of a smirk tainted her smile. "You could help me serve refreshments at tomorrow night's Gathering. We're going to have real cider from the Illini Orchard." Her voice caressed the word "real."

"I plan to be busy tomorrow night, too." Ria didn't bother to apologize.

"This refusal will go on your record. Every byte of data counts. If you want to risk being evicted, well, the choice is yours."

Ria stood silent, not trusting herself to reply. The blonde woman retreated down the corridor bearing the rejection of her benevolence nobly.

Ria closed and relocked the door behind her. If Hannah had just asked her to take her turn, she might have agreed, but no, she had to simper and weedle. She probably didn't know any other tactics. The sheer pettiness of the thing! But why had she resisted? Foolish to risk a bad report over something so minor. Being seen in Carey's company ought to be enough to silence critics—they might even imagine the relationship was sexual. On the other hand, eviction would be a calamity. She couldn't afford quarters as good as these elsewhere and to be cut off from the University's computer net would be literal excommunication.

Ria poured herself a glass of cider. The cold, fragrant drink did nothing to soothe her temper. She grimaced at the smiling Indian on the jug's label. Clearly, she was too furious to concentrate further on the Civil War. Perhaps a change of topic was in order, something completely irrelevant to her present situation. Mythology perhaps. She found the copy of *Rites' and Symbols of Initiation* that she'd meant to start last Monday. The stately cadences of Mircea Eliade's prose usually relaxed her.

But this time, the remedy failed. The restless, dreamless

night that followed made her regret reading so far past her accustomed bedtime. Next morning, she felt as dismal as the gray skies above although the overnight weather change had not left her with the expected headache. Not for the first time she questioned the necessity of her physical presence at the library. But home terminals like hers enjoyed only a limited degree of interface with the major nets that ran the world. The proliferation of personal computers hadn't restructured employment conditions after all. Society decreed that people work and even play in communal groups for their own good.

At work that day, her attempts to conciliate Hannah only aroused bickering too sharp for Ali to ignore. The supervisor's preference for peace over justice worked against Ria, but Carey was quicker to back her than before. It was comforting to be reminded that a friend made a warmer ally.

Once home, Ria tried to put it all out of her mind. She resolved to ignore any calls or knocks at the door and concentrate on unraveling her dreams. Best to get at it as quickly as possible before noisy partygoers clogged the hall.

She put the teakettle on the cook-surface while a frozen dinner heated. For want of something to do with her hands while waiting, she picked up a teaspoon. She stared at the utensil with rapt attention as though she had never seen a spoon before—how wonderfully smooth and shiny it was! Her caressing fingers warmed the cool metal. She caught sight of her own face unsteadily reflected in the bowl of the spoon. As she rocked it back and forth, the image of the ceiling light above her danced like the sun on rippling water. . . .

She drew her cloak about her rounded shoulders and leaned far out of the window. A damask banner fluttering from the sill shifted beneath her stiff, gloved fingers. Folly for one of her infirmity to brave January's cold, yet the glory of the day was worth the risk it carried and she would afterwards pay gladly in whatever coin should be demanded. She hailed

33

the neighbors who watched from windows opposite hers and applauded the brave display of hangings they had made.

Two storeys below her the silk and fur-clad merchant gentry of Cheapside awaited their new sovereign's coming behind railings draped with tapestries and other costly stuffs. The throng swirled against the barriers in clamorous waves. Men stamped their feet and women thrust their hands deep inside their sleeves to ward themselves from chill. Gems flashed in the afternoon sunlight and golden chains of office turned to rippling bands of flame.

Farther down the street a platform had been erected for the staging of a tableau. The district sought to flatter His Majesty's famed taste for allegory. Here they presented a noble tree like unto a Jesse Tree sprung from the loins of Father Time himself. In its branches sat children in stiff finery and gilt crowns who bore the arms proper to each royal ancestor. So grave the young ones' bearing, they might have been painted statues in some church. Below them musicians were gathered about a schoolboy orator primed to explicate the scene in both Latin and English verse.

A tumult of cheers and bells and trumpet blasts grew ever louder from the direction of Cornhill to the east. The assembled worthies craned their necks like lesser folk to descry the King and his attendants proceeding to Westminster for tomorrow's coronation. But she stood more still than they for her eagerness was an inward thing and age had taught her patience at the last.

A shout went up as the heralds came into view. After them strode a troop of halberdiers splendid in crimson doublets worked front and back with the Tudor Rose and the monogram of Henricus Rex. The monarch himself, clad entirely in cloth of gold, rode at the head of a thousand mounted courtiers. Fresh rejoicing greeted each smile the ruddy-faced young king bestowed. He has their hearts even as they had his. In him their nation's fortunes bloomed anew.

She counted herself well blessed to watch the cycle turn a

second time. She had cheered old King Henry and his sainted Queen Katherine as they fared to their crowning one Midsummer's Day nigh two score years ago. With more vigor than she would have believed she yet possessed, she raised her ancient voice to cry: "God save and keep Your Majesty. . . ."

Ria came to herself just as the teakettle started to boil. She was slumped against the kitchen table, far wearier and hungrier than she had been only moments before. No need to research this dream. The scene was obviously a Tudor coronation procession. No, not quite. What was the term she wanted? "Recognition Procession." The king would receive his crown the following day. But *which* king? No son of Henry VIII and Katherine of Aragon had lived past infancy—in history as she knew it. Yet if a Henry IX had reigned on some other time track, English history would have branched off in an entirely different direction.

So what did sixteenth century England have to do with a Mars rocket or the Civil War or that old woman and the giant otter who'd called her by name? She could see no common feature in the dreams. Except . . . in each of them people were waiting for some dramatic event to transform their lives. Was she being told to wait for some transformation of her own? Ria shuddered as if with cold.

Impossible! It was all impossible. Alternate universes didn't exist. Dreams only spoke for one's subconscious mind. It was insane to think otherwise. The madness she'd feared since childhood was sprouting, rooting, growing day by day. She stifled a scream.

The kettle bubbled on, indifferent to her anguish. She forced herself to rise and take if off before the water all boiled away. The oven buzzed to signal her dinner was ready.

# V

"You've almost got it, Ria. A little to the right now."

"How's that, Carey?"

"Perfect."

Ria stepped back to admire her newly hung poster. The glossy black and white image showed furrowed ridges thrusting out of misty lowlands. A single mountain faceted like a giant crystal soared beyond its fellows into the dark sky. The exhibition's title, "The Mountains of the Mind," was printed on the border.

"This one is called—" she bent down to check—"*Strange Peaks Above the Clouds*. Which one are you going to put up first at your place?"

"I like *Dense Snow in the Tai Mountains*." He held up a wintry landscape. "It reminds me of home, back in Cascade. I'm glad you talked me into splitting the cost of a portfolio."

"I'm the one who should be grateful. Attending that art show was your idea."

Carey scrutinized the remaining posters. He did not look

up as Ria sat down beside him on the studio couch. "The printing's not too bad for mass production—not that they can do much more than suggest the luminosity of the originals. I'll bet C.C. Wang's official rediscovery was decreed in the interest of ethnic balance. Some joke on the arts bureaucracy that he happened to be a genius, the last of the *wen-jen* painters. Most of their twentieth century choices were better left unexhumed."

"You seem to follow these things rather closely."

"So?"

"Don't bristle at me, Carey. No accusation intended. You sounded so authoritative at the museum. All that technical talk about atmospheric effects, dry brush technique—it was a revelation."

"Once upon a time I wanted to be an artist. I still play at calligraphy a little. Let's talk about something else." He squared the posters, slipped them back into the package, and resealed it.

"Would you like some cider?"

Carey nodded. Ria got a glass for each of them and returned to her seat. "Fastening the poster to the coathooks was a good suggestion, Carey. I'll see it there on the door every morning when I wake up." She traced the line of sight with the wave of an arm.

"It saves you a trip to the House Committee, too."

"I don't think they'd give me permission to hang anything on the walls. Hannah would make sure of it. She was snooping around here Thursday night but I wouldn't let her in."

"Hannah won't forget that. She has an exquisite sense of her own prerogatives."

"It's not that I had anything to hide. I simply made up my mind not to submit." Ria struck her thigh with her fist. "What a fine brave deed to boast of!"

"It's more than I manage to do." Carey's slight body tensed at the very thought of their co-worker.

"I didn't know you used to live in Cascade," said Ria gently. "Is it really as beautiful as it looks in pictures?"

Pride got the better of Carey. "Such a question! You can't begin to imagine it—the gulls crying over Puget Sound, walks through cool, wet forest, climbing snow-capped mountains. . . ." His voice faded out. "I'm getting carried away." He began combing his fingers through his curly hair. "It comes of trying to live on a child's store of memories."

"I was born and raised right here. I've never been near a mountain. I did see some hills in Indianapolis once but they didn't impress me."

"Seattle isn't Indianapolis."

"I doubt I'll ever get the chance to compare them."

"Nor I. Travel taxes keep rising faster than my savings. I haven't been back to Seattle since my father was transferred here ten years ago. He's in charge of commodities shipments for this entire region—reports directly to Leeds herself."

"Couldn't he use his influence to get you a job out there?"

"Bend the rules? My incorruptible father? He keeps a picture of Transportation Head Leeds in his office. None of his family. That might be construed as sentimental." He drained his glass of cider. "I bet you can't put a face to Ruth Ann Leeds' name."

Ria shook her head. "So, no way back to the mountains."

"None. I should learn to make do with the high-rise buildings of Chambana instead."

Ria winced. "There are still the mountains of the mind." She pointed at the poster. "In the long run, they may be the only ones worth seeking."

But once Carey left, Ria's anxiety crept back like fog. The afternoon's outing to Krannert had made no lasting difference in her mood after all. Ria thought of calling him back and making dinner plans. But that would only postpone the inevitable. No matter how long she persuaded him to stay, she would eventually be left alone to face herself.

What was wrong? She'd never minded being alone before. She'd actually relished every respite from togetherness. On the other hand, if she really craved company, she could go down to the lounge. But what good would it do to surround herself with strangers? Did she want companionship or solitude? Or both? Or neither? Why couldn't she make a simple choice? She'd been decisive enough earlier when Carey was around. (But who couldn't be more forceful than Carey?) The familiar pathways of her life were blurring and fading away before her eyes. Somehow, she'd lost her bearings since the accident and was blundering in panic through regions unknown.

Ria turned to the simplest remedy she knew: no problem is so large that it can't be nibbled away. She fixed herself a sandwich. Her appetite vanished after the first few bites, replaced by twinges of nausea. She wrapped up the sandwich and stored it in the refrigerator for tomorrow's lunch.

Then she tried to distract herself with a frenzy of housework. She scoured surfaces that were already clean. She rearranged the contents of every drawer and shelf. She laundered. She mended. She put all her books and tapes and spools in proper order. It was evening before she ran out of things to do.

A slight throbbing behind her eyes signaled a coming change in the weather although the ache was nothing like the ones she used to feel. Ria leafed aimlessly through books unable to concentrate on any of them. Between attempts at reading she prowled her apartment without knowing what she sought. The urge was as keen and compulsive as a pregnant woman's desire for exotic food. The fear of another hallucination likewise kept her moving. Too much quiet reverie might trigger another spell. And she mustn't let her gaze linger too long on shining metal. There appeared to be some connection. Danger was everywhere once one started looking for it, even in routine objects like doorknobs. What if she were found collapsed in the bathroom, thrown into a trance by the sight of the faucets? She'd wake up in a PSI ward—at the very least.

Ria decided that the safest way to avoid one thing was to focus on another. She put a cassette of Moussorgsky favorites in the player and settled down to stare out of her window into darkness. Lights atop a new building going up on Lincoln Avenue marked the horizon. Ria considered taking a walk in that direction—*Pictures at an Exhibition* always made her think of walking—but a storm was now gathering. Trees bent and pedestrians scurried on the street below. The lightning flickering to the west was still too far away for the sound of thunder to reach her. She turned off all the lights and watched the bright rumbling glory roll in. At length it passed, leaving insistent rain to pelt her window all night long. The white noise of it lulled her to sleep. . . .

She was climbing a rope hand over hand and biting back screams to save her breath. Acrid chemical smoke raked her lungs and eyes. Her arms—unmistakably her own weak, heavy arms—were pulled from their sockets by the strain. Her bleeding hands kept slipping on the cable. Every movement sent her sweaty hair flapping in tangles about her shoulders. Although she could see the flame erupting below, her refuge above remained shrouded in murk. Ria knew this for a dream. She struggled to awaken but some will more powerful than her own kept whipping her forward. She had no choice except to go on climbing up from Hell.

The nightmare faded with the dawn; the terror remained. Waking or sleeping, her mind was at hazard. There was no hiding place left.

Sunday was the kind of well-scrubbed autumn day Ria would have reveled in any other year. She walked for hours, all the way out to the University experimental farms. It was familiar territory. She'd worked there four summers as a stablehand. She'd loved it—animals accepted her better than people. Despite precocious scholarly interests, she'd even considered horse training as a career. She might've done more than consider it if her mother hadn't been quite so eager to get her "out into the fresh air and away from all those books." So she'd fled to the library instead.

Ria approached the pasture fence. Shading her eyes with one hand, she searched for familiar horses in the inner paddock. That red mare cantering on the fringe of the herd had to be Ember. She didn't recognize any of the others. No point in walking around to the barns—visitors were admitted only on official business.

How she ached for the chance to ride again! Just to touch warm, living horseflesh would hearten her. At this moment she would've gladly mounted any broken-down public stable hack. If she scrimped someplace else, perhaps she could afford the fees. She gripped the fence so hard the wire hurt her hands. Straining for sounds of distant whinnies, she tried to be glad for the beasts. A little crisp weather was all they needed to feel frisky.

Ria thought of buying a snack at a campustown food stand, but the first whiff of frying oil turned her stomach so thoroughly she fled back to the street. Watching Security Officers take a giggling woman into custody did little to restore her appetite.

After returning home, she started to punch out Ali's telephone number, then replaced the receiver. Ali would be all too curious about her gloom—tomorrow was soon enough to face her prying eyes. She thought of working out in the House gym—a drastic and distasteful remedy but vigorous exercise was supposed to ease depression. A check of the House calendar eliminated that plan. The choral dance group was scheduled to practice tonight. She did not care to encounter Hannah on hostile ground. With curious shyness, she turned at last to Carey. She half hoped her call would find him absent and thus spare her the necessity of admitting loneliness. However, not only was he at home, he was overflowing with

42

hospitable impulses and begged her to come over and inspect his latest calligraphic efforts.

Another time she might have enjoyed the visit and given Carey the praise he so obviously craved. At the moment she didn't have the strength to respond to his enthusiasm. She was so lightheaded from lack of food, she could scarcely sit up straight. She was still sweating from the long trek across the house and up to his floor. She found the mirror image arrangement of identical furnishings in his apartment vaguely disorienting. The lights were starting to look too bright while the shadows swelled. Was he going to show her every page he'd ever penned in one sitting? If he didn't offer some refreshments soon, she'd have to ask for some.

Carey was burbling on about the latest medieval hand he'd mastered. "Now look how dynamic the diagnonals make *littera batarda*. I pick up energy from the script itself when I'm doing it. On the other hand, the solemn verticals of *textus prescissus—*"

"Maybe you get energy from letters, Carey, but I require food. Tea would do no end of good for my dynamism right now."

Carey flushed and swept the stack of matted pages off the table. They slipped and scattered every which way at his touch. "Of course. This instant. How rude of me. Would you like some empanadas to go with?"

Ria nodded. She closed her eyes and imagined tea so heavily sugared it poured like syrup.

Carey put a sheet of frozen turnovers in the oven and set the kettle to boil. He made a clattery production out of assembling the tea things and managed to slash his left hand fixing salad. He excused himself to bandage the cut in the bathroom.

Meanwhile, the oven timer buzzed. By reflex, Ria sprang up to turn it off. The sudden move was too much for her. She staggered towards the kitchenette, blindly groping for support. She grabbed for the counter but touched the hot cook surface instead. Her recoil sent the tea tray flying and knocked over the kettle. Its contents spilled over her arm as she collapsed against the cabinet, gouging the side of her head on the drawer handles on the way down.

She came to as Carey was struggling to heave her upright.

"I'm sorry, Ria, I'm so sorry. Please try to get up—you're too heavy for me to lift."

"It's nothing. Don't pull at me like that. I can manage."

Ria sat up and felt a stickiness in her hair. She took Carey's hand and lurched up.

"Good thing you didn't yell when you went down or you'd have tripped the crisis monitor."

"Give me credit for some discipline. At home, I had to fend off Conciliators every time my parents fought."

"Let me help you to the couch."

"No, get me a towel first—not a bath towel, a paper one will do fine. I don't want to bleed over everything." Ria crumpled a paper towel over her flowing wound before lowering herself to the couch. "It's food I need, not fussing. I went too long today without eating and it's caught up with me. Have you got some milk, juice, anything?"

Carey poured her a glass of milk, still apologizing.

"Stop that. I'm the one who made the mess. How much mess did I make?" She winced at the pile of broken dishes beside the stove unit "I don't remember how many pieces you'd set out. What'll the damage charges be?"

"You let me worry about that. I'll report the breakage to the House Committee myself."

"I like to take care of my own obligations."

"Make an exception for once. I don't get many chances to be noble. I don't want you stuck with a tour of punitive work."

"You're sure you want to handle it this way? It's awfully good of you."

Carey quickly contrived an ice pack for Ria's head and cleaned up the broken dishes while she ate.

"Now will you let me look at your arm, Ria?"

"Trying to undress me, are you? I already told you there's nothing wrong with it."

"Why isn't there?" He was caught between a blush and a frown.

"I don't burn easily."

"That water had to be almost boiling hot."

"Oh no, not really."

"In any case, you can't go home soaked like that—with an ice pack yet. It would cause comment."

"I don't need any more of that. Do you expect me to stay here until I dry out? Is it a nefarious plot to get a captive audience for a calligraphy lecture? You can't be that enamored of my company."

"Ria, you are the hardest person to do a favor for. I was going to offer to take your clothes to the laundry for drying."

"Still trying to shuck me, eh?" The absurdity of the situation was brightening Ria's mood.

"You could wrap yourself up in a blanket. I'd offer to lend you my robe but it'd be way too small."

Ria complied. She showed him that her arm and shoulder were barely pink from the scalding.

"Ria, I don't know how to say this, but there are too many odd things going on. You haven't looked or acted quite, uh, normal since the accident. Make all the excuses you like, but I think there's something wrong. Are you afraid to find out what it is?"

"Yes."

"So afraid you don't even want to ask Medivise about your symptoms?"

"At this point, any inquiries I made for medical data would trip a monitor and I'd wind up with a summons." She shivered.

"Then why don't you punch your questions in on my ID number?"

Ria's eyes widened. "You mean that?"

"While I'm down at the laundry I expect you to use that console anyway you see fit." He wrote his ID number on a slip of paper and placed it beside the unit.

"If we're going to be conspirators, we might as well seal the pact in blood." Her tone was light but her meaning was not. She touched her oozing scalp and held out her bloody fingers to his bandaged one.

Later, back in her apartment, Ria studied the printouts of medical advice she'd gotten at Carey's. Both possibilities were chilling: either neurological damage from the electric shock or a budding psychosis. But whether brain or mind were at fault, PSI would catch her in the end. How much time did she have before someone reported her?

It took Ria a long time to fall asleep that night. But no sooner had she done so than the climbing dream returned. The rope and the smoky fires were exactly the same as before. The pain was worse. She struggled even harder to wake herself with no more success than the previous night. Although her will was tethered, her reason ran free. She deduced that she was actually dreaming, not hallucinating history this time. Her present situation had an arbitrary quality quite unlike her earlier adventures. It defied reality. Overweight and out of condition as she was, she shouldn't have been able to hold onto the ropes, much less climb for hour after hour. Smoke that thick ought to kill her outright instead of tormenting her. Since when did a dreamer analyze a dream in progress?

Ria was finally released to wakefulness. She started to gulp for breath as though starved for clean air. Her arms and back trembled with muscle tension. She slowed her breathing to a normal rate and willed her rigid body to relax. At least she seemed to have kept her misery quiet so far. Whatever happened, she mustn't trigger the alarm or alert the neighbors. That might raise questions for which she had no answers.

The trip to work might have been an ordeal but Carey chanced to take the same bus as she. He was not a morning person either. He was content to merely sit beside her without inflicting conversation.

They found Ali already in the office feeding data into her terminal. She wore the look of a mother about to surprise her children with a special treat. But her brows creased at the sight of Ria's haggard face.

"Is something wrong? You look ill."

"No, Ali, just tired. I had trouble getting my rest last night."

"You're sure that's all? We don't expect you to come in when you're not well. Maybe you should've taken off more time after your accident."

Carey halted this flood of concern. "If Ria says she lost sleep, then that's what happened."

Ali gave them both a slow, knowing smile and turned back to her keyboard.

Ria was spared the necessity of further comment by Hannah's tardy arrival. The petite blonde was favoring her right leg, yet contrived to limp gracefully.

"Fall at dance practice did you?" asked Carey.

"I twisted my knee yesterday," she replied. The tiny sigh as she gripped a chair for support hinted at pain bravely borne by a delicate constitution. "But we must expect to suffer for our art."

"Art can be very demanding," said Ria, trying to sound more sympathetic than she actually felt. She knew that trained body was as fragile as spring steel.

"But tell them your good news, Hannah." Ali motioned for her to sit.

"I'm taking orders for dream tickets today. Our session is scheduled for this friday evening. What'll you have, Carey, Up, Down, or Out?"

"Up, I always chose Up. You ought to know that by now." He took a step backwards and suddenly discovered a speck on the hem of his tunic.

"And you, Ria? You weren't here the last time we went."
Ali looked up awaiting Ria's decision.

"I'm not going."

"And why not?" Ali rose to confront her.

"I'm . . . allergic." Ria clasped her hands to keep them
from shaking.

"That's impossible. Dream drugs are perfectly safe.
Guaranteed safe. Health wouldn't certify them if they
weren't." Ali chose to regard Ria's excuse as a criticism of
Federation policies.

"Some people just aren't mature enough to avail themselves of the enriching experiences our society provides,"
murmured Hannah. "I always enjoy my sessions. They
make me feel so close to my fellow workers."

"But my problem is real."

"Then perhaps you should consult a doctor. We don't
want you to miss any of the recreations the rest of us share."

"Allergy treatments take a while," said Carey. "I
know." He touched the eczema on his neck. "She couldn't
be cured by Friday in any event." He beckoned to Ria. "If
you come over to my desk, I'll brief you for your appointment with Professor Clyde this afternoon."

There were no further discussions on dream tickets in the
office that morning. But Carey raised the issue again as he
and Ria walked over to the history department.

"I never heard of anyone refusing a ticket before. I wish I
had the guts to do the same myself."

"You mean you don't like going Up?"

"I like it all right, but I hate myself for liking it. Almost as
much as I hate the padded rooms at the center and those
flimsy paper costumes they give you to wear."

"Then why do you go?"

"It's easier to do what people expect, at least in public.
Why are we walking on the right-hand side?" He gestured at

the other pedestrians. "Because that's the way the traffic flows."

"No one's made me go back since I got sick my first time out."

"You really did get sick then?"

"Yes."

"I thought you were making that up."

"I'll tell you about it someday when the memory makes me less queasy." Would she ever trust Carey enough to describe what actually happened two years ago? She'd fallen into a state of hysteria so violent, she'd had to be removed from the Center and given an antidote. No lovely vision for her while Out. Instead she'd seen a magnificent black horse with all its legs cut off. It screamed horribly and long as its life gushed away in red torrents.

# VI

Carey departed for his own appointment, leaving Ria at Professor Gunnar Clyde's door. She needn't have worried about being on time. The eminent scholar wasn't at home. The minutes dragged by. Students thronged the corridor as classes changed. Ria thought of sitting on the floor but that would attract attention. She leaned against the wall and closed her eyes.

"So there you are."

The hearty bass voice brought her to instant attention. No wonder he was called "Boom-Boom" even to his face. Clyde unlocked his door, waved her inside, and was off again in a tornadic bustle. The big man could move surprisingly fast through the crowd.

Ria could at least sit while waiting. The office was an utter jumble. Books bristling with slips of paper were stacked everywhere, including the floor. A mound of microfilm boxes nearly hid the reader on his desk. Computer printouts were taped on the walls between framed documents and testimonials. An ornate silver plaque proclaiming Clyde a past president of the North American Historical Association hung directly behind his desk.

"You weren't waiting long." It was a statement, not a question. Clyde rammed a stack of folders onto a handy shelf and strode behind his desk. "I have a splendid prospect to put before you, Legarde. As the newest research staff member, you're ideally suited for my needs. You have the fewest standing assignments. You do right by me and I'll see you get performance points—maybe even a jump in grade for you—certainly will mean one for me."

"I'm sure I'll live up to your expectations, Professor, but what is it, please?"

"Remember that Lisbon earthquake biblio Newton did for me?"

"The one I was going to transmit the day of my accident?"

"You had an accident?"

"I was almost electrocuted."

"So that's why I got my data late." He glared at her for being so inconsiderate. "Well, that Lisbon study was the first test of my idea. I'm planning a new book, *Disasters and Destiny: The Impact of Tectonic Catastrophe on History*. I like that title, gets me itching to start work, just thinking about it."

"You're only interested in earthquakes and volcanoes?"

"Well, if I tried to cover every kind of natural disaster, I'd never get done. Not going to spend years tied down to one project—I have too many ideas need working up. One category this time but a panoramic overview. Breadth—I've always been in favor of breadth."

Ria thought he should speak up for girth, too. She didn't like the way the ponderous man flapped his arms for emphasis.

"Take your Lisbon quake," he continued, "50,000 people dead, whole city smashed. Tidal wave. Fire. The shock was felt all over Europe—metaphorically if not literally. Sir Kenneth Clark said it brought the Age of Reason to an end. I don't know but what he may have been right. So it started me thinking—I was buttering my breakfast biscuit when the thought hit me—what about other quakes? What about tectonic catastrophes generally? How did the Romans feel about Pompeii or the Indonesians about Krakatoa? Let's revive the old controversy about the Thera eruption. Did the destruction of the Minoans start the Golden Age myth?''

''I don't think so, Professor,'' Ria managed to slip in. ''The idea of a Lost Paradise is nearly universal. Eliade says—''

''That's as may be. If you want to argue, bring me the numbers. Bring me lots of cases. Pro and con. What about the rise of militarism in Japan after the Tokyo quake of 1923? Unrest in Latin America in the 1970's. Stress the majors— Tan Shan, Reelfoot Lake.''

Ria nodded at the mention of a familiar name. ''I've heard of the Reelfoot Lake Disaster. The New Madrid fault that caused it runs through Prairie.''

''I'm glad you're finally beginning to catch on. Now do you see the possibilities? A non-fiction bestseller. Maybe a TV documentary series. This could go Federation-wide.''

''But what's it got to do with me?''

''You're to write the research protocol, of course. But if you can't draw conclusions any faster than that, maybe I should try someone else.''

''I still don't understand why you want me. My specialty is medieval and Renaissance Europe. I can't think of any major disturbances—''

''Think harder.''

''The big Antioch quake in Byzantine times?''

''Aren't you ambitious, Legarde? You don't sound like it. I just said a minute ago I don't hold with narrow specialization. If you're a competent historical researcher in one period, you ought to be able to handle anything. You *are* competent? Newton assured me you were. I've worked with

Newton for years and she's right about most things. I offered her the job first but she wanted you to have it."

"She's always looking out for me."

"*Disasters and Destiny* will be an education for you. I want you to really burrow in. Don't be content with printouts and microfiche. Go over to the rare book room. Leaf through those sources yourself. Start with the ones you know: Bouquet, the *Monumenta*—"

"I don't think they have earthquakes or volcanoes in Germany."

"—Mauratori." He swept on unperturbed. "Find medieval Italian cases. There are twenty-four volumes of Muratori. I want you to have a look at them."

Ria wanted to say that they were quartos badly in need of rebinding but confined herself to replying, "I know the set."

"It's not every library that has the originals, worm-eaten though these are. When I was in school. . . ." He galloped off into an involved anecdote.

Ria's attention wandered from Clyde's bobbing jowls to the plaque behind his head. She stared transfixed at its glittering silver surface. . . .

It pleased him, here in barbarous Muscovy, to tread on bold crimson carpeting of English manufacture. With it beneath his feet, he could maintain his countenance fittingly composed, undaunted by the alien splendors of the Uspensky Sobor. Such a wasteful blaze of candles! ("Away with them," Gloriana had said. "We see well enough.") Incense and chanting hung heavy in the air. Sombre, large-eyed idols they styled *ikons* hung from gilded pillars. It outraged him more than the papistical abominations he had witnessed on the Continent.

Yet he had to grant that the young Tsar Ivan and his Tsarina cut imposing figures in their gemmy robes. Informants said the old Tsar Ivan had been a scarecrow of a man who favored monkish attire. He saw the infant Tsarevitch borne in with

due solemnity, escorted by those who were to stand as god-
parents to the heir. How did the Tsar's simple-minded
brother manage to keep his fair wife content? He could feel
the radiance of her even at this remove. He likewise marveled
that old Dionysii could move under the weight of his gold-
encrusted vestments. 'Metropolitan' his title might be, but he
was a prelate nonetheless and detestable like all his breed.
His heart rejoiced that no child begotten by him would be
christened with such mingle-mangle and mummery. What
end could be awaited from such a queer beginning? . . .

"Legarde, have you been paying attention? You should've
been taking notes all the while. Now go think catastrophe."

Ria stumbled getting out of her chair and knocked over a
pile of books. It took all her will power to keep from running.
How long had she been out? Had Clyde noticed? Would he
report her? It probably wouldn't occur to his chaotic mind.
But it was dangerous to make an ego like that feel slighted.
He'd forgive her only if she fulfilled her assignment well.

No more trances came that day, but at night the same
dream of fire awaited. Night after night it repeated, the
desperate climb to a goal that constantly retreated. She found
no way to break the dream's hold until it was ready to release
her.

Her face grew steadily paler. Her appetite faded. A permanent tension just short of pain settled below her cheekbones.
It grew worse in bad weather. Colors seemed to lose their
vividness, as though a filter lay before her eyes. Sparkles
danced in the air every time she changed position abruptly.
She could never quite get her breath.

Surely her co-workers would notice and act on what they
saw. She couldn't plead insomnia much longer. Fearing even
Carey's company, she refused his invitation to attend a concert of Australasian music. She was glad Professor Clyde's
order to inspect primary sources firsthand gave her an excuse
to absent herself from the office. By making a great show of

zeal for his project, she could avoid talking to the others while unavoidably present. At least no more trances attacked her during working hours.

By Saturday she was so desperate, she actually bought some cosmetics and experimented with ways to hide the ravages of stress. She was surprised at how much she liked the effect of makeup.

Ria managed to take a sound and dreamless nap Saturday afternoon. What would happen to the dream-cycle if she stayed up all night and slept during the daylight hours Sunday? She read and drank awesome quantities of tea to keep awake. She played music over earphones until her head ached. But by dawn, she felt herself losing the struggle. She fell asleep sitting up. . . .

The deck pitched wildly as another great wave smashed the ship. She nearly lost her footing on the icy mast ladder. Her body was as rimed with frozen spray as the metal rungs she clutched. There was more ice in the howling wind to sting her cheeks. The cold burned her lungs and froze her breath. Wetness seeped between mittens and cuffs and around the edge of her hood.

Step by treacherous step she climbed. She had to reach the crow's nest. She could see it through the sleet as a blur overhead. There was something she had to do there, if only she could remember what it was. The ship was depending on her. She was too exhausted to think. The heavy seas were churning her stomach sour. She was barely able to keep moving upwards. . . .

The force shoving Ria along finally released her for a stretch of dreamless sleep. It was Sunday afternoon by the time she awakened. This time she was more indignant than desperate. First scorched and now frozen, but seasickness was too much! She glanced about the apartment to make sure the furnishings were not tilted at crazy angles.

She was equally indignant with herself for failing to break the dream spell. If only she could marshal enough will power she could banish these symptoms—she almost called them visitations—permanently. Life had instilled Ria with an impenetrable stubbornness. She hardened under compulsion. But she had always been too busy repelling outside influences to be able to harness her will in any positive operation. Now passive resistance wasn't enough. She had to win back control of her own mind lest she be mastered by madness as her mother had been.

There was something exhilarating about anger. Righteous anger was healthy. The surge of adrenalin swept away her weariness. She needed that impetus to fight back. And she had to fight it by herself, not go crawling to PSI for help. If she put herself in their hands, the mind she'd get back might not be recognizable as her own.

The apartment could not hold her today. She dressed, ate, and was off into the crisp afternoon. The cold didn't bother her. It only made her cheeks tingle pleasantly. She wanted to be moving, to see how briskly she could walk. There were few pedestrians on the campus. No need to match her strides to those of slower folk. Down the broad sidewalks she sped, moving almost at a run, past the main quad, past the library, past Krannert. She turned away from the Assembly Hall and into the old Mount Hope Cemetery on Florida Avenue.

No need for speed here. She wandered about trying to read inscriptions on the weathered limestone markers. Bronze stars, now corroded green, marked the graves of Civil War veterans. No one had been buried here for decades but the University maintained it as an historic site. It was a favorite trysting spot for students in the warm months. Fortunately, no one else was around at the moment.

The long walk had tired her more than she realized. She looked about for a place to sit. There were no benches but the exposed roots of an old oak tree offered a dry seat. Most of the tree's branches had been lopped off after storm damage and the rest must surely follow soon. But she was grateful for the support of what survived.

Ria leaned back against the trunk. She took off her gloves to feel the ridgy bark. She tested its resilience with a fingernail. She contemplated the many subtle shades of gray it displayed and spied a tiny insect tunneling through the layers. She picked up a fallen leaf and rubbed it until only the lacy skeleton—the essence of the leaf—remained. She discarded it on the grass. Something glittered where it fell.

Ria flinched as if she'd seen a snake but refused to panic. Her new-found resolution wouldn't let her. Rather than ignore the object, she reached over and picked it up. It was nothing but a service button. Somebody had been rewarded with this trinket for faithful employment—seven years' worth by the seven stars that ringed the University monogram. Instinct urged her to throw it away but she wanted to test herself against the peril that lay in shining metal. She dared it to do its worst. It did. . . .

He swirled the urine flask and held it up to a candle for examination. Dark it was, malodorous and scanty. The humors were farther out of balance than yesterday, farther yesterday than the day before. He set the flask down to attend the patient. Only a feeble pulse beat in the bony wrist. Fever, not the normal heat of spring, spread an ominous flush across that sallow ancient face. The eyes flickered restlessly beneath their wrinkled lids. Was the crafty mind of the Doge busy with fresh webs of malice, even here on his deathbed?

Thanks be to Our Lady those eyes were closed. Never could he rid himself of the fancy that their blind gaze could penetrate his soul. Now, if he were still able, let Ser Dandalo attend to the state of his own soul. He would have much to answer for before the Judgment Seat of God: *"cui multum datum est, multum quaeretur ab eo."*

Were the priest delayed, the Doge would perish unshriven and unannointed, sending forth his spirit with all its stains intact. An evil thought, *absit, absit*. He would send for the priest as was his duty. The Council must be told and also the Marquis. The Crusade would set sail with one illustrious member the fewer. He motioned for a servant and drew the bedcurtains shut. . . .

The stuffy Venetian bedchamber vanished and Ria was back in the cemetery. Once again, the trance had lasted only a few moments—the bark had left no imprint on the back of her hand. The silver button still lay in her palm. She let it fall. So much for a show of bravado. Her teeth chattered as she walked home.

Nevertheless, Ria remained convinced that she was on the right path. These bizarre episodes must be fought and banished. She was certain that some way to control events existed, if only she could find it before she went mad.

She punched out requests on her home terminal for data on sleep phenomena. She studied alpha waves, REM sleep, circadian rhythmns, psychology and neurophysiology of dreams, even the effects of prolonged dream deprivation. She spent an anxious hour investigating whether dreams could be artifically induced. Was she the unwitting subject in some cruel experiment? PSI was powerful but surely not as omnipotent as people thought. If they could actually do such a thing, information on dream control wouldn't be so readily available, unless that was an especially devious cover. Lies within lies? Perhaps induction was possible after all.

But if not by PSI, then by whom? The mysterious old woman and her otter? Why had she spoken of teaching Ria new things? What was she supposed to learn from these dreams and trances—that she was crazy?

The only useful data she discovered were case histories of people who could stop and redirect their own dreams at will. The knowledge that such a thing could be done fired her resolve to try it herself. If she couldn't wake up, perhaps she could at least change the dream to something pleasanter. She fell asleep daring the sea-dream to come so she could alter it. . . .

It did but she didn't. The ladder was as cold and perilous as before.

Frustration made Ria angrier and in that anger lay a new reservoir of strength. A fury blazed through all her actions that week. As she flogged her weary mind and body to new exertions, the results were surprisingly productive. She designed a series of graphic displays to chart correspondences between tectonic and historical events. Enough were obvious to suggest that Clyde's thesis had some merit. How could such a blowhard be creative? Yet her resentment faded before the fascination of the material itself. She ran through a condensed course in earth science and conferred with geologists so that she could serve as liaison between them and Clyde.

Office squabbles receded in scale like events viewed from some great height. Ria felt a curious, almost mystical attraction for her subject. She longed to be at one with those titanic forces that moved continents, lifted mountains, spouted flame, and rent the rocks asunder while nations rose and fell with the fortunes of the land that bore them. She wanted her own share in those powers. A shred of prophecy came to her: "And in those days they will say to the mountains, 'Fall on us,' and to the hills, 'Cover us.' " But she would be above the crashing peaks, not under them. Someday she would transform the Ring of Fire into an arena of wonder.

The cautious part of her mind recoiled in abject horror from these fantasies. First paranoia, now megalomania. Surely it was time she surrendered herself to PSI. She had no right to try escaping treatment. Any day now she might go noncomp and slaughter her associates or wreck her workplace.

But her adventurous side, newly awakened after years of

stern repression, was not about to be stilled. Each night she did battle with her dream. Memories of the fire that burned at the Earth's core heated her body as she climbed the icy ladder. She kept trying to think herself back into her own warm bed without success. Yet the crow's nest came visibly closer.

Ria's glittering determination upset her coworkers even though they were ignorant of its cause. In the week following the librarians' trip to the Dream Center, Carey withdrew into himself to nurse some private humiliation. Hannah, on the other hand, was observed smiling languidly to herself when she knew others were watching, as though to suggest she'd been favored with some especially choice hallucinations. Ali treated Ria with an almost embarrassing solicitude. Ostensibly, she was trying to make her feel as normal as possible, but the results were just the opposite in practice. She glared whenever the word "dream" came up in any context. Ria's disability was not to be hinted at, much less discussed, so naturally it remained a matter of obsessive interest. Ria wondered if this wasn't Ali's real intention.

Ria suspicions were confirmed Saturday evening when she returned from a walk to find Ali waiting for her in the lobby. "What a nice coincidence, Ria. We haven't been getting together like we used to. I happened to be over here visiting my friend Linn from Cataloging and wondered if I'd run into you."

Ria doubted it was a chance encounter but pretended to accept Ali's explanation. "Perhaps we could have a cup of coffee in the snack bar. It isn't busy this time of night." She did not want to invite Ali upstairs, lest she have trouble getting rid of her, lest she see more than Ria cared to show her.

"The snack bar would be fine. I've been meaning to have a private talk with you outside of working hours."

The two women went in and got coffee from a vending machine. Ali also selected a cream-filled nutri-cake.

"Something nourishing to keep me going." She laughed too warmly. "I must tell you, Ria, I'm concerned. You haven't been quite yourself since the accident. Are you sure it left no permanent damage?"

"So the doctors said." Ria drank her scalding coffee.

"But you're looking downright ill. You didn't used to have such heavy dark circles under your eyes. Oh yes, I can tell they're still there, under the makeup. And you're not just tense, how can I put it? You're *fierce*. If you want a special leave of absence to really lick whatever's bothering you, I could make the necessary arrangements." Her first bite of cake exposed the creamy core.

"That won't be needed. I think I can solve the problem myself."

"Hospitals are full of people who thought they could take care of themselves, victims of that myth called self-reliance. There's no shame in getting a little counseling when it's needed. All of us need it from time to time." She finished the cake in quick neat bites.

"Are you offering me leave, or ordering me to take it?"

"Order? Who said anything about ordering you to do anything? I'm just giving you advice, as a responsible manager must."

"Has my work been unsatisfactory?"

"No, you seem to be accomplishing a great deal on Clyde's project. But you mustn't let him drive you too hard. That man has no sense of feasibility whatsoever."

"But if my performance is adequate, what's the complaint?"

"Frankly, you're upsetting the rest of us. Only yesterday little Hannah came to me on the very verge of tears because you'd snapped at her. Such a sweet child, I don't understand why you can't get along with her. And you seem to have set Carey off, too. He was a fine team player until he began hanging around you away from work—yes, we know all about that, don't we? Now he asks too many questions—or too few. Friction like that can't be allowed.''

"In other words, I might find myself looking for another job."

"Doctors do marvelous things these days, Ria, even about allergies. I knew you'd see things my way. Let me know which days you want off," she said, rising to leave.

Ria looked up with what she hoped was a docile expression. She remained seated until the other had gone. The coffee was now too cold for her to finish.

Ria stayed calm until she was safely back in her apartment. She chewed on her pillow to muffle the sound of her weeping. Threatening employment was the next thing to threatening one's life. Perhaps Ali was worried that a higher supervisor might drop by and be displeased with the atmosphere in their office—to Ali's discredit. Clearly, she was more interested in protecting herself than in seeing Ria helped.

If she were banished from the University, she'd be lucky to find work as a data processor in the local corn oil plant. She couldn't bear to part with the University. It was everything to her as it had been to her parents before her. This weekend was her last chance to regain control of her life. She had to stop the dreams.

She changed for bed and washed her face. Ali was right about one thing: there were hollows in her cheeks that hadn't been there before. Yet if she could get her color back to normal, the new contours would really be an improvement. What an uncharacteristically vain thought.

Inspiration struck just as she was getting into bed. If the dream could not be ended or changed, perhaps it could be finished. She lay down to commence the duel. . . .

\* \* \*

She pushed her gear and helmet before her up the passage. Her lamp showed red clay stains along the gray walls. They made a tidy scalloped pattern like waves on the limestone. Her jeans and shirts were slimy with mud. Her boots picked up more of it every time she dug in her toes. Her right pad had twisted around, leaving her knee to be gouged with every move. She kept crawling, pulling herself along at a jerky pace. It was sweaty work despite the underground chill. She tried to wipe her face on her forearms and only made it muddy. There was an itch at the back of her head that she couldn't reach.

The passage narrowed. The bedding planes' sharp edges raked her body. She thought for a moment she was going to get stuck. Her heart raced. She felt an extra surge of adrenalin boosting her progress. Her caving skills were equal to the challenge. She had chosen to explore. She knew where she was going.

A cool draft led her forward. She suddenly found herself heading down instead of up. A cavern must lie ahead. The draft blew stronger. She crawled faster, sensing the goal within reach. At last she slid out onto a mud bank, into the blinding light of torches held by unseen comrades.

# VII

Ria awoke about noon enveloped in langorous warmth. She snuggled back under the covers, trying to hold onto contentment as long as possible. The need for food finally drove her up but without yesterday's sick urgency.

This was no day for concentrates. Ria prepared lunch with slow precision, savoring her very hunger while she cooked. Putting cider instead of milk in the batter yielded uncommonly delicious apple pancakes. Or perhaps she had never really bothered to taste them before: sweetness, tartness, softness, crispness, blandness, spiciness resonating all together. Cinnamon was a marvel but apples were miracles. She picked up the one remaining fruit and caressed its glossy skin, red as any blood. The tree whence it came must have been planted before she was born, budded and blossomed long months past, set fruit and swelled without her notice. Its seeds could sprout into trees that would outlive her. Whence had she grown and what would she plant?

*Sartori* from an apple?

Ria laughed at herself. She buffed the apple and placed it atop her display screen.

She took a luxuriously long shower, enthralled by the caress of the water running over her skin. She could view herself in the mirror without cringing. There was something inherently fascinating about the human form. Why did her ego inhabit this particular kind of body rather than another? Why skin instead of feathers or scales or—her reverie was interrupted by her neighbor pounding on the door for admittance to the common bathroom. She swept up her gear and retreated to her own apartment.

She refused to feel guilty over this breach of House etiquette and concentrated instead on combing out her wet hair. Few people bothered with long hair any more but she was glad inertia had kept her from getting hers cut. Today she'd let it flow free like a mane instead of confining it to sensible braids.

Ria wanted to get drunk on beauty. She started with an old American vintage—Copeland. She dropped her tapes of *A Lincoln Portrait* and the ballet suites in the player. Then she opened a codex art book on C.C. Wang that Carey had brought to her attention. She contemplated the paintings without any conscious effort at understanding them. She did not even bother to distinguish mountains from clouds or water. She experienced the images only as ensembles of light and darkness. The whole universe seemed to lie before her in a single fuzzy drop of ink. The barrier between her and it was thinning. She could pierce it. She could see without seeing. Her essential self could emerge past the doorways of her eyes, could enter those hidden places on the other side of the painting—

The last tape had ended. There was no other sound in the room except her own soft breathing. Ria laid the book aside. The afternoon light was fading and with it, her euphoria. She was left with a mild, sweet ache of desire aroused and unfulfilled.

Later, as she finished her tea, Ria tried to set developments in perspective. A good night's sleep—novelty though it was these days—could not of itself have produced such joy. It could not explain her exuberant sense of accomplishment or confidence in achievements yet to come. If the doorway had been too small this time, why then she would enlarge it. It could not withstand her forever.

Seizing control of the cave dream had made all the difference: she had gone from patient to actor. Could she do the same with the historical trances? Could she induce one by choice? Light reflecting from shiny metal seemed to be the trigger. Since a spoon had worked once, it might again. Making note of the time, Ria lay down on her unmade bed and held the spoon before her eyes. Sunset rays gathered in the bowl like a burst of flame. . . .

The woman next to her plucked at her sari. She squeezed aside to give the other more room. A hundred or so people were gathered together this time in the chill dusk. Little tremors of expectancy flickered through the crowd. Soon Bapu would appear to lead them in evening prayers. Could they but raise sufficient truth-force, surely Hindus and Moslem must cease killing each other. Bapu alone held the key to the peace all—at least all here present—craved.

Ah, at last, there he was, hobbling along the pergola, a dear familiar wisp muffled in a white khadi shawl. His attempt at briskness was pathetic, for she knew his recent fast had left him weak. He had to lean for support on his two favorite walking sticks—his young kinswomen Manubehn and Abhabehn. People opened a path as they helped him up the garden stairs to address the crowd from the terrace. She rose with the rest in his honor. He returned their greeting with a humble *namaskar*.

All of a sudden, a man in European clothes lunged from the crowd. Manubehn raised her arm to bar his way. He shoved the girl aside but in stumbling, she dragged him down with her. After the gunshot came the screaming. Was Gandhiji hit? Men and women pushed forward trampling each other in their haste for a clearer view. She herself grabbed a faltering old woman and held her safely upright in the press. She saw that one man had thrown himself on the assassin. Then others dragged the unresisting fellow away lest the crowd rend him.

The Mahatma alone remained calm. He squatted on the grass and recited the *Ramanama* while the wounded girl bled to death in her weeping cousin's arms. . . .

Ria snapped back to consciousness. Her hands now lay crossed on her breast but still clutched the spoon. A glance at the clock showed that only 2 minutes and 35 seconds had elapsed during the trance. Yet events in that Indian garden had taken longer—fifteen minutes at least. Time seemed to run at a different pace within these imaginary worlds, just as legends said it should. A single night in the Hollow Hills equalled a century outside; an epoch passed on earth for every moment of eternity.

Clearly, her knowledge of myth was shaping these hallucinations as much as her knowledge of history. Realistic or fantastic, all were products of her own imagination and, as such, were suspectible to her control. If she cured herself, she could escape the notice of PSI. This very night she would take command of her own mind. Instead of waiting passively for whatever dream her subconscious might toss up, she'd design her own.

What should it be? Something as far from the cave as possible. She stood up and paced about the room thinking. Open air. Height. Man-made. Why not the new Lincoln Avenue Residence Hall? She stared at the skeletal building to memorize its structure, even to the tiny cone of the topping-out tree on its roof.

That done, Ria was determined to put the matter completely aside for the rest of the evening. She was now too hungry for further speculation and for once, dinner in the cafeteria did not seem such a daunting prospect.

The moon was her spotlight. She danced to the strains of half-heard music through bare unfinished rooms. She pattered down dusty spiral corridors and bounded up raw concrete stairs. She posed in arabesques at unglazed windows. Beyond one unwalled floor hung a steel girder that gleamed like polished bone in the moonlight. She lept upon it and ran its length. However slowly or swiftly she moved, the beam held steady: it was as if she possessed no weight at all. Untroubled by fear of falling, she could spin and balance at will for the sheer pleasure of feeling her gown swirl.

She gestured skyward and the crane silently hauled her perch aloft. Here was the roof, her proper stage, a shining platform so vast its edge defined the horizon. The music came clearer. She circled ever closer to the living tree at its center. She was leaping higher and higher at every turn. She could clear the tree if she chose. She could jump all the way to Polaris on a whim. Nothing was beyond her reach. Yet for now it was enough to dance and watch the evergreen grow.

At last she recognized the music. The hymn tune theme from *Appalachian Spring* swelled about her:

> *'Tis the gift to be simple, 'tis the gift to be free,*
> *'Tis the gift to come down where we ought to be,*

and the fir tree soared up to the stars. . . .

Her exaltation endured into the new work week. One especially welcome side effect was the confidence it gave Ria in dealing with Hannah. Monday afternoon Ria deliberately returned from lunch early to speak with her foe in private. (Hannah never ate lunch. She claimed to subsist on an occasional millet seed or bean sprout.) The petite blonde was sorting papers, performing even this simple task with ostentatious grace although no audience for her efforts was anticipated. Hannah did not crumple unwanted sheets. She folded them into rigidly tidy packets, running her thumbnail along to make each crease perfectly sharp.

"Back so soon, Ria?" she asked, not bothering to turn around. "I could tell it was you by your walk. Have you ever thought of dance lessons? They restructure your whole pattern of movement."

"I'm content to leave the dancing to you. Actually, that's what I want to talk to you about. I saw a notice for your group recital on the House calendar this morning. I'd like to buy a ticket."

"You would?" Hannah spun her chair around and stared up at her.

"Yes. Make that two tickets."

"Two?"

"One for me and one for Carey." Ria kept her tone carefully mild. She was satisfied merely to loom over her rival. How tiny the other woman was. She would be hard to notice on stage—just one small pale body among so many.

"I didn't think you cared for the dance."

"I'd rather watch old-fashioned ballet but I don't often get the chance since elitist art is in such disrepute."

"Quite properly so. All that unhealthy emphasis on soloists. Our modern choral dance on the other hand—"

"You don't have to sell me your style, just the tickets."

"I'll bring them tomorrow. You had no cause to snap at me." She swept her remaining papers into the wastebasket and slipped out from under Ria's gaze.

At that point Ali and Carey returned. They must have eaten together. Cary was scratching the rash on his neck again. He nodded at the other two women and retreated to his desk.

"I saw Professor Clyde on the way over, Ria," said Ali. "He's looking forward to your progress report Friday. How fares the project?"

"I think it's going well."

Not only was Ria's research progressing, she was actually enjoying it, even though she felt guilty about finding enjoyment in studying death and destruction. Human suffering appalled her even at a safe historical distance, but opportunities for patterning fascinated her. *Disasters and Destiny* ought to be a notable book—she regretted that she wouldn't be writing it herself. If she were lucky, perhaps Professor Clyde would acknowledge her contribution. Even so, satisfactory completion of the assignment would mean extra work points. One couldn't have too many of those.

She began investigating the role of human error in these natural catastrophes. How had folly and misjudgment made them worse? Pompeii should've had few casualties—Vesuvius gave ample warning—yet many residents had perished because they were unwilling to flee. Up until the last moment they kept hoping the deadly rain of ash would cease. On the other hand, the Minoans had evacuated Thera in time. There it was not the eruption that killed, but the flood, storm, and famine that followed. Ria wondered if memories of prudent flight had been much comfort to the victims.

Yet forethought did save lives. Modern building codes and emergency preparedness demonstrably lessened damage. Before the Federation had imposed uniform safety regulations worldwide, fatalists had rebuilt on the ashes of their forebears and died when their turn came. The wise and the foolish made their choices and reaped the results.

What sickened Ria were cases of choice denied. California cities used to conceal the location of fault lines lest fear inhibit growth. Politicians deliberately concealed the volcanic threat to Ste. Pierre because they wanted their supporters home to vote on election day. They'd burned along with Pelée's other 30,000 victims.

Perhaps it was best not to emphasize the role of politicians. A man in Clyde's position had to be politically sensitive. He wouldn't want anything controversial in his book lest he offend the powers that made grants and assigned privileges. But if the data were there, readers might draw their own conclusions and start wondering if the Pacific coast was as secure as the authorities claimed.

Matters continued in this positive direction for the next three days. Ria discovered that she could move Hannah about the office like a chess pawn on a board simply by standing over her or by invading her personal space too closely. The game was so easy, it soon bored her. Ria knew it was unwise to back an enemy into a corner, but her newfound confidence was making her a bit reckless. She walked taller and straighter now that she no longer cringed. When Ali remarked on her brighter mood, Ria let her imagine it was the result of counseling. The spell held until Thursday night's dream. . . .

The captain and the pilot had chosen to bicker in English, their only common language. He could make out enough of it himself to follow their arguments—and to wish he could not. They had been at it ever since the pilot had boarded off Ponta Munduba. To begin with, the Old Man had no sympathy for Latinos. Said they all had a *manãna* complex. (That should be an *amanhã* complex in the case of Senhora Pilot, no?) He didn't care much for women either.

Now they were arguing about the speed of approach. Everybody on the bridge could feel the tension. The captain was complaining that they'd miss their target time. He kept pointing to the digital clock. Did she have any notion of what it cost to transport liquefied gas. They were burning money by the minute. (Not to mention the captain's bonus.) Perhaps the esteemed *Capitan* would prefer to burn cargo? She explained that bay traffic was snarled by a recent wreck. The *Kyushu Maru* would have to wait its turn.

The captain fretted. He refused to sit in either of his chairs

but kept pacing the width of the bridge. The first officer had
sailed with him long enough to be used to his moods. He tried
to ignore the situation and stood ready at the pilot's side to
relay her orders when they came. But the rabbity *alemán* at
the helm looked as if he'd rather be anywhere else at the
moment. That pale thin body was visibly quivering. For his
own part, he was glad to be tucked safely behind the lines
with nothing more taxing to do than keep the log.

Vessel Traffic finally gave them the signal and they headed
up towards Santos. The pilot was conscientious, you had to
give her that. She watched the windows as well as the
displays. But she gave so many course corrections that he had
trouble keeping up with her. The captain's running commentary
was not helping anybody's concentration, especially
when he pounced on an ambiguous order. He made her
clarify that she meant "to 20°" and not "220°." This puffed
his ego at the expense of breaking her cadence. The
helmsman's face was turning gray.

No sooner had they gotten that squared away than the
collision warning sounded. Radar blips showed an oncoming
freighter veering out of her channel to cut around the wrong
side of the buoys marking the wreck. They blew the five
blasts at her. What was that cowboy trying to do? Pass them
starboard to starboard? Getting entirely too close. They ought
to be turning by now. Why weren't they turning? The captain
was shouting. Then he noticed. *O Jesús Maria!* The
helmsman was frozen in place! The pilot whirled to confront
him, repeating her order with horrible clarity. The first officer
heeded and wrenched the wheel free.

They went hard starboard.

With his own hands, the captain pulled the hapless seaman
out of the way and flung him in a corner. He stood at the
windows, his hands balled into fists against the glass, in
silence that was worse than any cursing. The freighter
skimmed by them at the last moment. The gap between the

two craft was so narrow they could read the name *Nelson Beak* on her bow. She was barely starting to swing back into her own channel. . . .

Ria awoke with uncontrollable shudders. The bad dreams had returned. She had only won a skirmish, not the war. This time she recognized the event she'd dreamed. It wasn't much of a feat. Almost any adult now living could recite the bald facts.

In 1985 the liquefied natural gas carrier *Kyushu Maru* had collided with vessel or vessels unknown outside the industrial city of Santos in what was then Brazil. The cloud of escaping fuel had enveloped the harbor and exploded, thereby detonating the huge gas storage facilities ashore which in turn obliterated tank farms, refineries, petrochemical plants, an air base, and every human being within a 15-kilometer radius. The world had never been the same since. The Holocaust had triggered anti-tech riots all over the globe. The Collapse followed. After a decade of depression, famine, and war, the Federation had emerged to impose a new order, an order that still reigned.

The causes of the Santos Holocaust had been investigated for 30 years without firm conclusions. Even the *Kyushu Maru's* role was only an assumption, although a highly probable one since it had been the only LNGC present at the time. The identity of the other craft involved was unknown. Until now. Ria wasn't even going to check on the fate of the freighter *Nelson Beak*. She was already unshakably certain she'd seen what really happened: a belligerent captain, a nervous pilot, and a catatonic sailor had brought down civilization.

The knowledge was more than she could bear. She huddled in a tight fetal ball. But the nightmare had to be true. The only alternative was to admit madness.

# VIII

For a long time, Ria lay huddled in bed, all her senses smothered by panic. When she revived, there was a taste of blood in her mouth. She rolled over numbly to look at the clock—somehow she hadn't heard the alarm buzz—and discovered she was already late for work. She jerked up and scrambled out of bed. Luckily Carey answered her hasty call to the office. He accepted her excuse of illness more readily than the women would've done. She made him promise to stay away until she announced she was better. Then she rescheduled her appointment with Professor Clyde and made herself a huge breakfast.

Food had its usual tranquilizing effect. She could at least start confronting her problems again. Watching the Santos Holocaust begin had been too devastating. No one should—insight struck so fast she knocked over her teacup. She didn't bother to blot the spill off her robe.

The disaster had *not* happened!

The two ships had passed safely in her dream—no collision, no million deaths. That was the single common factor in all her dreams of the past. Each showed a disaster averted: no Time of Troubles for Russia, no Fourth Crusade in Constantinople, no peacemaker slain, no city leveled. She'd been too entangled in the historical details to grasp the recurring theme. Were these dreams then mere wish-fulfillment impulses, yearnings for what might have been? But how could her subconscious generate output without input? She kept seeing things in her dreams she had never known. Besides, no delusions could possibly be that schematic. The four dreams of disaster averted dovetailed too precisely with the earlier trio of waiting dreams to be spontaneous.

Ria scribbled summaries of the dreams on paper. She attacked each as if it were a myth text. Applying structuralist methods, she extracted recurring motifs—fire, water, travel, ascent, birth, death, peril, victory. She reduced events to the simplest scenario—expectation, crisis, salvation. The patterns were so pronounced, they suggested a code. But who could send her such messages? Nothing in her dream research indicated that specific dreams could be induced. If PSI could beam images into her head wherever she was, day and night, then PSI could do anything. She might as well slash her wrists right now and have done with it.

Never! It might give her mother's ghost too much satisfaction.

Yet Ria could not escape the suspicion of being the subject of someone's experiment. She almost felt as if someone were cheering her on through the maze with joyful cries too faint to hear. "Joy" was not a word one associated with PSI. Neither was "cheer." Then who was conducting the experiment? The mysterious old woman and her giant otter were the only candidates left. Could phantoms design the illusions they appeared in?

Nevertheless, her glimpse of them had been every bit as realistic as her other historical dreams. Talking otters did not exist and had never existed but could she prove they would never exist in the future? Allow one impossibility and an army of others would rush through the gap. Ria was amazed at her own calmness. The neatness of her logic outweighed its sheer insanity. So beings possessed of vast and arcane psychic powers were tampering with her mind for some inscrutable transcendent purpose—ah, psychosis were paradise enow'.

Enough of the gallows humor. The beings in her dream—what were their names? Kara and Lute?—had seemed entirely earnest. They claimed they were going to teach her something but what earthly use was the power to dream on cue? Did it perhaps have some *un*earthly use? She'd spun all the theories she could on her own. The only way to get any more answers was to question her self-appointed instructors themselves.

Any form of communication had to work in both directions. If they were able to send messages, then they ought to be able to receive them equally well. Ria disdained to enunciate her request. Let the others read it directly from her mind. Let them show her another instance of a disaster averted, only this time let the example be drawn from her own research files—something involved with a volcano or an earthquake. Make that specifically a volcano. Are you listening, Kara and Lute?

Ria flopped on the unmade bed, folded her arms, and waited for results. Nothing happened. She had forgotten to trip the trigger. She needed the flash of a shining surface to begin a waking dream. She rose, grabbed a dirty teaspoon, and polished it on the sleeve of her robe. No sooner had she resettled herself on the bed than the bowl of the spoon dissolved into dark choppy waves. . . .

He could scarcely see the crescent of beach through the constant rain of ash. The pretty town beyond with its tile roofs and banana trees was completely hidden. Stifling dust had been falling for days. It lay in heaps on the *Roraima*'s unswept decks. It sifted into the fabric of his uniform and clung to his sweaty skin. He wiped his face once again in silence, too dispirited to curse. His collar itched abominably. His nose and lungs alike protested the sulfurous reek in the air. The filthy sky was empty of sea birds. What he would give to hear the white gulls crying again!

A babble of French drew his attention back to his duty. Another longboat crammed with excitable refugees was coming alongside. Not all of them would be spry enough to manage the jacob's ladder. He must see that the crew got them safely bestowed by other means.

Blue lightning flickered in the clouds above Pelée. . . .

Ria wavered back to consciousness to discover her phone ringing. She half-expected to hear Kara's voice on the line but it was only Ali, calling during her lunch hour to check on Ria's illness.

"It took you so long to answer, I was getting worried," said Ali.

"Sorry. I just got back into the apartment. I'd been out of it for a moment. You mustn't make so much out of a simple case of indigestion."

"Carey gave us the impression it was something more—he tried so hard to make it seem trivial. Now Ria, it's my nature to be fussy—and my duty as well. With what all's happened to you lately, I had to find out for myself how you were doing."

"A little bit better than when I first woke up. Please don't worry about me." Ria attempted to sound meek and grateful.

"Now if this continues, you will go over to Health Service?"

"It won't come to that really. I'm sure I'll be back at my desk by Monday." She could stall that long at least before an examination became mandatory.

"No chance we'll see you at the Library Halloween party

tomorrow night?'' Ali was in no hurry to release her. "I hate to see you miss all that fun.''

"You can have my share of the treats, Ali. Thanks for calling.''

She hung up before the other could prolong the conversation further. She'd forgotten about the departmental party but judged it fun well missed. She'd be under even more scrutiny there than at House festivities. These days she felt safer out from under the shadow of Ali's wings.

Ria munched an apple while rewinding her thoughts. Her order for a volcano dream had been filled briskly enough. She and her obliging instructors must have read the same sources. She recognized the scene as an evacuation of Ste. Pierre before the eruption of Mount Pelée on May 8, 1902. The disaster they called "The Day the World Ended" wasn't going to happen there. Wherever *there* was.

But what of the fantasy dreams, the ones that had nothing to do with history? What was she supposed to learn from those grotesque ordeals—climbing techniques? That was the sole recurring element she could identify in her struggles with the rope, the mast, the cave, and even the lovely interlude on the rooftop. If Kara and Lute wanted to cause distress, surely a nightmare about walking down Neil Street stark naked would've served as well. She recalled that as one of her commonest nightmares during her years at University High.

Whatever their purpose, let them give her something of her own chosing to climb now. How good were they at improvisation? Ria closed her eyes and pulled a book off the nearest shelf at random. Luckily, *Myths of Ancient America* was illustrated. She pitched her apple in the direction of the sink and riffled through the book. The pyramid of Queztalcoatl at Teotihuacán would do as well as anything for the experiment. She fixed the image in her mind and slammed the book closed with a crack. As she lay down she cried, "Once more into the spoon, dear friends. . . .''

The steps were treacherously narrow and steep. They were never intended for feet as large as hers. She could easily catch her heel on a clipped edge or a cracked tread. No proper balustrade either. It was such a long way down if she stumbled.

Why was she here? Would the view from the top be worth it? The calves of her legs were beginning to quiver already. She brushed vainly at gnats. The sun was making her dizzy. It hadn't seemed so hot when she started. She should have waited for a cooler day.

The feathered serpent heads beside the stairs shimmered in the heat. They were melting before her eyes, gaping jaws softening into blunt muzzles, scales flowing into fur. The whole pyramid was stretching and flexing like a living thing. The pitch of the steps rose ever steeper. She was crawling up them now on all fours, tearing fingernails as she clawed for purchase, yet the gap between her and the summit only widened. A broad bewiskered head as big as a temple appeared on the platform above. The stairway was no longer stone but rippling hide. She lost her grip and skidded down into darkness. . . .

Ria awoke more indignant than disappointed. The pyramid had shrugged her off as easily as a huge beast ridding itself of an insect. Was that all she was to them, a human fly who could be forced to scale impossible obstacles? Psychic sadists—that's what they were! But she'd get her freedom yet, no matter how many climbs it took.

She hurled her spoon down with such force, it bounced off the bed. Her apartment was too cramped to pace in properly. All her long strides accomplished was the bruising of her shin on the sofa bed's edge. When she bent down to rub the scrape she collided with the table and nearly knocked the flimsy thing over. Oh, to be someplace where she could safely scream!

Ria stomped to the window and pounded her fists on the sill. An autumn storm had blown up. Rain beat against the glass, mocking her fury. Wind shook the water-blinded panes. She heard faint sirens above the howling but could see nothing of the world outside. How small a thing her anger was. She pressed her forehead against the chill glass. She willed the coolness of it into her mind and tried to breathe in rhythm with the pelting rain. She poured herself into the water that ranged so free. The windowsill she leaned against felt like the rim of a chariot. She drove the pale horses of the storm before her: Rain and Sleet, Fog and Snow were the names of her steeds. Down they sped from high heaven, wheels that rolled thunder and hooves that flashed lightning. They galloped across an empty prairie that knew no bounds.

The rain slackened; her anger ebbed. She could again see traffic moving on the street below. They flowed hypnotically past, all those busses, trucks, and bikes. They traced bright tracks as the wet pavement reflected their lights. Raingear made pedestrians comfortably anonymous. Crowds were safe so long as everyone kept themselves shrouded. But she was alone, trapped in her cell by a fictitious illness and secret stubbornness. No one could rescue her except herself.

Tea and toast calmed her shivers and cleared her mind to attack the mystery once more. Determination, not defiance, would prevail. Perhaps she had been too arrogant in her choice of battlefield. Her mentors—tormentors, rather—wouldn't allow her to complete the climb in a hostile mood. So the pyramid had mischievously turned into a colossal animal. Not just any creature but an otter. A *smiling* otter. They were said to be a playful species—if the naturalists only knew. She wished the being called Lute would find himself some other sport.

Couldn't they permit her some other activity for a change besides climbing? What was so special about that? She remembered that in myth ascension was a well-nigh universal metaphor for spiritual progress—one had to struggle upward toward the Light. But a generalization that broad was little help. For specifics, she must tap data banks. Ria punched out a preliminary search program on ascent symbolism in world mythology, keyworded with motifs from all her dreams. She didn't allow herself to read the printouts until she had cleaned up the dishes.

This done, she hefted the paper, fanned it through her fingers, and pretended to estimate the amount of computer credit this research had cost. She read the hard copy with skittish glances, afraid to linger too long on any one line. She tried hard not to see the emerging pattern but truth trapped her before she finished. She'd known the answer from childhood without recognizing it, known it ever since she first rode a dream-horse with eight wooden legs.

Ria sat motionless for a long time. Desk and wall blurred out to her unblinking stare, like backgrounds viewed through a wide-open lens. There was no place left to hide from self-knowledge.

She sighed her assent and entered orders for the appropriate reference books. At least one of them was by Eliade, a familiar authority to guide her explorations. She needed all the briefing she could absorb before attempting more dream journeys. Tomorrow was soon enough to try again—assuming she'd be allowed to rest tonight. By now she was too numb to be anything but humble in her plea for a respite.

The morning found her no eagerer for confrontation. Unexpectedly, her schedule provided an excuse for delay: she was due to pick up her grocery order. This morning she groomed herself for this routine public appearance with almost ritualistic care. There was a cautious touch of self-assertion in the new way she twisted her hair and tinted her skin. If she could face a throng of housemates now, perhaps she could face those other two persons later.

The lines at the loading dock moved with their usual slowness. But instead of trying to shut out her tedious surroundings, Ria forced herself to observe the people around her as distinct individuals. The wearing of uniforms off duty didn't automatically make anyone a cipher, much less an enemy. Uniqueness persisted, could she but see it. She tried tabulating the body language displayed by the buyers—even the typical resigned slump had multiple variations. She waited as she did in stolid silence, others chatted non-stop flaunting their sociability. The voices of two women behind her stood out in the general buzz.

"So when the results were posted yesterday, Barby, I wasn't all that surprised. I always win at the first New Orleans meet."

"Nan, I know your luck holds at the Gulf tracks and practically everywhere else but the horses you tell me to bet on always run in slow motion."

"Some of us have that certain instinct. Don't look so glum, I'll buy you a drink out of my winnings. On my quota yet."

"Your quota?" She laughed. "You always know how to get round me." There were small nuzzling sounds. "I'll return the favor if my lottery ticket comes up. When I think of all the slop work I did around the House to earn that particular scrap of paper. . . ."

"But look at the payoff. Credit alone won't get you past the door of a restricted shop."

"That's what keeps me at it year after year. I want that admission card and the chance to dress like a department head."

"How exactly do they dress on their own time?"

"Come to think of it, I'm not sure. But I want to find out. This time it's going to work. Mind you, I didn't grab the first ticket I saw. I picked the number by this special formula, very scientific. First you take your birthdate. . . ."

At that point Ria reached the counter and missed the details of Barby's scheme. By the time she'd taken delivery of all her supplies, she'd stood in line three more times and was bloated with other people's intimacies. She wondered again if cooperative buying was really more efficient than private shopping. It didn't matter so long as its ideological basis was sound.

On her final haul she had the satisfaction of saving the pumpkin an old man had dropped on the stairs. She blocked it with her legs before it could roll all the way down and smash. The owner's gratitude almost compensated for her bruises. She regretted not ordering a pumpkin for herself—a cheerful jack o'lantern would brighten the apartment tonight.

Ria stowed all the food immediately instead of leaving it scattered about the kitchenette as she often did. She also washed the dishes promptly after lunch. Instinctively, she felt that her quarters ought to be in perfect order before she attempted further experiments. Cleanliness was the outward sign of inner discipline. However, there was a delay in achieving that state. Cleaning equipment was in heavy demand today so she had to wait her turn at the ultrasweeper.

Afterwards, while straightening stacks of tapes on the shelf over her window, she witnessed a street accident. An Illibus rammed a slow-moving delivery van with so much force, it hurled it into a tree. The van driver crawled out of her airbags and beat at the sealed door of the bus. Ria could imagine what language punctuated her futile blows. Security Officers arrived and subdued her before she could reach the other driver. They'd call it another noncomp incident in their files.

The damaged vehicle was soon removed. Ria had to admit that she'd run out of ways to waste time. She meant to reach the old woman and the otter today. She'd keep at it until she hammered down the barrier or her mind shattered.

Brave intentions were one thing, but what of the mechanics? Should she try to rig up some sort of costume? She decided she was most typically herself clad in the University's livery. But she ought to comb her hair again. And she wanted a more dignified instrument for inducing the trance than a teaspoon. She rummaged in the bathroom cabinet until she found a small steel travel mirror her grandmother had given her. She'd never had occasion to use it before. Lastly, she needed a focal image. What was the noblest thing she could mentally climb? Only a mountain would do. Make that "mountains"—the Mountains of the Mind.

Ria lay down on her belly this time with the mirror cupped in her hands. She flashed afternoon sunbeams in her eyes and fixed her gaze on *Strange Peaks Above the Clouds*. She was blinding herself to see more perfectly. A water shimmer glistened in the air between her and the door. . . .

She had left the gray village behind. The road sloped gently at first, then lost itself in a barren maze of folds and fissures. She could not have retraced her steps if she had tried. She chose the path that seemed straightest but it only led her along the mountain's flank to the edge of a wide crevasse. The sole route past the gap was slashed by clefts she had to leap. The crumbling stone trembled beneath her weight. Every step sent more fragments tumbling noisily into the depths. Once across, a series of meandering switchbacks brought her to the top.

From the summit she could gaze past a river of mist to the higher range beyond. Much as she dreaded the climb ahead, she had to reach those peaks or perish. Mist was too thin a barrier to bar her. It had no more substance than fear. A road she could not see would take her past the boundary. Blinded, drenched, and chilled, she trudged along the hidden way.

On the other side, all cracks ran upward. She followed one to the foot of the weathered battlements ringing the highest peak. The storms of years had beaten like surf against this citadel of stone. Its eroded walls rough as bark offered natural footholds for her hands and feet. She climbed through thinning air that seared her lungs with cold. At this height the wind blew without pause or pity.

SANDRA MIESEL

Layer by layer it scoured away her clothes, her skin, her very flesh. She was a snow-white skeleton toiling across a white mantle of eternal snow. Where the covering had blown away, ridges of pure crystal glittered and set rainbows dancing on the frozen waste. The final slope was as gentle as the first. At last she reached the ultimate pinnacle, a spur upraised against an inky sky.

There stood Kara and Lute awaiting her.

# IX

Kara and Lute were leaning over the bed. Ria was back under the same blue and white coverlet, animating the same young male body as on the earlier visit.

"How dare you smile!" she screamed. "After what you've done to me!" She tore back the covers and struggled to rise, but her borrowed limbs would not respond. Each movement sent pins and needles of pain stabbing through her. With a massive effort she managed to pull her torso nearly upright. Lute's furry arms barred further progress. She tried to squirm away from his touch. "Let go of me!"

"Rest easy, dear lady, rest easy now," he begged. He gently lifted her under the arms while Kara slipped pillows behind her back. Neither seemed disturbed by Ria's anger. Why should they be? She was scarcely a threatening figure, pinned against the headboard and wearing only a nightshirt hiked over grubby knees. She clawed at the sheet in short, jerky strokes.

"When you decide to sit still, child, Lute will release you," said the old woman.

"Do I have a choice?" Ria glared at her.

"We cannot allow you to move freely until you learn to control Julo's body."

"If you fall, Ria, he gets left with the bruises." Lute pulled the covers up to her waist, withdrew, and fetched a chair for Kara. Then he sat on his haunches beside the head of the bed. Ria sullenly counted the leaves woven into the coverlet rather than face his huge happy eyes. This wasn't the confrontation she'd planned.

"Ria, I'm so glad you're back, my whiskers are tingling." The otter's speech trailed off into pleasant burbles and the bells on his harness jingled softly.

"Your achievement stands," said Kara matter-of-factly, "whether you take joy in it or not."

"What was I supposed to enjoy? The electrocution? The seizures? The endless nightmare? You must excuse my lack of gratitude."

"Were all your dreams nightmares?"

"Of course?" Ria turned to snap at her white clad adversary. The old woman sat patient as stone. "No, not quite. Dancing on the rooftop was glorious. I wanted that dream to last forever." Her voice had fallen to a whisper.

"For every ending, a beginning. The seed dies so that the tree can grow. But for the moment your ears are closed to what we are saying."

"I'd prefer to hear some answers for a change." Ria's tone had sharpened again.

"Ask your question. Go on, ask us anything." Lute bobbed up and down making his bells jangle again. Kara stilled him with a tap of her staff.

"You're shamans, both of you."

Kara bowed and touched her broad bosom: "*Solexa*," she said. She pointed to Lute: "*Solexam*." He kissed the tips of his stubby fingers at Ria.

"I finally figured it out last night. My mind's a little slow—it had to be battered to the breaking point before it reacted. I should've guessed you were shamans right away, just from your gear."

"You mean Kara looks like some wisewoman's picture you've seen?"

"No, she looks like all of them." Ria took a deep breath before continuing. "Can't you get enough recruits wherever you are? Why the hell are you two trying to make a shaman out of *me?*" She slammed her palm awkwardly on the bed.

"But Ria," protested the otter, "you agreed to take instruction in *solarti*. We forced nothing on you against your will."

"I didn't realize what I was getting into." Kara's silence rebuked her excuse. "You promised to teach me marvelous things. You promised to show me the way over the mountains in my Dream."

"We are keeping our word. A journey can only be made one step at a time. You must climb ropes before mountain ranges. You did not ask the cost of the knowledge we offered," Kara said.

"It hurts too much to learn your lore."

"How else could you win it except through pain?" Kara's shrug expressed her opinion of Ria's pain threshold. "Would you argue with the hard-won wisdom of a hundred centuries?"

"Of six centuries among the *perfur?* More persons of fur have the soul-art than persons of skin." Lute was anxious to publicize the talents of his race.

"Neither we nor anyone else can teach you how to shamanize by rote," said the old woman. "We can only place you in circumstances that allow you to discover the core of the art for yourself."

"So you threw me in the water to make me learn to swim."

"To you, the initiation seemed a long and terrible ordeal, yet in fact it was among the shortest I have witnessed in my long years of practicing *solarti*.''

"Listen and believe, Ria,'' said Lute, stretching out every word for emphasis. "From sea to sea runs the fame of Kara ni Prizing. No greater *solexa* has been born into our age than she.''

"If you're so important, then why are you bothering with a nobody like me?'' Ria began to cry.

Lute started to reach out to her but Kara waved him back.

"You are the one least qualified to judge yourself. Your talent called to us out of a time not ours. We could not leave that call unanswered.''

"If you had a young one with a gift for making music, would you cultivate it or let it wither?'' said Lute. "Had my share of *gouar* lessons, I did.''

"Altruism always sounds fine in principle. What do you get out of this?''

"I get the one thing life has thus far denied me—a true daughter of my spirit.''

Ria's face twisted in revulsion. She covered it with her hands.

"Dear lady, we know why you're crying. You mustn't be afraid of us. Hands down, please, and look at me.''

Ria wiped her blubbery cheeks as best she could and turned towards the otter. Calm spread over her mind like a cool mist. She blotted her tears on a corner of the sheet, then realized she was now using the borrowed limbs as if they were her own.

Kara continued: "I had no child of the flesh. My niece who now counsels the Chamba in my stead is a good enough worker in her way but not the heiress I longed for. No apprentice—no *human* apprentice—'' she smiled at Lute, "has grown as tall as I would have wished.''

"And you think that I—oh no! I work with books and bytes of data. I can't talk with animals or summon spirits or sense weather or handle fire like a shaman is supposed to.''

"Can't you?" Lute snuffled merrily and shook his bells. Kara could barely suppress her laughter.

"What's so funny?"

"You." The otter gasped between snorts. "You don't seem to know yourself as well as we do."

"What Lute means," said Kara, "is that you seem determined not to recognize your own uniqueness. Consider but one example on your list of *solarti* powers—mastery of fire. You survived an electric shock unburned. Both heat and cold affect you less than other people. The fire you kindled with your mind in your tenth year drew us to you like a beacon. Ah yes, we know you were responsible for that incident. Deny your powers as much as you please but they are inborn, even as ours are."

"Once we had discovered you, we could not bear to lose you. Lute tracked you back to your beginnings and implanted that Dream of riding over the mountains. You had already taught yourself how to enter trances while astride the rocking horse. He merely placed the proper scenery before you on your flights."

"Imagery came right out of your own memory, it did. The art's all in the arrangement. Not such a bad job, eh? Dream wore like hardwood over the years, didn't it?"

"Lute is asking you to compliment his handiwork, Ria. He is proud—perhaps too proud—of his skill as a dream-shaper. It would not occur to him to wait until you had grasped the aesthetic canons governing that art. Now with your gracious leave, my dear *perfur,* I shall continue."

Lute pretended to ignore Kara's criticism. He sat meekly stroking his chin whiskers. It was Ria's turn to smile.

Kara went on. "Lute rekindled that Dream of mountains within you throughout your youth—we had to keep you glowing with desire for the heights. But once you were a woman grown, stronger measures were needed to drive you upward."

"For the present, I'll take it on faith that what you did to me was necessary. I can accept you as the source of those weird climbing dreams. I can even understand the symbolism behind them. But how could you make me experience unfamiliar episodes from history, episodes that in fact never occurred? How could you alter events in the past that happened before you knew I existed?"

"In theory, all leaves on the Cosmic Tree are equally accessible at any moment. There are limits in practice. About fifteen hundred years backwards or forwards in time is all we can attain."

"Is all any known *solex* has reached." Lute interrupted Kara. "Kara says I'm too proud but she's too modest. She's the first one who put some theory under the ancient soul-art, proposed that the places we reach are real but located in times branched off from ours." He pantomimed the growth of a tree.

"True, the notion was mine but mathematicians are the only folk who can write the equations describing those parallel worlds. It is the territory that holds my interest, not the map."

"Mathematicians?"

"Our university here in Chamba has several fine ones. Did you take us for barbarians?"

"More to civilization than plastic furniture, Ria." Lute's fur bristled.

"Do not judge in haste, my child. The University at Chamba is one of the finest in the Republic."

"I meant no offense." Ria swallowed hard. "But none of what you're saying makes much sense. Do you expect me to believe in the possibility of mental time travel?"

"Possibility? All those soul-flights and you still can't believe? What does it take to convince a human?" Lute snorted in puzzlement.

"I'm trying as hard as I can. While things are happening, they seem plausible enough. Afterwards doubt always creeps back on sly little paws. I can't escape my fear of madness."

"Debate is useless," said Kara. "You must seek the truth within yourself. Once you learn to trust your own experiences, then we can assist you to perfect your performance."

"Help's yours for the asking, Ria. Remember that."

"You're still talking in riddles. What is this soul-flight business?" Ria was alarmed at her own shrillness.

"Exactly what the name says—travel in the spirit." Lute was more puzzled than ever. His regard for human intelligence was plainly shrinking by the moment.

Kara turned toward him. "She is not comfortable with the word 'soul.' People in her world have forgotten that they have them." Then she asked Ria: "Would you prefer 'essence'? 'Persona'? Or the standing wave that is the sum of all one's living functions? However defined, this inmost self is what we who have the talent can project into the minds of other persons, wherever they may be."

Ria recited in a halting voice: "The medieval schoolmen said, 'An angel is where he works.' "

"Quite right!" said Lute.

Kara continued. "Angels are not the only ones to fly unseen. Once inside a host, we can tap memory and use senses without being observed."

"Then what's my body doing while the 'essential I' as you call it is here?"

"Running like clockwork. You'll return to it in a few moments of your own time. Eventually, you'll flash in and out in an eyeblink."

Rita shuddered. "It sounds like possession—a better pastime for devils than angels. If there were such a thing as demonic possession, of course."

"Devils indeed!" Lute sprang to his feet jingling in outrage. "Are you a devil? You're occupying Julo's body, seeing through his eyes, speaking with his mouth. And in what language, eh?"

Ria gabbled briefly in English. Lute had made her uncomfortably aware of using the boy's memory. She could not talk and think of how she was talking at the same time. "Sure of it you are I hurt him not?" she croaked.

"He enjoys being a host, says it's the soundest sleep he ever gets. We're not making him do anything we haven't done ourselves many times over—receiving and exchanging souls is part of *solarti,* too."

Kara motioned him to be seated again. "Julo is a special case. His persona slumbers while another is in residence. He is proud of his talent. It is the only gift he has—his waking mind is simple."

"He was kicked in the head by a horse," said Lute, tapping his own skull. "But he has enough wits left to be useful around the house."

"That he recovered and is able to work is also a testimony to *solarti.* I was a visitor at his parents' farm at the time of the mishap. I numbed the pain, controlled clotting, and reduced edema until he could be gotten to a physician. Lute still treats his bad headaches."

"You've lost me again." Ria had her syntax under control again. "What does soul-flight as you've described it have to do with medicine? Shamanic healing was all suggestion and sleight-of-hand."

"But those suggestions sometimes cured, although the old shamans didn't know the real reason why," said Lute.

"Think, Ria. Surely you know that pain, fear, grief, madness, and so forth have a chemical basis and that disposition affects recovery. With access to a host's nervous system, a *solex* can alter brain chemistry and stimulate individual cells at choice to foster a cure. When the subject is well known to the *solex,* this can be accomplished without soul-flight, as when Lute calmed you a few moments ago."

"We're asked for healing of minds and bodies more often than any other type of *solarti.*" Lute preened at the usefulness of his gift. "Taking away hurt, giving peace, those are the soul arts I love best," he said with unexpected earnestness.

"I've read that shamans can deliberately induce or stop seizures in themselves. Are you saying this is some kind of telekinesis on the molecular scale?"

"Down to the electronic scale," replied Kara. "Mastery of fire is achieved by similar means. Do not look so startled. I may well have a sounder understanding of the electron than you."

"Kara, I think she's getting tired." They were in fact rapidly overloading her capacity to absorb new revelations. "We don't have to explain everything at once."

"Very well. We will dismiss you in a moment." Her seamed old face turned solemn. She waved her staff like a teacher's pointer. "One more test awaits you before the fullness of the art can be yours. We will summon you again this night. You must go where you are sent. Stay there no matter what happens. And eat well before you retire—*sofli* requires tremendous energy. If you had a God, I would suggest you pray, but since you have none—"

"We'll do the praying for you."

Ria turned from one to the other. She fought the quaver in her voice. "I came here screaming for revenge but I might as well have tried to throw rocks at the sea: you've absorbed all the force of my rage. I will try to do whatever you ask." She wept quietly.

Lute dashed up, rummaged in a bureau drawer, and brought her a cloth handkerchief. "I keep asking you not to cry, my lady," he said, bending over her. "Will you do that for me?" Ria blew her nose. She noticed that his fur smelled like summer.

"You are using Julo's arms well enough," said Kara, smiling again. "Try the legs also. Carefully slide them around and sit on the edge of the bed."

Ria obeyed. Kara gripped her right shoulder and Lute her

left to steady her. She took a last look around the sunny bedroom. The forsythia branches still bloomed in their vase as before. . . .

She had consented and so it was done unto her. . . .

Early morning sun glittered on the water. He stared at it transfixed: he wanted the brightness to hurt but he had to yield to reflex in the end. A dark after-image hung before him like a tiny cloud as he stared fitfully around the hospital garden. There was still dew on the grass. A giant spider web outlined in silvery drops spread across one camellia tree. Patients sat in wheelchairs or walked along the brick pathways, renewing their strength from the freshness of spring. He could hear them laughing and chatting with staff members, some of whom he recognized. These people would recover. He did not want to look at them.

He focussed on the lily pond before him instead. Red-gold carp lurked under the pads, fanning their delicate fins ever so slightly. The haughty creatures would dash to the surface quickly enough at the first sign of bread crumbs. He used to enjoy feeding them every day after lunch. He had no food for them today. He hated them for being at home in the water. Carp were ageless; Vicky was only twenty-seven. His jaw muscles knotted. How could the Lord be so unfair, to let fish live and Vicky. . . .

A little black haired girl dashed up to the pond. "Fissie!" she squealed. The fish scattered in panic as her chubby hands splashed in the water. He grabbed the back of her pinafore just as she was about to leap in. He swooped her up in his arms and sought her mother. The woman had been too deep in conversation with an elderly gentleman to notice the child's absence.

"Hold onto her tighter, ma'am. It only takes a moment to drown." His voice strangled on the last word. He was gone before she could thank him.

He checked his timepiece. He could delay no longer. The issue would have to be faced. He stalked through the doors and down familiar hospital corridors, now grown alien overnight. He waited for an elevator to take him to Intensive Care.

Dot Schiele arrived from the opposite direction. He blanched at the sight of her. She was as tall and darkly regal as Vicky—people kept mistaking them for one another. There was a time he used to confuse them himself.

"I heard when I came on duty, Paul." She gripped his hand tightly. "Of all the goddamned luck. I couldn't feel worse if Vicky were my own sister."

"I know they've done everything humanly possible. I'm trying to hang on to that last thought. Hard."

"The kids?"

"With my parents."

"If you feel like talking about it, Jay Dub and I could stop by this evening. That's only if you want company, *cher*."

"Would appreciate it. Y'all give me a call first." His throat was tightening up again. The elevator door opened. Dot nudged him gently toward it.

"As I explained over the phone this morning, all the tracings have stayed flat another twenty-four hours. Lord knows I wish the news were better, Paul." Jake Russ had never learned professional detachment. He still died a little with every patient—and this was one of the Royal's own. His fleshy face sagged. Tiny broken capillaries flamed on his cheeks. Who should be consoling whom? Jake continued, "Doctors Guidry and Paine examined her this morning. I've got their opinions here for your inspection."

He forced himself to read the prognoses carefully. "So they concur that it's brain death?"

Jake nodded.

"I can face the term, Jake." Clinical language was a safe way to think the unthinkable. "I'm not going to crumple up and stick you with another case."

"I didn't expect you would."

"Where are the papers for me to sign?" He managed a bitter smile. "Handy that I already know the routine. You won't even have to decipher the organ donor forms for me."

"You're taking it well, man." Jake's eyes asked if he weren't perhaps taking it too well. "Sometimes hospital people are the hardest to handle at times like this. Do you want to see Vicky one more time?"

"Yes."

They walked around to the critical bay.

"Any change in Mrs. Tomasino's condition?"

"None, Doctor." The nurse stepped back.

The wan figure lay entangled in tubes and sensors that proclaimed its lack of function and response. He'd never thought to see his own hardware put to such use. Matted hair tumbled across the pillow. Vicky would never've let herself appear in public looking like that. There was nothing to be gained by postponing the inevitable. He signed a Cross on the body's forehead and walked out.

He couldn't remember how he got home afterwards. He found himself sitting at his own kitchen table drinking a small black. The coffee had no taste. He ought to pick up the phone and call Mama. No, let Petey and Marianna play a while yet in peace. Not that you could explain anything to children that young. That was the worst of it—they'd grow up without knowing their mother. They'd put flowers on her grave every All Saints' Day and forget her the rest of the year. Nothing he could do would keep her alive for them very long. But now there were the funeral arrangements to think of. Let Mama take charge of those. She would whether he liked it or not.

For the moment, he didn't want to talk to anyone, however dear, not while doctors were cutting Vicky to pieces. How easy and noble to donate her organs, easy to think of her doing good after her death, easy to speak of her living on as part of other people's bodies. Oh God! Then why was it so hard to accept when it happened?

They'd have been prepping the operating room before he left the hospital. Calls would be going out to gather prospective recipients—he nearly said "customers." This triggered the grisly image of doctors walking up and down Prytania Street hawking baskets of fresh organs, like the old-time vendors in the Quarter.

He put his head down on his arms and cried.

When he had no tears left to shed, he resolved to work the horror through, step by step—catharsis by flow chart. He forced his mind to picture procedures he'd witnessed many times. First divert the blood through the heart-lung machine. Lead it cautiously through yards of tubing, dictate respiration. Open the abdominal cavity to expose the dark liver and pink kidneys. Snip, snip, hoist on slings, perfuse, and chill. Watch their healthy color fade. Saw the breastbone, take the lungs, spleen, and heart—take particular care with that glossy heart. Less need for haste now. Strip the blood vessels, pluck the glands, harvest the corneas. Tidiness counts far more than speed. Don't overlook the bones. Spongy, red cancellous bone is always in demand, root it out. Last, but scarcely least, peel off the skin. Try for long, continuous strips—they make the neatest rolls for storage.

In time they'd find a use for everything but the squeal.

A thunder of velvet paws and a familiar stench roused him from his morbid reverie. The cat's scratch pan needed cleaning. Life, in all its grubby details continued on schedule without Vicky. He took care of the back porch chore and tried to coax Minet out of hiding. She stubbornly remained under the bed.

No use trying to take a nap, wrung out though he was. He knew he couldn't sleep. Vicky's scent was still on those sheets. When he washed them, he would lose one more bit of her presence. And what of her clothes? They'd fit Dot Schiele but she'd never accept such gifts. He'd have to call the St. Vincent de Paul Society to take them away. Rather than sit home and brood, he should do his daily stint of running. If he ran himself into the ground, he might be able to rest.

He changed clothes and opened the armoire to hang up his suit. As he swung the door out, the contents of the otterskin pouch suspended inside clinked sharply. It was a medicine bag Vicky's Red Indian grandmother had left her. He'd never peeked inside nor ever intended to. Although he had no idea of what it was for, he'd keep it for Marianna when she grew up.

It was a cruelly perfect day for running. The mild, rain-washed air was heavy with fragrance. The Garden District lived up to its name most fully in this season when azalea vied with magnolia, wisteria with honeysuckle. But he saw the flowers of spring only as pastel blurs as he sped along. The St. Charles Avenue route was so familiar, instinct sufficed to keep him on course down the middle of the old street car tracks. He concentrated solely on the act of running. Grief receded. His world shrank to a road bounded by steel: he was a breathing machine that pumped its arms and legs in strict mechanical rhythm mile after mile.

A flash of golden lettering caught his eye barely in time. He darted aside from a truck emblazoned Centre Builders, Ltd. A bit more absorption in his stride and the vehicle's wheels would've put a period to his sorrow. He crushed that cowardly thought before it took root and proceeded with grudging alertness to Audubon Park.

He followed his daily path along a well-worn public track. Its clay surface was still moist, spotted here and there by patches of slippery leaves blown down by the storm. It wound around the lagoon where swan boats and swans glided across calm water. He paused to rest under the moss-draped branches of his favorite live oak. He could hear faint music from the direction of the merry-go-round where he used to ride the "flying horses" years ago. A raffish blackbird challenged his right to stand under its tree. He whistled back. It flew off straight into the midday sun. . . .

Ria fought to break free of the blinding brightness but could find no way out. Then she sensed other presences restraining, then guiding her through the haze of light.

She was in a white tiled room that reeked of chemicals. Before her lay a woman's naked corpse stretched out on a slab. With sinewy black hands, she wrapped the flayed and sutured form. Then she bound up the jaw of the body that had once been her own.

# X

The arms of Kara and Lute still clasped her host body. Ria had returned to the same moment she had left hours earlier. Lute greeted her with an ear-shattering whoop and hugged her so hard thay both tumbled back onto Julo's bed.

"You passed! Dear lady Ria, you passed the last test!"

Ria thrashed feebly in the creature's embrace. He must be as mad as a human noncomp.

"A rowdy *perfur* will soon have my permission to celebrate out of doors." Kara's smile belied the tone of her rebuke. "Help our new colleague up so she can savor her triumph."

Lute complied with chittering streaks of apology that did little to soothe Ria. The old woman was standing now, her shaman's staff raised in salute.

"We are so very proud of you, child." She kissed Ria's forehead and then settled into her chair.

"Please tell me what I did," asked Ria in a small voice.

"I already told you," said Lute. "You just entered our ranks."

"He means that your initiation is completed. You are now a true *solexa*."

"All because I saw my own corpse?" Ria shuddered. "I was the woman who died in that dream."

"No," said Lute, "you will be that woman seven years from now on another branch of time."

"But that event is long past from our vantage point," said Kara. "Victoria Legarde Tomasino died April 4, 2022 in the Royal Hospital at New Orleans."

Curiosity distracted Ria from horror. "What's a 'Royal' Hospital doing in New Orleans?"

Lute snorted. "Being a great medical center, what else? No American Revolution on that time line. Most of our continent stayed British."

"There is a smaller hospital on the same site in your world. It is called Touro Infirmary."

"Back to my original question. Why did you force me to watch my alternate self die?"

"Your readings on *solarti* offer no clue?"

Ria's brows creased. She strained to remember the relevant details from Eliade's book. "My dream was equivalent to the death and dismemberment visions novice shamans must undergo before they obtain their powers."

"Quite right," said Lute. "Long and hard I searched for the right incident—had to sort out that one tragic case from all the others I could find."

"Then it wasn't a prediction of how I'm going to die?"

"'Course not!" Lute was getting impatient again with her slow human mind.

"You still fear that your life is no longer your own."

Ria nodded.

"Does a twig lose its identity because other similar twigs grow on the same branch? You are yourself and none other no matter what happens in another part of the Cosmic Tree. We have refrained from looking into your future to preserve freedom of action for all of us."

Ria relaxed a little. Success hadn't been inevitable. They'd been willing to take a chance on her. "But something more was involved besides death and transformation. Lute, why did you call it a test?"

"Can't you tell when you're being tempted?" He rubbed his chin whiskers in dismay.

"Review your feelings during the experience, Ria. How did you feel when you recognized Vicky as another self?" Kara was wholly mentor now.

"I wanted more than anything to make her live again. Her husband loved her so much, needed her so much. I felt a closer bond with him than with any other host. To watch him grieve was agony, and to be powerless to help him. . . ."

"Empathy carries a price. Go on."

"Seeing her in that hospial bed, I wondered if I could jump from his body to hers, stage a miraculous recovery, and live happily ever after. I thought I could reanimate Vicky's body the same way I'd operated Julo's."

"What stopped you, since you believed her life to be more favored and useful than your own?"

"Believed? I could see it was better all around than mine. She had everything I lack: people loved her. But because Vicky's life had been so wonderful, I could not bear to steal it."

"Does this not constitute a moral test?"

Ria was so embarrassed, she covered her face. "It didn't necessarily prove my virtue. Maybe I was just too timid to cheat."

"Ria, Ria, when will you learn to think well of yourself? You only want to accept unpleasant truths." Kara shook her head. "Perhaps you assume that truth is always unpleasant. In the long run, the right thing will prove to be the best thing. Here, the wrong choice carried its own punishment. If you had tried to take over Vicky's body, you would have trapped yourself in flesh you could not control. At best you could have attained a state of permanent coma, thereby prolonging the sorrows of her loved ones.''

"It wouldn't have been like this?" Ria flexed her borrowed arm.

"Julo's alive," said Lute. "Even damaged, there's still lots of unused capacity in his brain. Vicky really was dead by the time you saw her—the machines merely gave her the semblence of life. With her brain gone, you'd've had nothing to work with. You could've entered Vicky's cat with better results.''

"So you see, frightful stories about old shamans killing youngsters to usurp their bodies are only fables.''

"Could they swap souls instead to get a younger or better body?" Ria asked cautiously.

"Do you think yourself at hazard, child? After so many years of struggle, I begin to long for the eternal rest. I can pass the Door without regret now that I have seen you made a *solexa*.''

"I didn't mean to suggest. . . ." Ria stammered. "Aren't shamans ever dishonest?''

"One who used *solarti* as you describe would misuse it in other ways as well. He would be detected and destroyed. It happened sometimes in days past—an evil *solex* would have to be purged from the community of the art. But I have never heard of a body-stealing in my lifetime. It would appear that our testing does screen out unfit candidates.''

"You succeeded, dear lady. Accept it." Lute kissed her fingers.

"We may be asking you to climb too fast. Let us have some tea before proceeding further. Lute, find her a wrap and slippers.'' Kara left the room.

Lute retrieved a pair of wooly boots from under the bed. He searched a cabinet but was unable to find Julo's robe and muffled Ria in the coverlet instead. He offered her his arm for support. She stood up and took one cautious step. The conscious effort grew less with each attempt.

Lute led her through the bedroom door into a skylighted forest of potted trees and flowering plants. Vines growing in boxes near the glass ceiling fell in green torrents down the walls. The mingled scents of blossoms, leaves, and damp earth brought spring within four walls. She paused to sniff a bowl of hyacinths but Lute steered her across the ceramic tile floor to the kitchen.

Ria glanced about shyly, torn between curiosity and fear of rudeness. It was the largest private kitchen she had ever seen. Here, surrounded by pots and pans and shiny yellow woodwork, Kara seemed less formidable. She had taken off her shaman's costume and wore a simple linen blouse over her skirt. She had put a kettle on the fire—an actual fire, Ria noted, presumably gas. She was now slicing dark bread.

"Why do you hesitate? Look around." She laughed and swept the air with her arm. "Our world holds more than Julo's bedroom."

The whole wall opposite the atrium door was glassed with small bubbly panes. A miniature greenhouse jutted outward from the right side. Lute showed her flats of seedlings within. A few tiny leaves already peeped through the soil.

"When they're ready, Julo'll plant them out back, next to my pond." There was a strongly proprietary ring to "pond."

Ria looked where he was pointing. His pond fifty meters distant adjoined a grove of huge fan-shaped trees that were coming into leaf.

"What species is that?" asked Ria. "I thought I recognized all the common trees."

"They're elms."

"You have elms?" Ria yelped in amazement.

"Shouldn't we?"

"They've been extinct where I come from for half a century."

The notion of a land without elms plainly alarmed Lute. "What happened to them?"

"Disease. Could I go look at them up close some other

visit?'' Ria cocked her head from side to side trying to get the best view through the wavy glass.

''It would please me no end, my lady, to introduce you to these noble trees which happen to be my own totem. My *harnama,* the full name I took from my coming-of-age dream is Lives Under The Elm.''

''Lute has always been impressed by that coincidence, as if elms did not grow everywhere.''

''Sometimes, Kara, you're too hard-headed.''

''One of us had to be.''

Lute continued to mutter about the shortcomings of human dreamers while setting the table but Kara ignored him. Ria judged it to be an old argument. Kara motioned her to be seated, poured the tea, and pulled up her own chair. Lute removed a plate of peeled hardboiled eggs from the cold box. He was about to toss an egg up to catch in midair, reconsidered, and sheepishly put the plate on the table. He sat down on a padded stool and curled his tail about his legs.

''How many dozen so far this week?'' asked Kara.

''I haven't kept count,'' he replied between bites and reached for another egg.

''Behold the great weakness of the *perfur.* They are mad for a food their farms cannot produce—chickens and chittering do not mix.''

''Flighty birds drop dead at the least little noise.'' He consoled himself with yet another egg.

Ria stifled her giggles lest she choke while drinking. It was an herbal tea, pale and pungent, with a taste she couldn't identify. She tried only a bit of the bread, delicious though it was, because her host body wasn't hungry. She was amazed at how easily she was accepting the fantastic situation. She might have been talking to giant otters all her life. Now warmed by the tea and even more by friendship, she dared to ask, ''What year is this?''

''By your reckoning,'' Kara paused for a mental calculation, ''this is 2691.''

Ria drew a sharp breath, then forced herself to let it out slowly. "When did your world split off from mine?"

Kara replied: "The first break came when your world went to war in 1914, the year Western civilization cut its collective throat. But our branch—like all branches—had begun budding decades earlier, when the English queen Victoria abdicated in favor of her son. As a result, the nations of Europe wove different webs of allegiance in our past than in yours."

Lute interrupted her. "Nothing's sudden as it seems. Every moment grows out of those that went before. Every instant decisions 're made one way or another." He waved his hands in opposite directions. "Mostly they cancel each other out and the bud's reabsorbed into the original branch. But," he brought his hands together, "let enough of them line up in the same direction—affect enough lives—and there's a new branch on the Great Tree."

"I almost understand."

"Give you a simpler example: you know that the Santos Holocaust of 1985 made your world what it is."

"You forced me to witness the nexus point."

"Ah, but the world you saw where the ships didn't collide was already budding away from your own. For one thing, they were tapping petroleum out of the North Sea in the 1970s, something your people are just starting to do. Getting so I know your era's history better than my own." He shuffled happily. "But any learning's fun."

"You are wandering off the path, Lute."

He meekly contemplated his teacup. Leaf fragments floating within it seemed to require his utmost concentration.

"As I began to explain, Ria, our branch was spared the horrors of global war. Additional scores of millions lived out their allotted spans in the twentieth century. Their minds and hands created works your world never knew. Progress came swifter. When nations joined together, it was by peaceful choice. With the mastery of genetics and the conquest of space, mankind's ancient dreams of abundance seemed fulfilled. In those days, they shaped the stuff of life at will. They explored and built homes for themselves beyond Earth's boundaries.'' Her voice grew wistful. ''Our telescopes can still find their colonies in orbit—dry husks left after the whirlwind.''

''What happened?'' asked Ria.

''Their world was green and fair as any Eden—and equally lost to us through pride and malice. Flushed with success designing microorganisms, the engineers of genetics turned their attention to larger creatures. Law and custom barred them from tampering with human genes except to mend gross defects. They yearned to create useful new species of animals as the supreme exercise of their skill. Some even argued that humans had a duty to compensate for the animals they had exterminated. And so, with every good intention, they bred macro-rats—the hated macrats that trouble us to this day.''

''How large is 'macro'?'' Visions of elephantine rodents trampled through Ria's mind.

''Macrats're big as large dogs.'' Lute measured the air for emphasis. ''But it's their brains, not their size that makes them so dangerous. They're bright as apes—or so the ancient records claim—we've no apes left for comparison.''

''Are these ugly things around here?'' Ria shivered. A shadow had crossed the window. Perhaps Kara and Lute's world wasn't the cozy refuge it seemed.

''Chamba is considered secure, due in large measure to the watchful zeal of our *perfur* friends.''

Lute preened graciously. ''Even so, meet a pack of macrats in the wild or in a ruined city and you'll most likely stay for dinner—as the main course.''

''They eat people?'' cried Ria.

''And ever *prefur* when they can get them. Which is seldom.''

''Like natural rats, their food is anything you can find,'' said Kara.

''No peril here, dear Ria, nothing we can't handle.'' He

patted her shoulder. "But just think, without the macrats as trial, my people might not have come into existence." He could find a positive interpretation to anything.

Kara explained: "The *perfur* or macotters were the next step, a choice suggested by the needs of sea-farmers. A radically improved otter was the goal, not merely an enlarged one. They blended and adapted traits from many species: the size of the Amazonian otter, conformation of the Asian otter, clawless hands of the Cape otter—"

Lute wiggled his opposable thumb.

"This patchwork heritage shows in their breeding habits and social instincts."

"Hybrid vigor, yes, yes."

Lute jumped up and spun around ringing his bells as if inviting Ria to admire his graceful form. For the first time she realized he wasn't simply a giant otter. His cranium was higher and his legs were better adapted to walking upright.

"With the emphasis on vigor." Kara motioned him back to his seat. "The scientists wrought better than they knew. They brought forth an entirely new creature with a mind fully the equal of man's own—the fairy tales of talking beasts had at last come true. This discovery ripped the human sense of self to shreds. Only the arrival of beings from some other star would have caused more frenzy. Some viewed the macotters as rivals to man."

"They feared we might take their lordship over the earth away since we can speak your language, use your tools, walk your land." Lute covered his eyes to hide his sadness.

"The worst fools hailed the macotters as pure, unblemished beings who would show mankind the way to perfection."

"As if we couldn't sin, too." Lute clenched his jaws.

"Treated you like the Ultimate Noble Savages?" Ria was anxious to show sympathy.

"And consider what became of the continent's original Noble Savages." Kara nodded back at Ria. "It would have come to that, had not a group of conspirators decided to hand over the world to the new persons of fur.''

"They hated themselves because they weren't us.''

"They designed a lethal virus that was so slow to start killing, every human being on Earth—and off it as well—had been infected before the first symptoms of the deadly fever appeared. It was the Great Death.'' The lines on Kara's weathered face deepened as she spoke. "One in a thousand survived.''

"But a scientist on the macotter project got the colony into safe hiding before she died.'' He kissed his fingers, "To the memory of She Who Bled.''

Kara continued: "Once the Death passed, the macotters flourished. Soon hundreds of them were living along the now-empty shores of Chesapeake Bay. Then a man who had been a student of exotic cultures encountered them and joined his destiny to theirs. They shaped him as much as he shaped them, so much so, that he is commonly known only by his *perfur* name, Never Smiles. Although he had none of the talent himself, this scholar recognized the first stirrings of *solarti* in *perfur* and human survivors alike. He saw in it the seed of a new civilization.''

"Our great comrade, our brother-in-skin made the compact between our two peoples that endures to this day.'' Lute stretched out his hands to grasp Kara's and Ria's.

"May it be so forever.'' Kara sighed. "Much has been lost but much has been regained and we have climbed a few new mountains of our own—have we not, my children?'' She smiled at Lute and then at Ria as if she were in truth their mother.

Ria discovered her borrowed body could blush. To mask her embarrassment, she asked another question. "If that plague is your nexus point, then there must be other timelines—maybe a whole clump of them by now—where it never occurred. Do shamans explore there? Do they know what's happened on those branches since the Death?''

"No one really cares to know. I myself glanced briefly in that direction when I was young and proud. I would never chose to return. Nor would any of my fellows. Cherubim with flaming swords could not guard those branches half so well as our own regret for wonders lost. I have sufficient faults without adding despair."

"My world's hardly one you'd envy." Ria grimaced.

Lute shook his head. "There're worse ones, dear lady, wait till you've seen more branches before you judge. Point is to make yours the best it can be."

"Each thing in its season. Your talent is a flower newly opened. You have much to learn before it can bear fruit. Come to us like this each night for more instruction."

"But how can I find the way to the right moment every time?" Ria was beginning to grasp the magnitude of what lay before her.

"We can't tell you in words—you've got to confront the Great Tree for yourself. Afterwards, you'll no more lose your way than a bird could forget how to fly."

"Bear in mind, Ria, that what you will behold is merely a symbol, a symbol cut to the scale of mortal minds."

Ria nodded. " 'Humankind cannot bear very much reality.' "

"Neither can *perfur*," said Lute, serious again.

"However, we strive to bear as much of it as we can." Kara rose and led them back into the atrium. On her previous passage, Ria had failed to notice a circle of huge cushions lying on rya rugs in the center of the room. These surrounded a small, floor-level fish pond and were in turn surrounded by tall potted plants. Kara's shaman costume lay on one cushion. She donned it and sat down, motioning Lute and Ria to take places beside her. Sensing Ria's worry before she could voice it, she took a silver ring from her own finger and slipped it on her pupil's. Then she raised her shamanic emblems skyward and intoned:

"By sunlight, starlight, firelight, reflections of the Light

113

Eternal, forward we fare together.''

Kara struck her drum with her staff. The leather disk gave a sharp, dry crack like snapping wood. She beat a brisk, unvarying rhythm. Ria's heart pounded in synchrony. She breathed in steady counted measures. Hearing was all. Her other senses guttered out like spent candles. Sound became substance, silence void. Between them, they defined creation.

A sudden jangling overrode the drumbeat. Ria's eyes refocussed on Lute. He was running his hands over his harness, ringing brash cascades of bells. He glided up from his cushion and danced to the shifting tempos of his own music. His body flowed through rippling arcs along the narrow margin of the pond. His tail brushed against Ria's bare leg as he passed. He dipped so close to her, she could smell an exciting new muskiness on his fur. She longed to shed her wrap and rise to partner him. Instead, she watched his shadow flicker across sunlit water. Brightness and darkness meshed with sound and silence. She flashed Kara's ring before her eyes bespelled by the liquid sheen of the silver. . . .

She could see neither herself nor the others, yet the presences of Kara and Lute enfolded her as if with shining wings.

Furrowed ridges of exposed root loomed before her like gray mountains. She could have easily lost herself among the peaks and canyons of the bark but the party kept moving upwards in a rising clockwise gyre. They circled the mighty trunk, seeking its smoother, higher reaches where curving branches defined a globular crown. They sped through networks of ever finer branches out to the terminal twigs.

On each stem grew seven oval leaves arrayed pairwise with a singleton poised like a lance point on the tip. Some leaves were pale translucent green; others shaded off to bronze, magenta, wine, and gold. Frizzy clusters of reddish flowers sprouted next to winged brown seeds. Bare twigs bore blunt dark buds and leaf scars notched like crescent moons. Supple fresh twigs and rotten ones sprang from a common branch. Where whole limbs had broken off, new bark swelled to seal the wounds. Budding, leafing, blooming, fading, the Eternal Now held every season. They spun the cycle closed.

> *To turn, turn will be our delight,*
> *'Till by turning, turning we come round right.*

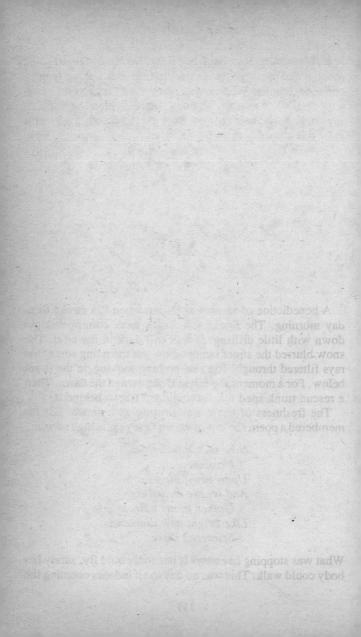

# XI

A benediction of snow was falling when Ria awoke Sunday morning. The thick, soft flakes were coming straight down with little drifting. It was still dark in the west. The snow blurred the street lamps' glow yet the rising sun's first rays filtered through. Ria saw nothing moving on the street below. For a moment she felt as if she owned the dawn. Then a rescue trunk sped by, leaving deep tracks behind it.

The freshness of snow was fleeting as a dream. Ria remembered a poem she'd written her first year in high school:

> *Now that I am grown,*
> *I cannot walk*
> *Upon new-fallen snow*
> *And let the snowflakes*
> *Gather in my hair*
> *Like bright new diamonds*
> *Scattered there. . . .*

What was stopping her now? If her soul could fly, surely her body could walk. This was no day to sit indoors counting the hours until she could return to Kara and Lute. She ought to celebrate her victory out where trees grew.

After breakfast she phoned Carey and invited him to venture forth with her before the snowy wonder faded. Groggily, he agreed.

As she dressed in her warm lined pants for the first time of the season, she was startled at how loosely they hung. She'd lost more weight during her ordeal than she'd realized. Shamanizing must burn calories at a prodigious rate. However, she did not foresee it becoming a government-approved weight control technique.

The snow was half a meter deep by the time Ria and Carey got out of the House. Footing was treacherous on the unplowed walks. Ria lent the small man her arm lest he flounder.

"I could always pick you up and carry you," she offered.

"Don't you dare!" He straightened up and slogged forward with new determination. "I was crazy to come along. You were crazy—" he stopped short, abashed at his tactlessness.

Ria laughed. "On the contrary. I'm perfectly sure I'm sane. Don't you recognize healthy joy when you see it?"

"So how often does one see it?"

"All too seldom. But happiness has to be shared. You're the only person I can share mine with." She squeezed his arm so vigorously she nearly knocked him off balance.

"I'm flattered—I think. A less muscular expression next time, perhaps? We'll never make it to Crystal Lake Park, Ria. Wouldn't Carle Park do as well? It's a lot closer."

"But so much smaller. Where's your trailblazing spirit? Look, Green Street's been plowed. If we walk along the curb the going'll be easier. Security is much too busy at the moment to bother ticketing us."

Carey saved his breath for walking until they reached their destination. When Ria led him under snow-decked trees, he compared their white branches to Venetian lace. This launched a highly pedantic lecture on the evolution of European lacemaking, delivered with much handwaving. Nevertheless, Carey had neither energy nor enthusiasm for romping. He refused to join Ria in making snow angels beside Boneyard Creek.

"Carey, I don't think you ever learned how to play."

"What do you mean? I always got passing marks in my playgroup."

"Did you now?" Ria stood up and dusted snow off her clothes. "I couldn't say the same myself. Were you a model of cooperation like those children over there?"

She pointed to a nearby band of preschoolers. Their counselors had lined them up to throw snowballs at a target. None hit it because each was muffled so tightly against the cold. One child who'd been building a snow castle alone was marched back to the group.

Ria clapped with exaggerated vigor. "Glory to sociability!" she cried loudly enough for the counselors to hear. There was no danger of them recognizing sarcasm.

"Carey, your nose looks alarmingly red. Mine probably is, too."

"No, not really."

"Well, I'm feeling chilled inside. Let's go look for something to eat along Main Street."

They left the park at a faster pace than they had entered it.

Ria was comfortably weary by the end of the day, glad to be tired from exertion instead of anxiety. She prepared for bed, then lay down holding her grandmother's steel mirror. It became a radiant pool she could stir with her own hand. . . .

It was night when she awakened in Julo's bedroom. Kara and Lute stood waiting as before but this time neither wore shamanic costume. They welcomed Ria with kisses.

"How do you feel now, child?" asked the old woman.

"Amazingly good," answered Ria.

"That's as should be," said Lute. He snuffled quietly.

"I expected the sight of the Cosmic Tree to leave me delirious with ecstasy. Instead, I'm calmly merry. Now I know who I am, even if I don't know where I'm going yet."

"That will come in its own good time," said Kara. "Your joy in *solarti* gladdens us. More training will deepen your joy."

"To the kitchen for your next lesson," said Lute.

Ria got up from the bed in one fluid movement. She stared disapprovingly at her nightshirt-clad body.

"One small favor, please."

"Anything, m'lady."

"Could you possibly have Julo fully dressed next time I'm due to occupy his body?"

"We can ask him," said Lute. "His hosting stints're usually scheduled for times when he's asleep."

"Thanks. I feel silly wearing these nightclothes." She smoothed the hem of the gown.

"My people don't have to worry. We're always correctly dressed in our sleek fur." He ran his fingers over his gleaming pelt.

"Enough," said Kara. "Come along. Lute, turn out the lights."

Ria found she could walk easily this time without assistance but she slowed her pace to keep in step with Kara. When they reached the kitchen, Kara said to her:

"On your previous visits, we had to bundle you carefully for warmth. But by now you should be able to control the temperature of your borrowed body."

"I'm comfortable, if that's what you're asking."

"Control of inner fire goes beyond mere comfort. Sit down, child, and roll up your sleeves."

Ria obeyed. Lute brought an enameled bowl filled with crushed ice and water out of the cold box. He dipped a linen towel in the water, wrang it out, and wrapped it about Ria's right arm.

"That's freezing! Take it off!" She jerked away from Lute.

"Warm your flesh, *solexa*." Kara's eyes were blue flames.

"Do *what*?"

"Your supposed to dry the cloth with body heat, Ria," Lute explained. "Feel your way. Concentrate. Burn those calories quicker."

Ria fought the cold, drawing energy from sources she couldn't identify. She sensed vibrations quivering at a faster rate; felt mutual attractions broken and reformed.

The towel was no longer wet.

"That'd save me money at the laundry," said Ria with a nervous chuckle.

Lute snorted. "Time was, naked shamans got wrapped in dripping sheets and put outdoors in the winter wind. Or they were plunged into frozen lakes. They mastered inner fire in one galloping hurry."

"Our ways are gentler today," said Kara. "This simple exercise required you to alter metabolic reactions in a specific area. Feel your arm."

It was feverishly hot to Ria's touch.

"Now do the same with the left arm," the old woman commanded.

Although the towel was wetter this time, Ria dried it even more quickly.

"Both arms at once."

Lute produced a second towel and the experiment was repeated.

"What's next? Self-combustion? This lady's not for burning."

"You can heat more'n your body," said Lute. He poured most of the water out in the sink, then folded the dry towels into a pad and set it under the bowl.

"Bring it to a boil." He tapped the container's rim.

"How?"

"Apply the same technique you used on your flesh," said Kara patiently. "Energize the molecules of water to raise their temperature. If we did not know you had the capacity, we would not expect you to perform the deed."

Ria struggled with the task. At least she knew what the structure of $H_2O$ looked like, even though her description of 'flapping hydrogen wings' had pained her primary school science teacher. She was sweating with effort by the time the first tiny bubbles appeared in the water. Lute invited her to confirm its hotness. She held her hand above the steaming surface, then abruptly plunged her fingertips in. The hot water did not scald her. As she'd correctly reasoned, the same power that warmed her flesh could also cool it.

"So this is why I've never been badly burned," she cried.

"You have been using your gift instinctively all your life, child. Now you can do so with full understanding." Kara glowed at her pupil's progress.

"Some tea while you're thinking that over?" asked Lute.

"As long as I don't have to boil the kettle myself."

"'Course not, Ria. We don't use *solarti* for everyday things. We'd wear ourselves out."

After tea had been served and the dishes cleared, Lute set a small brazier on the table. It held bits of crumpled paper.

"I suppose you want me to set that on fire," said Ria.

The macotter nodded. "You can do it. Treat the tinder the way you did that dry grass when you were little."

Memories flowed back to Ria—stifling rooms with locked windows, sun-rotted curtains gray with dust, dry weeds billowing in a brisk wind, a single milkweed pod exploding in flames.

A nervous tongue of fire licked the fuel in the brazier.

Other experiments followed. Under her mentors' direction, Ria induced static electricity, drew an electric spark across an open switch, and even persuaded a tiny motor to make a few revolutions.

"I assume you two are experts at all this," said Ria with studied casualness.

"Quite right!" Lute did no more than glance at the motor before its vanes were whirring too fast to be seen.

"This is how you caused my accident. No wonder Repair couldn't find anything wrong. The terminal didn't try to electrocute me—you did!" She glared at one and then the other.

Lute snorted back at her. "Don't you blame Kara. It was my idea and my doing."

Kara was unconcerned. "You took no hurt of it, child. We caused you no more pain than was necessary. You must be ready to face worse suffering than that in your life as a *solexa*."

"Granted. But I still owe this dear *perfur* something for his trouble." Ria flicked a spark at Lute's muzzle that made his whiskers stand straight out.

He yipped and rubbed his injured nose. "Not nice!"

"A child's trick is unworthy of you, Ria."

Ria was aghast for yielding to a violent impulse. "I'm sorry," she said. "I remember grievances too long." She touched his face gently. His stiff whiskers folded back as he tilted his cheek against her hand. She let it rest there for a long moment.

She raised her next question in a chastened voice: "What you're teaching me is dangerous. Aren't you worried that I'll misuse these powers, misuse them worse than I did just now?"

Kara replied: "We know your heart to its core. How could we not know it after all these years? If you should give us cause to doubt your character in the future, we would instantly take measures to disarm you."

Ria wondered what was meant by "disarm." "But you've never tried to initiate a subject on a different timeline before. You say no one here has. Surely it's risky?"

"We count the prize worth the risk. There is some purpose

at work in you that I feel but cannot clearly see. It will not let me rest.'' These last words were almost a sigh. The old *solexa* closed her eyes and rubbed her forehead as if to smooth away its furrows. ''But is this Providence in action or merely my own pride? Has my wisdom deluded me at the last? I was always so quick to see what needed to be done. Now I have done it all and do not know what remains undone.''

It came to Ria that initiation continued throughout one's life. She wanted to say something that would comfort Kara but no words came.

Lute jarred the table getting up. He paced back and forth nibbling on his fingers. ''Know the risks? Don't we just! You've reminded us of something we wish we'd never witnessed. Yours wasn't the only great talent we found exploring on your branch of time. Tell her, Kara, tell her about the self-made *solexam*.''

Kara chose her words slowly. ''This man—may his evil name perish unremembered—was born in China at the end of your eighteenth century. He came of an ancient and distinguished lineage and was amply equipped to pursue the life of the mind. Although being a righteous Confucian he despised both Buddhists and barbarians, nevertheless he mastered the mystical practices of Tibetan Buddhists and learned the ways of tribal shamans dwelling beyond China's borders. He became, as Lute said, 'a self-made *solexam*.' He showed a notable flair for dream-shaping. In this barbarian art he saw a means of destroying the barbarian Manchus who had conquered his homeland.''

''Through *solarti* he discovered a fitting instrument for his plans, a youth named Hung who had been driven mad by repeated failures in the imperial civil service examinations. For forty days he smothered Hung with visions until the lad believed himself to be the chosen Son of God and King of Heaven.''

''All at a distance, you understand,'' said Lute. ''The old

adept never met the disciple face to face nor explained what he was doing to him. *We* played fair with *you,* Ria.''

Kara continued. ''The cunning *solexam* died suddenly before completing Hung's initiation. But who can halt a boulder once it begins rolling down the mountain? Hung proclaimed himself a prophet and messiah, blending misunderstood scraps of Christianity with his own delusions. His message won so huge and rabid a following, he dared lead a revolt to replace the Manchus with his Great Kingdom of Heavenly Peace. By the time this T'ai P'ing Rebellion was put down—''

''Twenty million people had died.'' Lute snapped his teeth together. ''That's the low estimate.''

Ria's face twisted in horror. ''You say you watched all this happen. Couldn't you do anything to stop it?''

''No, child, we could not. That war lies in our past even as it does in yours. It is therefore fixed and immutable. We cannot lop off the branch whence we ourselves sprang.''

''Yet you feel free to interfere in my life.'' The bond of mutual trust stretched dangerously thin.

''Don't make it sound like a game, m'lady.'' Lute stood behind her and laid his hands on her shoulders.

Kara regarded her with weary patience. ''Have you forgotten your previous lessons so quickly? We are free to intervene because you yourself are not part of our past. And since we have no certain knowledge of your future—or of our own for that matter—all possibilities remain open.''

''But what if my training backfires like Hung's did?''

''You're being trained right and your heart's right. Makes all the difference.''

''We would have never touched your soul if we did not believe you will use *solarti* wisely. We cannot avenge the actions of that scheming *solexam.* But it may be that the debt incurred through one man's sin will be repaid through one woman's virtue.''

Ria slumped. ''Forgive me. I've been afraid so long.''

"You can stop being afraid of yourself right this minute." Lute's hands lifted her upright again.

Ria observed that an ugly pallor was creeping over Kara's face. "I'm tiring you."

"In truth, you are. I begin to feel my years late in the evening. Let us continue this tomorrow night."

Lute led Ria away.

Kara and Lute taught Ria new skills every night that week. The mastery of fire prepared her for the mastery of bodily processes. Soon, not only could Ria make electrons dance to her tune, she could alter the rates at which her lungs pumped, her heart beat, and her blood clotted. Once her preliminary survey on earthquake and volcano disasters had been delivered to Professor Clyde, she had more free time to pursue her own research. Discovering how little she knew about the life sciences, she set about remedying her ignorance by ordering some computerized courses and signing up for training in biofeedback at her House. It was daunting to realize how many different disciplines, from medicine to meteorology underlay shamanism. Much would be required of Ria in her vocation as a *solexa*.

By Sunday, unseasonably warm weather had melted the deep snow into mud puddles although icy heaps left by the plows still loomed like miniature glaciers along streets and walks. Ria and Carey emerged from the Man Library's east door at lunch time. The noon sun was so warm they left their coats open, but the nude sculptures flanking the doorway remained chastely concealed by packed snow.

Ria grinned. "They look better covered up, don't you think?"

"Who?" Carey hadn't been paying attention.

"Laredo Taft's ladies—*I Haven't Got a Thing to Wear* and *I Can't Do a Thing with My Hair*." Generations of students had handed on these nicknames for the statues, the one hugging her bare body, the other clutching her tangled locks.

Carey returned a wry smile. "Possibly. I've better things to think about than stone females—the winter cinema series, for instance. Since you dragged me out in that awful blizzard last week, the least you can do is let me coax you to watch some films."

"Depends on what they are."

"Swashbucklers."

Ria looked blank.

Carey explained: "Rare adventure classics from the last century—sea battles, sword fights, guys swinging from chandeliers." He thrust an imaginary rapier at her. "And no pretense at offering anything except entertainment."

"Mindless films full of violence? No social message? We'd better see them before they're suppressed. I wonder who let them out of the archives?"

"The daring bureaucrat probably went noncomp right afterwards. If we're going to catch *The Thief of Bagdad* tonight, we'll have to. . . ."

They almost collided with the crowd before a scowling Security officer waved them back. She and her team ringed a throng of smartly uniformed University dignitaries. These clustered around a copper-haired giant of a man who wore servicable denim overalls and stout boots.

"Can that be? Yes, it is. Ria, that's the Head of Resources—Ivan Mackenzie-Frazer. I read he's in town for a high level Ag conference at Allerton House. He has to leave Washington once in a while to inspect the hinterlands, but in his case I gather he actually enjoys it: direct communion with the land is a sacred tradition in Wheatland."

"I've never seen anyone that important in person before. Let's take a closer look."

"But not too close or we'll make his escort nervous."

"They're heading for the Morrow Plots." The continent's oldest corn testing site was an obvious attraction to show the continent's agriculture chief.

Ria and Carey prudently remained on the sidewalk while

the dignitaries cut across the soggy lawn and into the soggier field. Ankle-deep in mud, they surged between the rows of standing corn like so many foraging hogs. They knocked over a few cornstalks while jockeying for position. One man fell down. Mackenzie-Frazer inspected the memorial plaque, read the signs recording last year's yields and even husked a few dry ears for the cameras' benefit. He seemed more impressed with the corn than with his hosts.

Ria turned away. "If that's power, Carey, I don't want it."

"What makes you think you have any choice?"

Ria awoke from her next transit out of doors. The scent of bridal wreath hung in the late afternoon air. Blackbirds whistled overhead. She was lying in a hammock near Lute's pond. The macotter put aside a curious musical instrument to greet her.

"No, don't stop. What's that thing you're playing?"

"We call this a *gouar*."

He held it up to give her a better look. The neck was carved and painted to resemble a cock pheasant and the two globular sounding chambers were gilded. It had more strings than she could easily count.

"A *perfur* instrument?"

"Our favorite—my favorite, anyhow, Some of us favor the boat harp or the chalice drum but nothing thrums like a *gouar*." The chord he struck buzzed with complex reverberations that raised the hairs on the back of Ria's neck. "It's all in the sympathetic strings that run under the melody ones, see? Kara doesn't like thrumming. Makes me play outside."

"Perhaps the *gouar*, like the bagpipe, is best appreciated under the open sky."

Lute gave a good-natured snort and ran through a complete melodic line.

Ria spoke up quickly before he could favor her with an entire composition. "Do you mind if I take a look at your elms? They've leafed out nicely.''

Lute walked beside her among the handsome trees. ''It's an old grove, older'n Kara, even.''

The stand extended beyond their fence and into the surrounding yards. Ria traced the sawtoothed edges of an elm leaf with her fingers and admired the proud, high arch of the branches.

''May I?'' she asked and climbed up on a low hanging limb. Her perch gave her a better view of Kara's boxy-looking brick house. The atrium skylight rose like a bubble from the center of the deeply hipped roof. Outbuildings she hadn't noticed from indoors clustered on either side of the kitchen greenhouse. All that room for just three persons! Ria swung lightly down from the branch, something she couldn't have done in her own body.

''Easier time moving now, eh? Everything comes in time. Want to help feed my carp?'' Lute pointed to a pot full of table scraps on the pond's banked margin. ''But watch this first.''

He sat down on his haunches, completely still except for slight twitchings of his whiskers. Scorces of fish churned the surface in a swirling frenzy of color—red, gold, black, bronze, and white. Their mouths gaped wide for food before any of it had been thrown.

''You called them with your mind.''

''Tickled the brains of a few and the rest followed. Now give 'em their reward.'' Ria crumbled a stale roll and scattered it over the surface. Lute dumped the pot's contents into the seething water. ''Most *perfur* can herd fish—in ponds or out. Human *solexes* find it hard. Guess they don't know water creatures well enough.''

''There's the medieval legend of St. Anthony preaching to the fish.''

''Why'd he do that? They haven't got souls that need saving.''

Kara called to them from the kitchen door.

Lute threw back his head and gasped in silent laughter. "Must admit, Ria, must admit, I've been stalling you out here until our surprise arrived. Come meet her."

Kara waved them into the atrium where a female macotter stood waiting. Numerous black leather pouches and a skirt of thin gray fringe hung from her body harness.

"All hail," cried the newcomer. She whistled at Lute. He threw his arms around her neck and kissed her nose. After repeated nuzzlings and snufflings they separated.

Lute started to make introductions: "Julo is playing host today—"

"Could tell that right off. Walks different," the stranger muttered.

He continued as if he hadn't heard the interruption, "—to the soul of Ria Legarde, a new *solexa*."

"Honored," said the visitor. She held up her hands palms out. "What's your *harnama*, Ria, 'Rides In Air'?" Her choppy cadence was hard to understand.

"I'm not . . . from here," said Ria. "I don't have a mystic name."

"Do now. The naming gift's mine. I'm 'A Mountain Red In Sunrise.' Amris."

Ria bristled at the other's presumption but had the wit to raise her own hands in *perfur* greeting.

Lute said ruefully, "My sister's used to giving orders. She's the Ranger Captain of the Wabash Valley."

"Easy work, compared to minding Lute as a cub."

Not only was Amris older than Lute, she was larger. Her ears were chewed to rags and a wide scar slashed across her nose. She reeked of roses.

"Just show m'calling token." Amris opened one of her belt pouches. "No sense giving it, since only your soul's here." She held out a stamped and dyed leather disk for Ria's inspection. "My mark." She pointed to a stylized peak and rising sun, then flipped it over. "My Twin Stars clan mark."

This was a star of six points counterchanged. Ria instinctively applied the medieval terminology. She wondered if the *perfur* had a college of heralds to keep their emblems in order.

"Now you've met me proper and true." Amris replaced the token.

"That pouch new?" asked Lute. "Like that silver clasp." He bent down to admire it.

Amris nodded. "Basala's work. Lined with tree tiger fur, too." She let the others see how her disks fit into cunning rows of pockets. Rough Amris might be, but her taste was clearly elegant.

"Basala made m'new scent bottle, too."

"Don't open it." Lute sniffed ostentatiously.

Amris glared back. "Happen to like m'scent. Can't wear it on patrol."

Kara had been watching the byplay in amused silence. "Will you take some whiskey with us, Amris?"

"Pleased to, Lady Kara." Amris turned to find a seat among the floor cushions.

Ria's eyes widened at the sight of a sheathed knife hanging below the nape of the ranger's neck. She stared at Amris' gear piled beside the atrium door. Could that long, leather-covered object be a gun?

Lute got filled glasses into their hands with a surprising minimum of fuss. Then he set out a plate of chocolate meringue puffs. He looked so smug and Amris so gleeful, Ria concluded these were a rare treat. Although she and Kara declined the confections, within moments nothing was left of them except a few sticky crumbs on the macotters' fur.

Kara glanced from plate to glass and back to Ria. "How dull it would be," she said, "if their tastes marched with ours step by step." She offered a toast: "To our differences."

Ria took only the merest sip. Prohibitive taxes had effectively barred her from hard liquor and she was unsure of its effects on Julo's body. Having sipped, she wished she'd asked for a dilute drink like Kara's.

Lute noticed her hesitance. "Something wrong?"

Ria handed him her glass to finish.

Amris wrinkled her meringue-smeared muzzle. "Least she's not wasting Quail Cloud's best."

"None could bear to waste a drop. Your kinfolk on the Kankakee are justly renown for their corn liquor," said Kara. She took another swallow. "How fares your hunting?"

"Too well." Amris touched the fringe hanging from her belt.

Lute and Kara nodded gravely.

"Worry much more, I'll start shedding," continued the ranger. "Every circuit sees more rat-sign. Record, report. Can't sweeten words enough for Fort Wayne to swallow. What're they paying me for? Upriver and down, talk to sheriffs—those sons-of-cousins. One says his county's been clean twenty years. 'Nother says a rat drive's too dear. Railroads, canals, manufactories not too dear! But what use the day they find crunched bones 'stead of their kin?"

"On that day, they will listen," said Kara. "Until then, your very competence makes weak humans feel weaker."

Lute refilled his sister's glass. "Where's the major build-up?"

"Mouth of the Wabash. Macrats're eating Posey County bare. Everything below Fort Vincennes is a-crawl. Lost a ranger near there last spring."

"Who?" asked Lute.

"A Burning Hills, nobody you'd know." Amris briefly kissed her fingers to her comrade's memory. "They lost more'n one in Kentucky of late. Fort Louisville's talking grim. Word'll get north sooner or later. Humans heed humans better. Shouldn't complain so much while bounty money's good."

Amris brushed again at her fringe which Ria finally recognized as dried macrat tails. She was glad she'd eaten nothing.

"And what will you do with this wealth?" asked Kara.

To Ria, such a question was unacceptably personal but

*perfur* seemed to appreciate opportunities to boast.

"Invest in cross-cousin Rakam's pork-packing outfit."

"Is he still chittering about the perfect ham?" Lute snorted. "If he ever finds it, he'll probably eat it all by himself."

"Eats his share, he does, but sells enough to line both our dens right well. Live to retire, I'll be one rich *femfur*."

"Careful somebody doesn't try to marry you for your money, dear sister."

"*Masfur* tries that, I tear his head off."

Ria pitied the male macotter who roused the ranger's temper. Indeed, she was anxious not to rouse it herself. Her clenched hands betrayed her nervousness to Lute. He bent over to give her a reassuring pat.

"She's never actually ripped the head off any person—of fur or skin."

"Lute's still got his. Keeps it 'less he spills m'drink."

Ria tried to justify herself. "Where I come from, violence is taboo. It's bad taste even to joke about it." She did not want to admit that she found Amris unnerving.

"Then you will have to adapt, child, if you are to continue working with us," said Kara without a trace of sympathy. "Violence is very much a part of our world."

"No macrats, how'd I earn m'living?" said Amris, ever the strict pragmatist.

"You'll hear rougher talk than my sister uses when we take you to the Midsummer Feast," said Lute. "*Perfur* aren't tame people."

"When you take me to what?"

"The gathering of the season, when we all go to our clan homes to celebrate summer." Lute's whiskers quivered with excitement. "More food than you ever saw! Torchlight dances! Races! Music contests!" he trilled.

Amris snorted. "Just like you: talk of food 'stead of ritual."

Kara blocked his retort. "The treaty Never Smiles made

with the first *perfur* is also renewed at this time each year. Certain humans are invited to attend as witnesses. I am honored to serve in this role, an honor I extend to you as my guest.''

''You are kinder to me than I deserve,'' said Ria meekly. She forced her hands to relax. If she could endure the trials of her initiation, surely she could endure the rigors of macotter merriment. But a whole village full of them. . . .

## XII

November wore on. Every spare moment Ria honed her shamanic skills but the manner of the honing was now hers to choose. Kara and Lute mostly confined themselves to evaluating her progress and suggesting new directions during her brief nightly visits.

Ria discovered for herself how to extend the mastery of fire to electronic devices. Such apparatus did not exist in her mentors' world nor had they ever had occasion to investigate it while visiting technologically superior timelines. Ria spent an amusing afternoon running her tape player through its paces without touching the controls. Revelling in this small achievement, she felt like an undergraduate who'd published a scholarly paper. It proved that she could contribute to *solarti* and would not always remain under tutelage.

This success also gave Ria the confidence she needed to practice medical procedures on her own body that Kara and Lute hadn't permitted her to try with Julo's. She designed simple experiments to accompany the programmed course in basic physiology the data bank offered. Scientific knowledge was indispensible but *solarti* let Ria experience the chemistry and physics of life with absolute immediacy. When enzyme embraced substrate, when helix begot helix, when antibody duelled with antigen, she was there. Her delight was to contemplate the energies of her own being. Her duty was to master these interior fires.

Ria waged her first campagin against the heart. She quickly learned to spur or slow its beating, pinch off circulation or restore it. Breath control came as easily. She was attaining the powers of a yogin without tedious yoga discipline.

The endocrine system presented more of a challenge but adjusting her appetite was also a more useful accomplishment. She could actually monitor *solarti'* s energy demands burning off excess weight. Fine-tuning her menstrual cycle was equally satisfying—no more moody spells. By controlling adrenalin flow, she could drive herself past the normal limits of exhaustion or relax despite provocation.

Improved work performance drew reluctant compliments from Ali. Ria began to entertain hopes of a promotion in the spring. And if her hopes were denied, she had grown bold enough to lodge appropriate complaints. (However, too much boldness manipulating insulin levels gave her a nasty episode of hypoglycemia. Perhaps smoothly functioning systems were best left alone.)

Ria attacked her immune system cautiously. She gained the knack of raising and healing allergic rashes. How gratifying if she could treat Carey's chronic eczema. Ria preened over her plans for secret benevolence. But secret vengeance would be equally simple. She pictured Hannah's smooth, pale skin turned scaly and oozing, clawed raw by frantic nails. She heard her foe's asthmatic gasps and felt the fatal spasms of anaphylactic shock.

Ria wept for shame. The old fear of misusing her powers

came surging back. She plunged through troubled waters of thought to consult Kara and Lute. . . .

A cold spring afternoon shed dismal light on the atrium. Fresh earth and wool rugs smelled pungent in the dampness. The old *solexa* listened to Ria's self-accusation with a sign of pity or disgust.

Then she said: "Your strength and stature far outmatch your enemy's. You could slay her with your hands as readily as with your art. But you have not done so."

"Certainly not!"

"So the ease of killing does not determine whether you do murder or not."

"No," sobbed Ria.

"Then why are you in turmoil?"

"I don't really want to harm Hannah. It's just . . . I'm ashamed of myself for gloating over it. Violence goes against everything I was ever taught."

"Of themselves, thoughts do not kill, not even the thoughts of a *solex*."

"But my revenge fantasies were so ugly."

"Ah! There we have it. It is the ugliness of your desires that offends you, not the malice they express." Kara glowered so fiercely Ria cringed. "You confess one fault in order to conceal another."

Ria buried her face in her hands.

"People of your time fancy they can scour the heart clean of every blemish. They labor in vain, child. Accept your weaknesses and go on. The more you struggle to deny unworthy thoughts, the more they will bedevil you." She coughed heavily.

When Ria dared to meet Kara's eyes, she saw in them the scars of a lifetime's private battles.

"I'll see why Lute's so slow with the tea." Ria stumbled off to the kitchen.

Hot tea—and Lute himself—lifted Ria's spirits. She could not despair for long with him beside her. She eased her tense body against the rippling warmth of him and restated her problem.

"Try to understand, Lute, I've grown up in a strictly guarded world."

"That didn't protect you too well, m'lady." The *perfur* snorted.

"It protects most of the people most of the time. But you two have thrust dangerous powers into my hands. What if I kill someone with a medical trick? What if I burn down the House by accident? I'm terrified that I'll abuse *solarti*, even without meaning to."

"Stay frightened and you're sure to falter." Lute chopped the air with his hand. "From early years our cubs handle knives and fire—tools they need to stay alive."

"They don't hurt themselves?"

"Not often," he answered with casual pride.

"Lute fails to mention that the elders carefully instruct the young ere they arm them."

"Still . . ."

"Self-control's the only kind that works."

"They learn to fend for themselves or they perish." Kara had another fit of coughing. "We think you have more sense than a *perfur* cub but perhaps we have misjudged you, Ria. Either you will deal with your fears or you will forfeit my attention. At this moment you weary me. Depart."

Ria returned to herself chastened. Kara and Lute had in effect said: "Naught for your comfort and naught for your desire." They were right, of course. She would never gain self-confidence by refusing to explore. But she appeased caution by concentrating on positive uses of the art.

Since she could alter the rates of biochemical reactions, she could mend torn flesh neater and quicker than she could mend torn cloth. Yet it was easy to see how the satisfaction of repairing tiny wounds might lead to deadly aberrations. Kara had mentioned mad *solexes* in past centuries who cut their bodies to pieces and restored them for show. Her own world held legends of adepts tearing out their eyes or removing limbs at will.

Surely controlling pain was a safer skill to cultivate. Now when Ria slipped on ice—as she too often did—she forbade her body to ache or even show bruises. From numbing she moved to pleasing. No pharmacy potion could rival the subtle euphorics she coaxed her brain to make. Maintaining herself in a steady state of well-being smoothed out the peaks and valleys of daily living but Ria found it surprisingly difficult to adjust to contentment. She kept testing her mood like a new dental filling: was she as happy now as she'd been a moment before, an hour before? She searched in vain for signs of old familiar anxieties seeping through the calm and searched all the harder when none were found.

The nightly visits to Kara and Lute lost their excitement. She began resenting her mentors because they asked questions and set goals. Their demands stirred pools she preferred left still. On Thanksgiving Day, she did not bother to report to them at all, enjoying a forbidden thrill as if she'd cut a class. Throughout the starless night and the bleak day that followed, she lay cocooned in her blankets, too enraptured to move.

Friday evening Ria stoked herself with sufficient biochemical cheer to face a House party. She wanted to show off the new dress she'd bought recently to celebrate her slimness. With the luxury tax, this had taken most of the money she'd been saving for a bicycle. Still, the flame shaped hem swished against her knees in the most delightful way.

Ria emerged from her apartment just as her bathmate was leaving his. She hadn't seen the gangling, thin-lipped man since their initial introduction eight months earlier. Her imitation of a neighborly smile went unnoticed. She ought to have realized he was no more sociable than herself and perhaps equally sensitive about it. She pitied him briefly before stroking away her concern. Her long strides left him behind as she swept down to the party alone.

The lounge was painfully bright. Gape-mouthed plastic turkeys strutted on long tables laden with refreshments. The leftovers from yesterday's feast returned as sandwiches and sweets. Ria entered into the spirit of the evening, proving she could squeal and cheer as well as any other resident during the approved games. Whenever her glow threatened to fade during the frantic rolling of balls and passing of ribbons, a slight neurochemical adjustment brightened it. No such stimulation was needed later when she asked men to dance with her yet none attracted her enough to invite further attention.

Afterwards she found Carey talking with Hannah beside the buffet.

"But I like cranberry jelly, Hannah, honest I do. Hardly ever get to taste the stuff."

The petite blonde gazed reproachfully at his plate. "Eat it if you must," she sighed. "Sad enough that people desert sound nutrition for outmoded customs at Thanksgiving dinner, but to compound the error. . . ." She sighed again.

"Don't let her make you feel guilty, Carey," said Ria. "Fill up your plate if you like. It's our social duty to eat what's put before us without complaint." She took a mince-meat tart and bit the sticky little morsel in half.

"I understand perfectly why you'd break your diet, Ria, in the face of sweet temptation." Hannah gestured with her carrot stick. "But we dancers can't allow ourselves even one fattening meal."

"When did I say I was dieting?" Ria ate another tart.

"But you've lost weight," said Carey, looking as frantic

as a civilian trapped on a battlefield. "You might perhaps consider wearing skirts more often. Becoming, highly becoming. I should've said so sooner."

"Some ladies have to wear pants all the time because they can't afford sheer hose." Hannah's soft blue eyes focussed on nothing in particular.

"So you're as solicitous for my bank balance as my waistline, Hannah. Try not to wring your hands too hard. They might wrinkle." Giggling at her enemy's outrage, Ria nearly missed the measuring stare that briefly hardened the other's features. "Are you ready to be rescued, Carey?"

"If you don't mind, I'd rather eat. You don't mind, do you, Ria?"

Ria scooped up a handful of cookies and left, still laughing. Later, when she was about to retire, a note slid under her door. Although it was unsigned, she recognized Carey's tight, round hand. She sat down on the bed to read it.

> I'm writing instead of calling so we can't
> be overheard. Are you going noncomp,
> taunting her like that?? She told me
> she thinks you're taking illegals. What
> if she reports you to PSI? Please watch out!
> I'm afraid for you.

Ria shrugged sadly. Carey was entirely too nervous. He lacked the means of scaling her lofty plateau of calm. Perhaps she could do something for him. Or perhaps not. As she let the note fall, her gaze flickered across a gleaming doorknob. A huge wave smote her down into roiling surf. . . .

A floor loom dominated the cluttered, book-lined workroom. Ria was sitting bolt upright in a hard chair. Her hand was cranking a yarn winding frame. Beside her, Kara was spinning wool on a wooden wheel. Lute hovered in front of them brandishing a pair of heavy shears.

"We are most pleased to welcome you this morning,

Ria.'' Kara barely inclined her head in greeting. Her wheel sped steadily on.

"Why'd you do this? I thought you were through dragging me to and fro.''

"We were,'' said Lute. "But you swim out of your depth, we'll haul you home every time.''

"Explain that!'' Ria sprang up to confront Lute.

Despite his stooped posture she had to look up to meet his unsmiling eyes. She hadn't reckoned on the stiffness of Julo's body from prolonged sitting. She automatically moved to erase the ache.

"Not so fast.'' Lute pushed her back into her chair and stood over her with his left hand still on her shoulder. The shears were uncomfortably close to her chest.

"That hurts.''

"Meant to. You're not going to muffle every little twinge today. Or flit home till you've heard us out.''

"We do not beg your pardon for our harshness,'' said Kara. "Your present danger requires rough measures.''

"What do you mean? I'm feeling fine. I've never felt so fine in my life.''

"In a few days you have come close to unraveling all the months and years of effort gone before.'' The spinning wheel slowed to a halt.

Said Lute: "You're addicting yourself to those pain killers your own brain brews. Cunning compounds, enkephalins. Can't get enough of them now, can you?''

"What's wrong with stopping pain? I thought that was a major use of *solarti*.'' Ria tried to squirm out of Lute's grasp.

"Yes, we comfort those afflicted in mind and body. That is Lute's special work. But we do not seek to shield ourselves or others from every pinprick life inflicts.''

"Will you listen with a clear head?'' Lute's tone softened.

"And if I won't?''

"Be warned, m'lady,'' he was grave again, "you're not

meddling with one molecule in Julo's body while I'm standing here. I can follow you into your world and do the same. Waking or sleeping, I'll stay with you till you come to your senses. Otherwise, touch your brain here, touch it there and—"

"I'll go no more a-roving. I understand." She clamped her lips together.

"Some new *solexes* get drunk on their power over pain," said Kara. "Those who passed through bitter times in childhood like you, Ria, most often fall into this trap. They forget whose well-being their art exists to serve. How can you guard your people if all you watch is yourself?" Kara's words rolled in steadily as the tide.

"Don't I deserve some pampering? If you're my friends, why don't you want me to be happy?" Ria glanced from one to the other until tears blurred out the sight of them.

Lute's hand slid across to stroke her neck. "May all beings be happy," he said.

"May they also be strong enough to endure unhappiness when they must," said Kara. "My child, wool kept hidden in a sack will never be spun and woven into useful goods."

"Achievement's joy, not making molecules or mischief."

"Tell me about joy, Lute. It's built right into your genes isn't it?" She knocked his hand away. "Your precious *solarti* has brought me damned little joy to date. Pain and pitfalls, that's all it is. So what if I can run up and down the tree of time like some misbegotten monkey. I've got books and pictures. Why should I go poking into other people's minds for information? I've got as much conventional medical care as I need— you don't but I do—so what's the use of self-healing gimmicks? I wish you'd never found me!" She hunched up and wept in great, tearing sobs.

When Lute tried to soothe her, she batted his hands away. In the process, she cut her left hand on the shears he still held. Kara came to her side. "That is quite enough, Ria. Stop that bleeding before you stain the wool."

Focussing her attention on healing the injury stopped Ria's crying. Self-consciousness made the task go slower than it would at home but the results seemed to meet their professional approval. Kara lifted Ria's bowed head so that their eyes met. The old woman's narrowed to blue slits lost in wrinkles. Her words battered at Ria like pounding surf:

"Hear well what I say, daughter of my spirit. The hands sweep round the clock and the shadows lengthen even as I speak. I thought I could die content once you were made a *solexa* but was never easy to content. Now I pray to see you perfected in the art, outgrown your need of me before I pass through the Door. Each foolish crisis of yours delays that glad fulfillment. The patience I pride myself upon wears thin. Either take up the challenge of your calling without tears or cease pretending to be a *solexa*. I grow weary of telling you: the purpose of your art and your life is yours to seek. Only you can answer the questions you have raised."

Lute said, "Maybe you're struggling too hard with the art. More to living than that. You think Kara and I practice *solarti* every waking minute?" He snorted.

"Other forms of learning and making also give us joy," said Kara.

"Let me show you," said Lute. "You haven't been in this part of the house before." The *perfur* bobbed around like a spring with its tension suddenly released.

Ria followed him to the bookshelves that covered one entire wall. She felt a twinge of nostalgia for the days when librarians had routinely dealt with actual books, not bytes of data. She groped for a response to Lute's obvious pride in the collection.

"These wouldn't begin to fit in my apartment. I have to depend on printouts or microfilm."

"The University library's at hand but we like to have our own copies of basics." He pointed to the labels identifying

144

each section. "We've got the full range of arts and sciences—'most anything a *solex* needs." He gave Ria a confidential nudge. "Get my tail trod if the lot's not kept neat."

"*Perfur* require encouragement on matters of order." Kara's voice was mellow again. "As his desk yonder bears witness."

Ria scanned the titles, chuckling when she recognized Eliade's *Shamanism,* the same text she'd studied during her initiation. She pointed to the book: "I never expected to find that here."

"Why not?" asked Kara. "Good work outlives the world that bred it."

"But this copy looks fresh. It can't be from before the Great Death."

"It isn't." Lute bit out his words. "Books do crumble after six centuries. We reprint 'em. Even publish new ones."

"Pleasure reading is commoner in our time than yours, Ria. One of the many thriving presses in the Republic is here in Chamba."

"Were you visiting longer, m'lady, and someday you will, you could read things that don't exist on your timeline."

"Such as?"

Lute pulled volumes from the literature section and handed them to Ria. "Wonderful stories like *Sabbath Candles* by Anne Frank or *Ezana's Memoirs* by Mikael Yekuno. And here's Kara's favorite, *The Flowers of December* by Wilfred Owen.

"The poems of his deep age," the old woman explained. "They take on fresh meaning for me as each year passes."

"What's your favorite, Lute?"

"My taste's more modern. Kara and I could argue till evening, but won't—don't frown m'lady. Can't be faulted for favoring m'own people's words. Take *Nightscents* by Manis Ghost Claw of Tidewater. Bought it at last year's

Midsummer Feast.'' He showed Ria a bundle wrapped in a black suede covering like a medieval book chemise. ''Nothing but the best for her song-poems.''

He untied the covering and riffled the pages of the black calf volume inside. Each page was tinted and printed in different colors and bore a single lyric bordered by exhuberant interlacings. The whole book smelled of gardenias. It was something William Morris might have published after dining on moldy rye bread. But before Ria had gotten a good look at it, the volume was closed, sealed, and reshelved. Lute chirruped on, rather too eagerly, about good reading.

''Lately we've been getting access to works that aren't in our own past. Clever *solexa* out east—a 'word-huntress' she calls herself—reads the best books on other timelines and brings 'em back page by page in her memory. Bought one, didn't we, Kara? What's that author's name, can't pronounce it?''

''Alexander Solzehnitzen.''

''Grim going. Didn't understand enough to finish it.'' He nibbled his fingers briefly. ''Must visit those times and places till I do understand.''

Ria shuddered. ''Spare yourself. Prison camps and firing squads aren't for your kind.'' She handed the books she'd been holding to Lute. He crammed them back on the shelves in no particular order but Kara did not protest.

''Lute, show Ria the rug you are making.''

He took it out of a cabinet beneath the *gouar* hanging on the opposite wall. Only a few tufts of wool had as yet been tied on a canvas backing marked with swooping curves. ''Kara's reminding me I'm slow getting started this time. Made all the rugs in the atrium didn't I?''

''When the impulse strikes again, you will return to the project with zest. There is ample time to cover my floor before next winter.'' She turned to Ria. ''I have tried to interest Lute in weaving but it bores him. He confines himself to dreaming designs for me.'' She displayed pattern sketches on Lute's desk while he stowed the rug.

Ria tagged behind Kara and peered over the old woman's shoulder at the floor loom. She hadn't been near one before and feared to touch it lest she tangle something. Kara seemed to sense her thoughts.

"Dressing the loom and tying up is far more tedious than weaving the web. Once each warp thread is secured in its proper place, the work goes swiftly.''

"What will this be?'' asked Ria. "It has the same shades of red and blue as Lute's rug.''

"It will be a tapestry for my bedroom. See, the Tree of Life design is reversible. I mean to finish it off in white fringe.''

Ria frowned. "But it's only June here. A little while ago you. . . .''

"Spoke as if I might die at any moment?'' Kara smiled. "In the event I am mistaken, I do not wish to fare cold weather with bare walls. One does the task at hand in the moment at hand. Would you care to throw the shuttle once?'' She tightened the warp tension and pressed a treadle.

Ria hesitated but Lute urged her on. She obeyed.

Kara beat the new thread into place and relaxed the tension again. "You did it correctly, child. If you had not, I would have pulled your thread out and bade you try again. Go home, Ria. Think well on everything we have said this day.''

Back in her own body, Ria lay stiff and sleepless. Her mind flew back and forth like a busy shuttle, but what it wove was hidden from her sight. After Kara and Lute's scolding, she feared to induce sleep biochemically. She tried counting threads and imagined an endless array of parallel fibers stretched so tightly that they hummed.

The humming turned to moaning. She wasn't imagining these sounds. They were coming from next door. Her bathmate was having a bad night. Had the party gotten the better of him this early? The moans grew louder, mingled with short guttural outbursts that must be curses. Ria listened for other noises in the corridor. The other residents were still downstairs. But if he were still ranting as they drifted home, someone would surely report him to the authorities. Then he'd be cited for disorder and drunkenness. He had to be drunk to be carrying on that way.

She heard him come into the common bathroom. She expected sounds of retching but there were none. Now his complaints came through hideously clear. Hiding her head under the covers did not blot them out. No one should overhear such a litany of anguish. What was wrong with the crisis monitor? Was his voice too deeply pitched to trip it? Ria stood up and timidly knocked on the bathroom door.

"Are you all right, citizen?"

"Go away!" he screamed. "No help. Don't need help!"

"If you say so."

She backed away and sat down on the bed again. The hysterical edge in the man's voice slashed at her. She remembered where she'd heard it before and shivered. Her neighbor must not be allowed to go the way of her mother. If she called Suicide Prevention, he'd be sent to PSI for treatment and their cure might be worse than his disease. But *solarti* might save him. Could she wield her shaman's powers when they were really needed? She grabbed her steel mirror from under her pillow and broached the swelling waves. . . .

He gagged on the last swallow of *Amaretto*.

"My god, Gin knows I hate the stuff. Why'd she give me a bottle? Throwing her money around. Why couldn't Gin have given me gin?" He guffawed and flashed a death's head grin at the mirror. "Last laugh is, I won't be here to feel the hangover."

He poured a spoonful of white powder into his empty glass. Who'd ever miss ten grams of cyanide from that teaching lab? Who'd ever miss him? He filled the glass with water and swirled it to dissolve the poison. He raised a toast to bid himself farewell. The mirror exploded in sparkling darkness as he fell. . . .

Ria lay quivering on her bed. She staggered up and put her ear to the bathroom door. There was silence except for the noise of the running tap. The fainting spell had felled him like a tree, just as she intended. With luck, his glass had dropped in the sink and the water would wash its contents away. The ventilating fan ought to pull off the suspicious odor. Anything left would be attributed to the amoretto. She need only alert the House manager to her neighbor's accident.

# XIII

Saturday afternoon Ria's neighbor came calling. Territorial instinct flared briefly to deny him entry. But seeing the poor fellow's shoulders tensed as if expecting a blow, she had to let him in.

"My name is Leigh Franz. From next door." He waved feebly in that direction. "They told me you were the one who summoned help when I . . . last night . . . my fall." He tugged at his knobby fingers. "I want to thank you for getting the medics here." He stressed the word "medics."

"It was the obvious move when I heard you hit the floor."

He reddened. "You can hear a lot through that door."

Ria kept her voice carefully light. "Not all that much. The fan's noise blurs most of it. I was about to fix some tea. Will you join me?"

While Franz sat waiting for his cup to cool, Ria delicately nudged biosynthetic pathways in his brain. Her brief occupation the previous night made this feasible. He'd attribute any brightening of his mood to the tea.

"You must've gotten quite a bump," said Ria.

"Don't remind me." He winced. "But no concussion or anything worse than a citation for drinking. Filling out the accident forms'll be more of a pain than the fall itself."

"Can't be too careful, can we?"

He nodded warily.

"But we can talk sometimes. Would you like that?"

The ringing of his telephone jabbed through the wall. Ria let Franz out through her bathroom door. When he returned, his tight face had loosened into a grin.

"That was my lab—I'm a biochem tech—I've got to get over there right now."

"On a Saturday?"

"You harvest your bugs when they're ready: they don't keep University hours. The new fermentation route did scale up. Yesterday I was sure the batch was ruined."

The news meant nothing to Ria but he seemed pleased. Franz didn't look as pathetic when he smiled. He turned back on the threshold, suddenly sober. "Last night if . . . I'd've never learned our experiment worked. When you need a favor, any favor at all. . . ." He shook her hand hard and left.

Ria decided to visit Kara and Lute at once. She couldn't sit through *Captain Blood* this evening with such news bubbling inside her. Mirror in hand, she flashed through waters that glowed like molten steel. . . .

The warmth of her friends' greeting overwhelmed Ria. Lute hugged her so hard, they tumbled out of the atrium cushions and rolled across the shaggy rug together.

"And who lectures me about damaging Julo's body?"

"What damage in a good romp?" Lute snorted with injured innocence.

Had she dared, Ria would have held his supple body against hers a moment longer. She straightened her cushions and sat next to Kara. Lute sprawled at their feet.

"There are a few blind paths on any mountain. Once you saw that, child, you abandoned the false turning quicker than many who stray." Noontime sun shone down on the old woman's face.

"Don't fret over temptation," said Lute. "Without testing, you don't learn."

"So glib now, Lute? After your fears that Ria might fail and forfeit her powers? But *perfur* cannot stay gloomy long. This denning up in self tempts your folk far less than ours. Joy is as much a part of *perfur* as their fur." She smiled to see Lute preen. "To us slow humans they proclaim: 'Living is dancing.'"

"But we miss the dancing more when it stops," said Lute so softly only Ria heard him.

"Ria, your perilous crossing is one I myself once faced." Kara was being uncommonly expansive. "Unlike you, I was marked out to be a *solexa* from my earliest years. Since my elders expected great feats from me, I drove myself mercilessly to perform. When I discovered how slight manipulations in brain chemistry brought blessed relaxation and then oblivion—" She stared past Ria confronting the memory as if it were fresh.

"First the craving, then the loathing, until the craving for solace doubled and redoubled. But my master—" she kissed her fingers to the memory of a man decades dead—"spied the danger quickly. He actually did to me what Lute threatened to do to you: he overrode and blocked my powers. He did not permit me to use *solarti* again until I had learned other means of easing tension and understood why I felt so tense. How it stung my pride to have my swift progress stayed! In time I could stand aside a bit from that pride and fix my sight on the art instead of what I, the soul-artist, meant to achieve. That is the secret I bequeath to you, Ria. (Lute knew it already without being taught.) Lose yourself to find yourself. Then the happiness you receive will outshine the pleasure you reject as the sun above does a tallow candle."

"I begin to see it, Kara. I saw it in my neighbor's living eyes." Ria bent her head. Her gaze slid past Lute's face. "Perhaps you can teach me other ways to help Franz. But please," she continued timidly, "may I take a break from medical experiments for a while?"

"Don't have to beg, Ria," said the *perfur*. "You've learned most of what a *solex* who isn't going into medicine needs to know."

Ria squared her shoulders and raised her head. "If I decide to halt my current line of study, what do you suggest I put in its place?"

"You should practice placing yourself in time and space," answered Kara. "Blaze a trail along certain branches so you can climb the Cosmic Tree alone with surefooted steps."

"No climbing just now, dear lady. Stay here a moment, this day's so far." He rippled upright and stared expectantly at Kara.

"Before you start weedling, I will grant your wish. Just this once, to celebrate Ria's recovery, you may play your *gouar* for us inside the house."

Lute chirruped with glee.

Ria approached her new assignment bristling with earnestness, determined to prove herself cautious and humble. But as the week passed, absorption in the challenge distracted her from worrying over attitudes. She felt like a fledgling bird as she clumsily beat her way from branch to branch of the Tree. However, she spun and crashed less when she returned to points she'd visited previously. The congenial minds she'd entered during her initiation made attractive targets. She could travel up and down these persons' lifespans, scrabbling at first, then moving securely.

Ria climbed one branch to see the nervous young journalist grown into an esteemed editor, old and mellow as a chess queen carved out of bone. Up another branch she found Captain McCauley become a bearded patriarch enthroned on a horsehair chair reading Kipling to a parlor full of round-eyed children. Down a third branch she beheld the aged Englishwoman as a young wife proud of her new matron's wimple, singing while she weighed gold for her husband to cast.

No instant Ria shared was ordinary. Every particle of every cell in the Cosmic Tree was someone's personal universe, none inferior to any other. She could have spent a lifetime exploring each one. Kara had answered her rightly: not the artist but the art—and the limitless reality it revealed. Surely she would discover hard tasks awaiting her, tasks uniquely hers, yet she was equally sure of returning here to contemplate beauties ever ancient, ever new. The hand that stirred the water in the pool had healed her at last of the need to be useful. One step nearer to mastery, she sped to Kara and Lute with swift, sure strokes. . . .

Evening shadows and soft humming filled the atrium. Lute was playing the *gouar* with unaccustomed delicacy. Since Ria could not see his face clearly in the darkness, she touched his arm to signal her presence.

"Know you're here, Ria," he whispered. "Been expecting you."

"Let me tell you what I've learned." She kept her own voice low. "Kara—"

"Kara's asleep."

The old woman lay back on her cushions breathing raggedly.

"This moment's for listening, m'lady."

Ria curbed her eagerness for talking. She stretched out beside him and closed her eyes. The *gouar* thrummed like a chorus of insects. Anxiety ebbed away. The urgency to report her insights faded. Surely Lute could sense the new peace in her spirit without being told. She savored the aromas of fish stew and fresh bread wafting in from the kitchen. They must have eaten earlier. She could taste the stew on Julo's lips. She

sorted through the damp green smells of pond and plants—
there had to be lilies somewhere in the room. The fishy,
flowery, musky scent of Lute himself beckoned her. She
brushed his fur.

"Would you sing for me?" She asked softly.

"A song by Manis please you?" He bent toward her and
sang in a thin, shivery keening:

> The sickle moon
> Shears through thin clouds
> To harvest stars
> Like silver blooms.

More Tidewater melodies unrolled beneath his fingers.
Luminous waves rode the glowing sea, mingling as they
crashed on dune-ringed shores, and falling back in drops of
living flame. She trembled on the threshold of his mind.

The doorbell jangled.

Lute sprang up, tripped over his *gouar*, punched on the
lights and dashed off to answer the front door. Kara awoke in
a fit of coughing. Ria helped her sit up straight.

Lute returned glaring and making flapping motions with
his arms.

"Her?" Kara winced.

Lute nodded. "Her. The Buzzard Lady herself. Can't get
rid of her."

"I will see her exactly one time more." Kara set her jaw.

Moments later the caller swept in with a rasp of ruffled
petticoats. She was dressed entirely in black and decked in
heavy jewelry. Tight, unnaturally black curls topped her
pale, wrinkle-netted face.

"I told the otter you would see me, Lady Kara. He actually
attempted to send me away."

"My colleague has a name, as well you know Wilamine
Hork."

Kara did not rise or offer a gesture of greeting. Ria remained kneeling at Kara's feet and tried to keep her expression blank.

"Luke, Lute, whatever you call him was distinctly rude." She adjusted her massive gold necklace. "A woman in my position is not accustomed to such treatment. When my late husband was alive he saw to it I had respect. As a client I insist—"

"When were you ever a client of mine?" Kara chopped her off. "I refused to treat you while I was still the chief *solexa* in Chamba and I will go on refusing you while life and breath are left to me."

"I can pay any fee you name. Besides, you have to accept me for treatment. It is your sworn duty. My condition baffles everyone else. If your niece or that fellow Lerrow over in Lafayette were half as good as people claim, they would have cured me long ago."

"No *solex*, however gifted, can cure an ailment that does not exist."

"I have not spent a single day free of pain since my husband died. Not that I care to discuss my symptoms in front of your servants."

Ria struggled to look meek but she saw Lute's muzzle wrinkle to expose his fangs. A rank scent spread from him. Hork was too intent on impressing Kara to notice. The old woman folded her arms tightly as if holding her body together.

"If healing were in truth your goal and not the healer's fame, you would be seeking Lute's aid instead of mine."

Hork shrieked, "Let one of *them* touch my soul?"

"Another such outburst, foolish woman, and more than your soul will be touched." A fit of coughing seized Kara. Lute rushed to attend her. When she found her voice, it was as grim as her face. "Julo will show you to the door. Never return."

"I can find my way there without the half-wit's help."
Hork stalked out.

Ria did not need to be told to leave.

That night Ria's dreams were troubled. She saw an un-
horsed knight, weaponless and lame. He staggered across the
bed of some vanished sea towards a mirage of cool mountains. Clouds of powdered salt raised by the wind seared his
throat and burned his skin. A vulture spiraled lower as he
faltered. Gems glittered on the beak and claws that would tear
out his eyes. A dainty golden bell hung about the bird's bare
neck.

Ria awoke to a fresh snowfall. The view from her window
was as sere and white as the desert in her dream.

Carey stopped by in the afternoon, burbling about the
wonders of the evening's film series offering, *Four Feathers*.
Ria was in no mood for cinematic crises, much less an epic of
the sun-baked Sudan. She introduced Carey to Leigh Franz
and sent them off to the theater together. Perhaps the needs of
the two lonely men would dovetail and free an extra bit of
energy for use in her art. Well-rested and alert, she pierced
the disk of brightness. . . .

Lute's back was toward her as she sat at the kitchen table.
He was working with a shelf full of fishbowls along the
window wall, chirruping as he added and subtracted contents. His expected grace and unexpected concentration held
her silent for a few moments before she felt obliged to
announce her presence. She stood up quietly, stepped behind
him and touched his neck.

"Heard you coming Ria. Can't take a *perfur* by surprise."

The caress turned into a message.

"Feels good. Keep it up," he said.

Ria was happy to give comfort for a change instead of
receive it. "Who was that dreadful woman—last night or
whenever it was?"

158

Lute's body stiffened. He turned around. "She's the biggest lamprey in the lake—richest woman in Chamba. A whiskey maker's widow. Keeps trying to force Kara to treat her. Can't understand why Kara won't. Gets nastier each time she's refused."

"Hork's illness isn't real?"

"Only to her." He snorted.

"Kara said you could cure her."

"Straightening bent minds is one of m'gifts but that one wouldn't call for me on her deathbed. Nobody's making her suffer but her." He cleared the shelf of used equipment. "Makes me want something stronger than tea." He fetched a dark bottle and pointed to the label. "Quail Cloud's not Hork's."

Ria cut her drink with water but Lute took his neat.

"Your people don't always love mine," he said, "not always."

Ria was embarrassed for her species. "Surely there aren't many like the Hork bitch?"

"And may the Most High keep them few." He took another swallow. "Kara keeps them at bay. But without her. . . ." He chewed his fingers. "Kara's still resting from last night. She's persuading her lungs to clear."

"May I see her?"

"No. Not till the spell's past."

Ria accepted his stricture. "It was you I dreamt were in danger." She described the knight menaced by the vulture. Lute did not object to being called a man.

"You're right. Hork may try to harm me when I'm left alone, as I must be someday." His tone was detached. "But a dream only shows thoughts, not the real future. Must ask Kara what she's been dreaming lately."

"And if she saw a vulture, too? I think I've shared dreams with others in the past."

"Quite right. So've I, with Amris when I was small and she was still at home. Those were accidents. You and I ought to try it on purpose. An experiment's the very thing.''

Ria knew he was trying to avoid discussing Kara's health. Did he doubt her ability to withstand bad news? Such doubts might be justified.

"How can I share my dreams with you," she asked, "when you don't let me into your mind?"

"Matter of meeting, not entering." He poured himself another glass. "We'll give each other cues before going to sleep, compare results afterwards. Never heard of it working across timelines but you and I. . . ."

Their eyes met for a moment, then Ria looked away. "I don't think I could break into your mind or Kara's no matter how hard I tried."

"Not yet. Our skills're still greater. We can block you or pull you here at a particular moment but you can't do the same to us." He swallowed again. "Before you go wailing about weakness, let me tell you there're some humans— never met any myself but records say they exist—*solarti* can't affect. Tempting to think they lack souls, no, not right, everybody's got a soul, everybody."

The notion of soulless intelligence upset Lute. Ria tried to turn him back on the track. "It does hurt to be kept out of your mind. Will you ever let me in?"

"Someday. Not now. Take it on faith we've got reasons. Don't frown so, m'lady. I've been dreaming about you already, without needing to host your soul."

Ria brightened. "What did you dream?"

"I was climbing a spiral stair in a darkened lighthouse. Those metal treads weren't meant for *perfur* feet. Climbed for miles. Not a minute's rest." He rubbed his back, remembering the ache.

"Oh the anguish of it all! After some of the things you put me through in dreams." Ria tried to snarl like a *perfur*.

Lute twitched his whiskers. "When I got to the top, I couldn't turn on the light until you appeared and hit the switches with me. Beam clove the darkness like a shining sword.''

Ria offered an interpretation: ''You must be thinking of joint projects. But I don't stay here long enough to pursue any.''

''You'll get the chance during Midsummer Festival, two whole days at least.''

''Is that enough time for anything worthwhile?''

Lute chuckled and offered to refill her glass. She declined.

''While you're with us, you've got the use of that ring Kara gave you. Should have a silver ring in your own world. Can't count on having bright metal around when you need it. Can work without a trigger if you have to but it takes extra effort.''

''I can't afford silver.'' Her meager savings, depleted by the purchase of a dress, wouldn't cover jewelry.

''Steel, then. Anything shiny.''

''No taboo on cold iron?''

''What?'' Lute snorted. ''This isn't magic, Ria. Unless everything is.'' He swept his arm around the kitchen. ''Plants flower. Fish breed. Descendants of apes and otters think. Just as magical to be a poet as a *solex*.'' He planted a bourbon-scented kiss on her nose and waved her home.

The next day, Ria put the question of a ring before Carey. Surprised as well as gratified by his enthusiasm, she let him take charge of designing and make the ornament.

The following Saturday they returned to her apartment after an enjoyable evening viewing *Cartouche*. Carey pressed a small box into her hand. He scarcely seemed to breathe while she opened it. His efforts quite surpassed her expectations. Although the ring was merely a steel disk set in clear plastic, it achieved an austere elegance worthy of its purpose.

''It's magnificent!'' She slipped it on her bridal finger.

"And it fits." Its massiveness rode well on her large hand. "Thank you, Carey, thank you so much." She clasped the small man in a fervent hug.

"Glad you like it," he gasped.

"Now what do I owe you?"

"Owe? Ria it cost next to nothing." He was more grateful for her gratitude than she was for the ring. "All I did was sniff around the hobby room, talk to some people taking the plastic crafting course, and cobble it up from various kits. The resin came from an off batch one guy was about to throw out—perfectly durable, don't worry about that. It sparkled too much to suit him."

"Doesn't our world need more sparkle, not less?" They laughed together.

After her friend left, Ria sat admiring her new possession. She had never owned a ring before. The mirror-bright metal within the shimmery bezel cried out for use. She composed an image, flashed it in Lute's direction, and dived into liquid stillness. . . .

The mountain stood alone, rough and black as doom. In a riot of lightning and roiling ash it split asunder. Lava streamed down its flanks to cool in streaks like clotted blood. Its crater caught a century's rain until clear waters lapped a rim grown green with trees. This sky-hued lake reflected clouds and Lute's bewhiskered face.

# XIV

Winter vacation brought the Library Research staff the welcome prospect of its annual professional outing. Trips were especially prized employment bonuses because the University paid all expenses and the usual travel tax was waived. Ria was eager to visit this year's destination, Chicago, a place otherwise beyond her means.

The week of departure opened with a blizzard that heaped fresh-drifted over the existing ice encrusted snow. Bone-deep cold set in. As the bitter days passed, Ria sensed even worse weather coming. Her instincts were confirmed by the posting of an official winter storm watch on the morning they were to leave. Although travel was clearly becoming hazardous, the staff was required to go enjoy themselves on schedule.

Despite her forebodings, Ria was reluctant to beg off the expedition. The Health Service would have to verify any plea of illness. Would self-induced symptoms fool the doctors well enough? She must avoid further signs of deviance that would draw unfriendly attention. She decided to defy her anxieties and gamble on taking the trip.

The west wind was already rising by the time Ria staggered into the central bus depot. She was convinced that not a single tree grew between Chambana and the Rockies. Carey spied her through the glass doors and offered clumsy assistance. They walked to their boarding gate together. Since they no longer felt self-conscious about being an odd match, Ali and Hannah had given up smirking at them.

Carey gave his luggage to the baggage handler but the sight of the woman stunned Ria. She recognized the worker in the greasy uniform as her senior English teacher from University High School.

"Instructor Russell!" she cried. "What are you doing here?"

"Pu ah on nah bus." The grinning woman croaked back at her.

"Aren't you Marie Russell?"

"Pu ah on nah bus." The other repeated her gibberish. She tried to tug the suitcase away from Ria.

"I'm Ria Legarde. I was one of your pupils five years ago. Don't you remember me?"

Ria seized the woman's shoulder trying to make herself understood but the other jerked away. She backed against the side of the bus with hand upraised to shield her face.

"On nah bus," she whimpered.

Carey tugged at Ria's sleeve. She bent down to hear his whisper.

"Let it go, Ria. Maybe she was your Marie Russell once but she isn't now." He mouthed a single syllable "PSI."

Ria stumbled up the steps into the chartered bus.

Snow showers burst upon them before they were out of Chambana. The wind rose even higher in open country. The bus wobbled and shuddered under its attack. Ria stared grimly at the snow pelting her window. She stared till the swirling gusts became rampaging stallions, death-white steeds with eyes like frozen stars. She let their screams blot out the fresh memory of Marie Russell's tortured voice and the older memory of that voice declaiming poetry in tones like singing steel.

The bus skidded off the road and rammed into huge snowbank. Although seat belts had spared the passengers serious injury, the cold now threatened them. They were marooned midway between the Buckley and Onarga exits, too far to walk to shelter in either direction. Rescue vehicles would take a while to reach them since the closest were based in Paxton, more than 20 kilometers distant. Although one man suggested they attempt to right the bus themselves, he was hooted to silence. It was far easier to huddle together until help came.

Ria tried to draw Carey close to warm his body but he turned rigid at her touch. Ali fussed over Hannah as if she were a tropical bird, even lending the younger woman her scarf for extra protection. Ria withstood the temptation to blast Hannah's perfect cheeks with frostbite. Why couldn't the others cope? With so much body heat available, they were in no real danger even if they were stranded for hours.

Ria had faced a nastier winter emergency in her childhood. She'd been riding with her father in a University truck—a flagrant breach of the rules—when he lost control on an icy country road and overturned the vehicle in a ditch. He was knocked unconscious. Unable to call for help on the truck's radio, she trudged five kilometers to the nearest farm station through searing, crackling cold. The trek did not harm her in the least but contact with the frigid cab door had left her father's face badly frostbitten. The accident also cost him his rank as chief campus arborist. He never recovered from the humiliation.

But why bore (or worse, alarm) her colleagues with the anecdote? They were unlikely to believe her. Ria settled deeper into her coat as if going to sleep. She turned her head toward the wall and cautiously slid back her glove to expose the ring. Sliding the setting around to the back of her hand, she blinked rapidly to make the center flash. Then she gratefully plunged into the shining waters of her own mind. . . .

Ria awoke to scents of macotters, water, and sunbaked wood. She was lying on cushions spread between Kara and Lute. He playfully brushed a damp lock of hair from her forehead and helped her sit up. They were riding amidships in a small motor launch operated by two *perfur*. An awning shaded them from the sun but the glare off the river hurt Ria's eyes. Her clothes were streaked with sweat. Their vessel was approaching a dock where an adult macotter and three cubs waited.

"All hail," cried Lute. He waved madly at the shore. "Look, it's Amris come to meet us."

Kara waved in a more restrained manner which Ria copied. They docked and debarked. Kara thanked the boat-handlers while Lute sprang ahead to a warm reunion with his sister. He sat on his haunches to fondle the squealing cubs. Amris briskly introduced them to Kara and Ria. The loudest and liveliest of the trio was called Dasher. He was the eldest child of their cousin Rakam the entrepreneur. Dasher's playmates were merry-eyed Mossy and her plump younger brother Puff. Mossy was eager to show the newcomers her stuffed toy duck but Puff clung to Amris' leg. The *femfur* dislodged his tiny hands and held them up in the polite *perfur* greeting. Kara knelt down and gravely returned the gesture. Puff squeaked with shy pleasure.

"Made your manners, off we go." Amris swept Puff up in her arms.

Dasher and Mossy scrambled ahead to lead them up to the village proper on the bluff. The cubs raced up steps beside the dam separating the Tippecanoe River from Evening Star Lake. Dasher reached the top first, a feat that seemed to impress him more than it did Mossy.

"Catch us, Amris," he cried.

She hastened after them. Meanwhile Lute spoke quietly to Kara.

"If the steps bother you, I'll—"

"You show too much concern."

"With reason." He gave Ria a sad look and left them.

Despite Kara's preference for walking unaided, Ria kept close behind her as a precaution. It was a slow climb for the old woman even though the stairs were broad and shallow to suit *perfur* feet. Ria glanced back over her shoulder. Their crew was unloading the moored boat while another craft neared the shore. Upward and eastward from the dock ran a gravel road lined with clapboard buildings painted red. Beyond them near the river loomed a windmill. Farther south lay fish ponds, gardens, and a paddock where draft horses grazed.

Kara and Ria joined the others at the rest of the dam. They stepped down to the village, a single large complex of buildings with polka dot walls. The several square blocks of patchy grass surrounding these structures swarmed with *perfur*. Scores of them rushed to and fro yelling and chittering in happy chaos. They carried lengths of lumber, wads of bunting, armloads of evergreen boughs, hand tools, baskets of fish, and outlandish musical instruments. A placid nanny goat and two kids ambled through the uproar.

The nearest macotters were setting up booths for craftworkers to sell their wares during the festival. If a plan guided their efforts, Ria was unable to discern it. Dasher broke away to hurl himself at a thick-bodied *masfur* who was trying to mediate a standbuilders' dispute. The cub's squeals sliced across the adult macotters' angry humming. All three glared at him.

"Asked you to keep him in hand, Amris," said the macotter in charge.

Amris ignored his rebuke. "Father's busy, Dasher. Let him work."

"Busy for days," the cub complained. "Him'n mother

both.'' He trudged back to Amris with a sideways plea for sympathy.

Rakam noticed who else had come. ''Oh, Lady Kara, an honor.'' He greeted her with excessive deference. ''Pay m'respects soon as duty permits.''

''I understand your position,'' said Kara.

''Wouldn't want to distract you from duty, Rakam,'' said Lute.

They left him to his executive labors.

''Pompous,'' Lute muttered.

''Cures a good ham,'' replied Amris.

''Comes of his closeness to the pigs.''

Ria tried not to smile out of consideration for Lute. She could afford to find Rakam amusing since she didn't have to share his world. How would Lute react to a Professor Clyde?

Past the clamor of standbuilding, they came to the main polka dot structure.

''Our *koho*,'' said Lute proudly.

''It is the clan's community house,'' Kara explained. ''The Festival dinner will be served inside tomorrow.''

The cubs snuffled at the mention of food. Lute went on boasting: ''It's roomier than Quail Cloud's, finer than Burning Hills'—''

''We've been here longer,'' said Amris.

Now they were close enough for Ria to see that the dots were cross-sections of logs set in mortar. These were painted in madly clashing colors—scarlet next to lemon yellow, magenta beside orange. The corner posts were carved and painted like flower stalks. The turfed roof slanted down to a south wall filled with small, thick glass panes. A ridgepole in the shape of a tree branch jutted from the northwest corner to support a weathered brass bell. Before the great western doors stood twin pillars with deeply carved bases. These pillars bore the emblems of the Twin Stars clan and the Rolling Shores tribe to which all the clans of the region belonged.

A single large ash tree stood between the *koho* and the

lake. Ria was startled to see a man talking with a *masfur* and a *femfur* in the shade of the tree. These three welcomed Kara and Lute like old friends, then turned curious eyes toward Ria.

The human, a comfortably shabby bespectacled man in his fifties, spoke first: "That is your servant Julo's body, Kara. Whom does it guest today?"

"The soul of my pupil Ria Legarde, a *solexa* of great promise," she replied.

"The one you told us of? The very one?" The *femfur* murmured sounds of awe and approval which the man echoed.

The short, white-muzzled *masfur* came alert. Amris seemed on the point of asking a question but kept silent.

"Herself," said Lute.

Kara continued the introductions. "Behold Ellesiya, the prime *solexa* of Twin Stars, Gemai their clan chief, and Wan Lerrow, prime *solexam* of Lafayette."

They raised their hands formally and the *perfur* showed her their personal marks. Ria wished they knew her well enough to embrace her the way they had her friends. *Perfur* friendliness stirred her old hunger to belong.

Knowing less of rulers than shamans, she naively asked Gemai: "How were you appointed, sir? By the tribal elders?"

"By them? Away off on the Michigan dunes? We chose our own chief, Lady Ria. You must come from far not knowing that." He stroked his white whiskers. "I'm not an actual mayor like Oren Henderlund of Lafayette—we're waiting on him and his folk now. *Perfur*'re wary about power. Rituals keep me busy but m'job's mostly keeping calmer than m'clanmates so they'll let me lead 'em in a crisis."

"Gemai," said Ellesiya with a fluid wave of her arm, "you're the only one in the clan who doesn't preen over talents."

Ria half expected her to pirouette. The graceful creature

looked as if she were dancing while standing still.

"Pride's the only thing Doc Lerrow here can't cure," said Lute.

"You'd know, Lute," said Amris, drawing a hurt look from her brother.

Gemai struck a pose of downcast modesty and everyone laughed. The cubs laughed loudest to see their elders at play. Yet to Ria, Lerrow seemed the humblest of the lot. Important persons in her world did not mingle with such easy intimacy.

Kara got them moving again. "Let us leave you to your council, mighty or modest as it may be. Come to me at the guesthouse afterwards, Wan. We have much to discuss."

Quarters for human visitors lay past sprawling flower beds on the north side of the *koho*. The cottage and surrounding out buildings were connected to the *koho* by covered walkways. The complex reminded Ria of a medieval manor house. However, the guesthouse interior was arranged like Kara and Lute's home with a square of rooms grouped around a solar atrium. Thick walls made it pleasantly cool. Ria and Kara found their bags waiting in the chamber they were to occupy.

The whole party relaxed in the atrium while Amris handed out mugs of warm beer. This brew was sweeter and darker than the one Ria knew. Mossy and Puff held their mugs carefully in both hands. Dasher tried to drink like his elders and spilled beer on himself. As Lute was drying him off, he squeaked:

"Guess what, Lute, guess what? Amris let me watch her shoot her gun. Bang!" He sighted and fired an imaginary weapon. "Macrats, look out! And I got to hold it, too. Bang!"

Ria blanched. "You actually let a little one handle a gun?" Guns were rigidly controlled in her world. She'd never touched one herself.

"What harm?" asked Amris. "Empty. Safety on. Got to

start learning self-defense young. Where you come from humans don't?''

''We're not allowed—we don't need to,'' she corrected herself. ''No macrats there.''

Amris wrinkled her muzzle in disbelief.

Before she could reply, Kara said, ''Show Ria your rifle, Amris. Ria is suspicious of what she does not know.''

The cubs chittered as Amris unslung the weapon for Ria's inspection. It was not unlike pictures she'd seen of old guns but images hadn't conveyed the lethal efficiency of the thing.

''A genuine Colson,'' said Amris beaming. ''Don't see many nowadays. Can throw a 7 millimeter slug 900 meters in a second.'' She stroked the brown-toned barrel.

''It's a family heirloom,'' Lute explained. ''We've been rangers for generations.''

''Stock's new, made to m'measure,'' said Amris.

It was burl walnut, carved with the *femfur*'s mountain-and-sunrise mark. Ria almost felt like touching the satiny wood but her social conditioning held.

''I'll be a ranger, too,'' said Dasher. ''Found the rifle sign last Yule.'' He pointed to a tiny silver charm hanging from a chain around his neck.

''Game doesn't always hold true, young one,'' said Amris. ''Kept finding cradles every year I played.''

Lute guffawed.

''What will your calling be, Mossy?'' asked Kara.

''Music-making,'' she replied. ''Maybe.'' She showed them her harp charm.

''And what of Puff?''

''He's too little to play Find-Your-Life.'' The other two cubs giggled.

''Do not be so quick to claim pride of age,'' said the old *solexa*. ''It may be that Puff has the makings of a *solexam*. He may be the one to find the silver tree next Yule. At the moment, allow me to find some rest while you find some food. I will eat with Wan when he comes in.''

Amris and Lute took Ria and the cubs off to share the midday meal with their brother Siote and his kin. They explained to Ria that the *koho* was a refuge in bad weather but during the summer *perfur* families lived by themselves in the woods near their village. These individual earth-sheltered huts, called *warums*, were scattered all around Evening Star Lake and its northern counterpart, Morning Star Lake. Ria mistook the first *warum* she saw for a grassy mound until its occupant popped out of a low door to wave at them.

Siote's people were already outdoors when they arrived. Once encircled by her hosts, Ria felt a shiver of panic—those powerful furry limbs, those heavy fangs within the smiles. The cacophony of scents they wore—cedar and mint, sassafras and honeysuckle, fennel and roses—mingled with the odors of mud, fish, and leather. Beneath it all, their natural muskiness came through. She remembered that they were mustellines, thinking cousins of the mink and the wolverine, and she was merely human.

The introductions confused her. How could she tell *perfur* apart? She clutched at distinctions in size, coat color, or markings. Siote was shorter and darker than Lute. His wife Nirena was plumper than Amris and unscarred. Nirena's younger sister Mania and her husband Tahar showed their newlywed status in constant scuffles that drew ribald jokes from the rest. Ria didn't catch the names of a neighbor couple and their half-grown daughter.

They were all talking at once in voices louder and shriller than Ria was used to. At first they tried to slow down their speech for her sake but soon forgot in their haste to tell Lute all the family news since spring.

The meal of grilled fish served in grape leaves calmed them somewhat since they couldn't talk as much with their mouths full. Dasher nearly choked on a fish bone but Lute pulled it out and treated the scratch inside his throat.

How could a dozen *perfur* seem so many?

Walking back to the village afterwards with Lute, Ria savored the quiet. There was nothing but a few snuffles from him, the crackle of twigs underfoot, sounds of birds and insects. She would have lingered longer if she could. They were back into turmoil too soon.

During their absence more *perfur* had arrived, raising the noise and confusion level higher. Would the festival be the luncheon party writ large? The fever of action infected Lute. His darting eyes and quivering whiskers told Ria he wanted to be with his clanmates instead of her. When he hailed a passing work party, she bade him join them.

"Why don't you go with your friends? Wan Lerrow's coming out of the guesthouse. I can talk to him."

Lute chirruped his thanks and scampered away. Ria watched him hoist a plank on a platform being raised beside the lake. She turned around to find Lerrow standing behind her.

"It must look chaotic compared with what you're used to."

"How do they get anything done? Obviously they do: these buildings didn't grow from seed. Kara and Lute didn't explain much."

"Your work's going to require you to diagnose situations for yourself."

"Can't I have some hints?"

"This time, m'lady." He grinned and straightened his steel-rimmed spectacles. They were held together with a bit of wire. "You'll have to take this on faith, but *perfur* festivals do come off nice as you please every year. Just the setup's noisy. You know they can't walk across a room without raising a ruckus. Main thing is, *perfur* won't take orders from on high. They've got to see and smell whomever's in charge. Takes lots of tail-twisting to persuade them to act, but once committed, they work like hell's merry imps—until something distracts them and the persuading has to start all over. Let a rare butterfly flitter by this minute and half the workers on those booths would rush off to chase it.''

"Rakam wouldn't like that." Ria pictured the pudgy macotter huffing in irate pursuit of the deserters.

"Daresay not. Next year he'll be pounding nails while someone else's in charge. He'll resent it all the more because his wife's a dance dreamer and runs her show every time.''

They dodged a *perfur* who couldn't see for the bundle of pine branches he was carrying.

"Comes time for ritual, though," said Lerrow, "they'll get more solemn and reverent than a church full of humans. That's obeying the voice of tradition, not any one individual.''

"You seem to know them inside out.''

"Might say that." He smiled at some private joke. "It's part of my job, in fact, as you'll see tomorrow night.''

"How many *perfur* attend the ceremony?''

"Five hundred, maybe. Good weather's bringing everybody in. That sounds like too many *perfur* in one place to you.'' He smiled.

"I'd only met Lute and Amris before.''

"And Amris takes some getting used to.''

"Yes.''

"I keep forgetting your world doesn't have *perfur*. Me, I can't picture doing without them.''

"I think I could do with less of their galloping good cheer. It depresses me.''

"Let's get indoors then, away from the worst of it and out of the sun. We could go back to the guesthouse. Kara's resting there now. Or would the *koho* interest you more?''

"I've already been in the cottage.''

They sidestepped a troupe of choristers. Ria assumed that's what they were. Each was singing a slightly different version of the same shrill tune. Ria's ears protested.

Past the *koho*'s double doors, Ria felt as if she'd fallen into a page from the *Book of Kells*. Every bit of woodwork, from the pillars to the balcony running along the north wall, seethed with carved and painted patterns, swirls of abstract interlacings as restless as the *perfur* themselves.

The noise inside the community house was an equally apt expression of the *perfur* spirit. Trestle tables thudded on the brick plank floor as a work party set them up down the empty middle of the hall. Shrieks interrupted happy chitters when feet got in the trestles' way. These tables would hold tomorrow's feast. The length of the rows promised something immense, even by macotter standards.

Lerrow led Ria to a sprawl of cushions and tabourets clustered in front of the great hearth on the east wall. Three elderly *femfurs* tossing gambling counters on a cloth covered board didn't bother to look up from their game as the two humans approached. Lerrow awakened an even older *masfur* who was dozing beside racks of kegs and bottles. He ordered beer for himself and Ria. The bartender shrugged when they declined hard candy as an accompaniment and set the bowl beside the gamesters instead.

Ria asked Lerrow a question. "If you're a shaman, why do the others call you 'Doc'?"

"Medicine's my special *solarti* gift. I'm both *solexam* and physician. Yes, we've got doctors here, not as advanced as yours to be sure, but soul-art makes up for some of the equipment we lack."

"So the medical exercises Kara and Lute put me through have practical use."

"Wouldn't make you do them otherwise, m'lady." He took a long swallow of beer. "You've met a young *femfur* named Manita? She was born with a septal defect—"

"A hole in her heart."

He nodded. "Such heart surgery's beyond our resources so I patched the defect, cell by cell, through *solarti*. Manita's a fine fit *perfur* today."

"Now wait. You keep saying 'my world' and 'your

world.' You seem to know my real origin though Amris and Gemai don't.''

"Kara's told me—and Ellesiya—all about you. You're unique, young lady.'' He toasted her with his mug.

"People keep saying so.'' Ria squirmed.

"But Kara wants to wait a while before publicizing the results.''

"Until she sees if the experiment worked?''

"Partly, but initiating a *solex* on another timeline isn't something we want everyone with a smattering of the art trying.''

"But she told you.''

"She's consulted *solexes* in foreign parts, too. I'm the nearest thing she's got to a peer in this corner of the land—not that anybody living's quite the peer of Kara ni Prizing.''

He continued. "It was Lute insisted Ellesiya be told. They grew up together and he knew she could be trusted. If he'd stayed home instead of going to study with Kara, he'd be the chief soul artist here, not her, which she well knows. But someday when she's the prime *solexa* of all Rolling Shores and he's still in private practice, who's to say which choice was best?'' He shrugged.

"Didn't Lute want the post?''

"He's too much the scholar. Day-to-day responsibility for the clan would hobble him. You look surprised, Lady Ria. Don't you realize yet what a powerful talent Lute has? I can see that you don't.''

"Are you saying I've been entertained by an angel unawares?''

"Well put! Not an angel—the mischief he used to make! But a new piece in our world's game. I'll not live to see all the plays he makes.''

Ria frowned. "You sound like Kara talking about me. What exactly's wrong with her, Doc? It seems serious but Lute won't discuss it. Instead he says things like 'I should get her a kitten to boost her spirits.' Kara's faded just in the few months I've known her.''

"Truth is," he looked grave, "her heart's giving out—chronic congestive cardiac failure. Our drugs and treatments can ease it but not cure it. Even if we mobilized a whole team of medically gifted *solexes*—which she'd never permit even if they could be found—the prognosis would still be poor because of her age.''

"Why would the operation take so many shamans?''

"Because each of us can only leave our bodies for a brief interval. Remember I said I'd patched Manita's heart cell by cell? Damn slow work it was, too. Stimulating tissue growth in an infant's a vastly simpler problem than the corrective intervention Kara needs.''

"Could I make a difference? I'm here in a host body. I can leave it for as long as I want.''

"Maybe if you were a trained surgeon and could handle the operation yourself. Maybe.''

"Tell me what to study!" Ria cried. "Please, I want to help. Kara means so much to me." She couldn't lose her mentor so soon after finding her.

"You're a generous lady." He ordered more beer. "But Kara and Lute tell me your talents don't lie in the medical area, even though you can do some basics now. That's why they haven't said anything. They don't want you wasting time you need to prepare for your proper specialty, the mastery of fire.''

"Couldn't they let me choose for myself?" She drank to mask her agitation. They're still not treating me as a colleague."

"You almost said 'equal.' That's what I'm curious to learn, Lady Ria, exactly how equal you are.''

Once more Ria felt manipulated by forces beyond her control. "A moment ago you called Lute a gaming piece. Is that all we are, he and I, nothing more than gambling tokens like the ones those old *femfurs* are tossing?''

''Their game's played with peach stones.'' The eyes behind the spectacles grew enormously gentle. ''A fruit stone is really a seed.''

''I think I'm up to facing the *perfur* multitudes again. Alone, if you please.'' Ria left her beer unfinished.

## XV

Ria exited through the back door which was connected to the separate kitchen building by a covered passageway. Outside, five *perfur* were unloading baskets of eggs from a wagon. Ria ignored the workers and their cargo but stopped to admire the draft horses. These four glossy black beasts wore harnesses festooned with tassels. Seeing, touching, even smelling horses again thrilled Ria. Shyly, she traced the delicate contours of their nostrils and combed their forelocks with her fingers. The horses endured her attentions as patiently as they did their masters' noise. (Shrieks over a dropped basket drew no more than ear flicks.) Ria left the macotters busy working and the horses brushing at flies.

Ria walked west staring across the roofs of the red structures she'd seen earlier. These, she'd learned, were warehouses and workshops built into the side of the bluff. Faint sounds of whirring and hammering came from that direction.

More booths had been set up in rows flanking the lake.

Some of the jolly proprietors were already doing business. Customers excited by the first offerings hampered the efforts of others to lay out their wares. How could hagglers hear one another above the chittering and humming? Ria let the crowd carry her along, seeing what she could through the tangle of furry bodies. On sale were pebble mosaics and packs of dye, body ornaments and schools of marzipan fish, gaming boards and gleaming knives, pine needle baskets and lean smoked hams. A lutier was playing a peacock-shaped *gouar* to a drummaker's accompaniment. A book dealer and a seller of spiced fish paste were quarreling over the clashing scents of their products. Ria tried one of a honey merchant's free samples. It tasted like mustard. She was sorely tempted to spend some of the pocket money Kara and Lute had given her on a present for them. But Quail Cloud bourbon, being another clan's specialty, was not available. She didn't know if her friend drank the locally made maple syrup liqueur.

Beyond the booths, close to the edge of the lake, Ria spied a crowd of *perfur* clustered around a red striped tent. They were listening to a feather-decked *femfur* chant:

> So every spring
> She counted time
> For kindred sped
> Beyond death's Door.

The audience howled approval. The performer bowed, accepted the contents of a bag passed among her listeners, and retired into her tent. Ria wondered what the poem had been about. She'd have to ask Lute.

Here and there, limestone stairs led down to the surface of the lake where latecomers were still unloading their canoes. So absorbed was Ria in the bustling processions, she collided with two heavily laden *perfur* before she'd noticed them. After mutual apologies, she helped them pick up the bulky leather boxes they'd been carrying. Noticing that the *masfur* was bent with age and the *femfur* had a badly crippled foot, Ria insisted on taking part of the load herself. She was glad Julo had a strong back.

Upon reaching their booths, the pair introduced themselves. They'd instinctively recognized that another soul resided in Julo's familiar body. The elderly *masfur* was Habale, a scent mixer, and his daughter was Basala, a leatherworker.

"I've heard of you, Basala," said Ria. "And I've seen that exquisite token pouch you made for the Ranger Captain Amris."

Basala snuffled. "Honor to serve the brave Captain. Pleasure, too, with her sure taste."

"Honor also to serve you, Lady Ria," said Habale. "Want to watch while we unpack? See our full stock. Won't last long. Not at all, not at all." He chirruped at the prospect of brisk sales.

This innocent pride persuaded Ria to stay. Having a longer reach, she hung canvas that would shade their booths from the next day's heat. Today's sun was already too low to be annoying. The slow-moving old *masfur* set out measuring gear, gauze bags, racks of tiny stoppered bottles, and stout glass jars. He fussed and muttered getting the array into an order that pleased him.

Yet Ria found the aroma of Basala's leathergoods more enticing than her father's stores of herbs, petals, bark, and essences. The beauty of the *femfur*'s work dazzled Ria. Genuine leather was an expensive rarity in her world. Here, finely made harnesses and containers were commonplace. Basala showed Ria her pattern book from which other items, such as a curiously constructed saddle, could be ordered. The artisan offered to design a personal emblem to match Ria's *harnama*, Rides In Air. After several sketches on a wax tablet she smoothed with a mere touch of her finger, Basala produced an image Ria liked. Fluid curves suggested a horse and rider galloping above a cloudy mountaintop.

"Can you remember the look of it, Lady Ria? No use stamping actual calling disks you can't carry home." The *femfur* refused payment. "Fair exchange for your help setting up. Favor to a visiting *solexa*'s good for business, same as a favor to a ranger. Though any that fights macrats is my friend. Raiding party killed my mother. Working on me when Amris' uncle drove 'em off." She closed her jaws with a crunch.

Basala's terseness chilled Ria. Not only was most of the *femfur*'s right foot gone, there were scars on both legs and her tail was missing its tip. She was ashamed of herself for staring but the other did not mind.

Basala patted Ria's arm and said, "I'm proud o'surviving."

Habale shuffled over to join them. After admiring the design for Ria's mark, he studied her so narrowly she felt uneasy.

"Experiment," he murmured to himself. "Yes, yes, fine experiment. Must try it."

"Try what, father?" asked Basala.

"Mix a scent with only the soul to work from. Lady Ria's soul." He pointed to her, then he grasped her hands firmly and stared at her with eyes that were watery and a little sunken.

"Is that enough to go on?" asked Ria.

He nodded. "Come by tomorrow afternoon for a whiff. Coriander'll be the base note. Show you the recipe so you can have it made up at home."

"Thank you but I must tell you, where I come from, nobody wears perfumes."

The two *perfur* were shocked into silence. Ria left her new friends to their customers. She continued along the curving lake bank, past the ceremonial platform and the last stretches of turf. Canoes glided south on the sunset waters. Some macotters were swimming while others called fish into weirs to be held for tomorrow's feasting.

At last she found Lute sprawled on a jetty down at the lake's edge. His harness lay beside him and his fur was wet. She descended the stairs to be with him. They sat together for awhile without speaking, merely letting their fingers trail in the water, watching leaves drift by in the gentle current.

"My own waters," he said. "I don't swim in them often enough."

Ria gazed out across the darkening lake and recited:

> *What color are the waters of evening*
> *Lit by the evening star?*

"Lovely."

She laughed nervously. "My attempt to rewrite Ausonius."

"What's that?"

"*Who*, not what. A Roman poet. He sang of a quivering leaf afloat on a quiet river while the Empire crashed around him."

"Now I remember." He nodded. "Fall of Rome's a lot farther back from us than from you. Too far for *solexes* to reach. Once made it all the way back to fourteenth century France. Wasn't easy." He looked smug. "Sat in a bowman's mind at some battle—what'd he call it? Poitiers. Didn't like to watch the killing. Never went back. Wonder what became of sergeant Jack?"

"You've taught me to take *sofli* for granted too well. I keep forgetting the time gap. Keep forgetting that in the here and now I have been dust for six hundred years. If I searched long enough in Chamba, would I find my grave?"

"I haven't seen it, m'lady," he replied softly.

"Nor looked?"

"Only your body's dead here, not *you*." He looked at her with terrible earnestness.

She snorted. "You believe that?"

"Don't need to believe. I know where eternity begins. Show you sometime." He fell silent for a moment, then brightened. "Till then, want you to feel comfortable whenever you are, in whatever body."

Ria tried to lighten the mood. "I'm uncomfortable enough in this body to want a cooling swim. Come with me?"

"This instant."

"Let me undress first. Lute pulled off her boots. Ria squinted at her reflection in the water but it was rippling too much to show a clear image. "What does Julo's face look like? You've never let me see it."

"We thought it'd be less awkward for you in the beginning. Forgot afterwards. Could find you a mirror here or next time we're home. It wouldn't show Julo as he is naturally, only yourself looking out of his eyes. That's all I saw when I guested in his body."

"So I need another vantage point." She stood up and took off her shirt. She admired her muscular male chest with its little flat nipples and fair curly hair. She was unbuttoning her fly when a *perfur* cub's head bobbed up beside the jetty. It was Dasher.

"Lute 'n Ria! Come to the *koho*. Tahar 'n Manita're going to Build the Bones."

After Lute lifted him out of the water, Dasher drenched them shaking himself dry. Ria glared but put her damp shirt and boots back on. She hoped she could change clothes before the *perfur* swept her up in new activities.

Dasher chattered all the way back to the community house. "Tracked you down so quick, shows I'm meant to be a ranger. Gonna track macrats." He mimed a search and fired an imaginary gun. "I get places first. Bet Mossy's still looking." He scuttled around their feet, nearly tripping them.

Mossy was, in fact, sitting quietly with Puff near the main doors of the *koho*. Dasher joined them, boasting of his prowess and complaining that cubs were excluded from the ceremony.

Sun shades were drawn across the window wall but there was just enough light inside the open doors for Ria to recognize Amris, Gemai, and some of the other *perfur* she'd met earlier. About two dozen of them were gathered in the aisle between the buffet tables. The crowd parted to let them reach Kara's side. The old *solexa* had a chair but Doc Lerrow and the *perfur* stood. Tahar, Manita, and Ellesiya crouched on a richly embroidered cloth in the center of the ring. The mates faced each other with Ellesiya between them confronting a tree-shaped candelabrum. Ria felt the press of strongly scented furry bodies. It was not the dampness of her clothes that made her shiver.

The ceremony began.

Ellesiya lifted her hands. She and all the perfur present intoned: "By sunlight, starlight, firelight, reflections of the Light Eternal." The candles burst into flame of themselves.

The *solexa* continued alone: "May the Most High bless this new-pledged pair: make him bold as Rue, her wise as Lis, first parents of our people. May they found a clan that lives till every leaf be fallen and every bough be dead."

The crowd responded: "Till all the seas shall fail and rivers no more run."

Ellesiya handed the couple a beaded white bag and stretched herself on the floor face down. Manit and Tahar shook the bag three times and turned it upside down. A rain of tiny colored flakes scattered over the design of concentric circles on the cloth. The crowd sighed with a single indrawn breath. Each *perfur* craned and squinted to get a look at the pattern. They did not seem to like what they saw.

Ellesiya raised herself again and studied the array. Her tone was guarded. "There's nothing to be seen on time's nearest branch. Manita died young there. Tahar never was born. These fish scales tell us what we think will be, not what must be." She pointed to specific circles. "Blues on the water ring, green on the woods ring—fertile country where they're settling."

"Not fertile us?" asked Manita. She traced a brown ring where no scales lay.

"Reds for danger, reds for rats," said Tahar. "Too many."

Ellesiya nodded slowly. "Oracle says two things at once: prosperity and peril. Now Build the Bones together, to show you can meet all fortunes well."

She untied a black pouch from her belt, loosened its strings and set it before them. Tahar and Manit took fish bones from the bag and lay them in the center of the design. Layer by layer the dainty stack grew higher, a skeletal tower that a breath might blow away. The crowd prickled with tension. Hands spontaneously joined all around the ring. Ria feared Lute would crush her fingers, he gripped them so hard. She sensed everyone was trying to will a favorable sign into being.

Screams tore the stillness. Tahar's hand twitched. The bones scattered.

They ran to the doors, jamming against each other in their haste to get out. Ria elbowed her way through. Dasher lay bleeding but unmoving against the foot of the pedestal that supported the clan emblem. Puff kept shrieking, "Hurts! Hurts!" Mossy only whimpered. Amris gathered them in her arms while Doc Lerrow examined Dasher.

"What happened?" asked Amris.

Mossy pointed to the ridgepole. "Climbed up there. Going to muffle the bell so it wouldn't ring tomorrow. Fell—"

She wailed and set Puff crying again. Even in the dusk a white cloth could be seen fluttering overhead like a small winding sheet.

Kara joined Lerrow and Lute beside the injured cub. "Will it be the Door?" she asked calmly.

Lute gulped before answering. "Better if it were. His neck's broken."

"Third cervical. Cord's severed," added Lerrow.

"He's not suffering now. Doc stopped the bleeding and I'll hold the pain. Puff was feeling it more than Dasher. Give 'em here, Amris." Puff went limply quiet in his arms. "Dasher'll never move again."

"Merciful God," whispered Kara.

The clamor grew. More *perfur* ran up to the accident scene demanding to know what had happened. On learning, they wailed and gnashed their teeth. Ria's own were chattering uncontrollably. Quadriplegia was tragic enough in a human, but for a *perfur* cub. . . . She slammed her hands together so loudly the others stared at her.

"Are you just going to stand around snarling? If *solarti'* s so wonderful, let's heal him with it. There's too much talent on hand not to find a way." Ria made no move to wipe away her tears.

Kara turned slowly to face her. "There may be a way, daughter, if you will open it." She raised her voice to address the crowd. "Hear me! Lady Ria whom you see before you in the body of my servant Julo has not simply exchanged souls with him in the usual manner of *sofli*. We who know her secret have held it close: this *solexa* has not come from distant parts but from another branch of time entirely."

The crowd murmured.

"Thus she is free," Kara continued, "to move from body to body without displacing the soul within. This spares her host the huge expenditure of energy needed to make an exchange. Therefore, let Ria enter Dasher to oversee his healing while the rest of us who know the art bear her up moment by moment."

"I see it, Kara!" Lerrow slapped his thigh. "Four experienced *solexes*, maybe a hundred others with measurable talent, enough to pull it off. Get those nerve fibers rejoined straight, inhibit scarring—that cub'll swim again!"

Ellesiya did not bother to comment. She took command. "Find a pallet for Dasher. Get torches. Rouse the village. Summon every pattern dreamer, art maker, beast tamer, every lighter of the family flame.''

The crowd exploded in all directions to obey. Ria watched in a daze, hoping her small medical knowledge would prove equal to the task. She heard Lute pleading with Kara. His words came as if from a great distance.

''You can't take the strain, Kara. It'll kill you.''

''So? Better I should die than he live thus.''

''Ellesiya, Doc Lerrow, and I can handle it. No one would blame you for staying on shore.''

''I would blame myself.'' The finality in her tone brooked no argument.

''You lie down to work, it'll be on a blanket. You'll listen to me that much.'' Lute hummed as he walked away.

Events moved too fast for Ria to ponder the burden of power. Dasher was cautiously moved to a clear space in front of the doors. In petal-like rows, scores of *perfur* lay down on the grass between the *koho* and the ceremonial tree. The four *solexes* were closest to the patient. Ria did not see the final preparations. Three half-grown cubs escorted her to the guesthouse where they would keep Julo safely occupied during the treatment.

These young *perfur* offered nervous encouragement. Ria tried to make Dasher's face appear on the surface of her borrowed silver ring. Then she dropped like a stone into unknown waters. . . .

Ria hit her target. Once there, she perceived with the passionless immediacy of an angel. The being called Dasher was an array of cells, a concert of energies, each one subject to her ordering. She focussed her awareness on the tangle of severed neural fibers that was his spinal cord: had she eyes to see them, they would have looked like unbleached yarn. Time to redress the loom mischance had wrecked. Sley the reeds, tie the harnesses, every warp thread in its rightful place before the weaving could commence. Kara had shown her, was showing her, would go on showing her until the task was done. There were more threads than she could number, each one more fragile and elusive than the last. She fastened them all. Lute upheld her, Lute and a host of others surrounded her like breaths of brightness. Raise, lower, throw, beat, went the rhythm of the loom. Crews of weavers sped to and fro in time to Dasher's heartbeats, the pattern makers themselves a pattern.

It was full day when she woke. She felt rested and so vigorous and alert she stared for a long moment at part of last night's dream. She stretched herself, then went rigid when she looked down and saw she was still slightly rumpled. Was it so old woman on the afternoon.

She jumped up, of course, no hesitation. She needed to find the kitchen, eating hard.

"What's happening, Kara—" she said as—
"Were out, there all night."—
resting in the long, she said.—
you eat.

"How's the baby?" she said hastily, to cover it. She leaned over Kara.

Should recover...? Kara, who, having just made the difference... the baby... that of her said... mother's eyes and seemed to say that all is held.

# XVI

It was full day when Ria awoke. She was astounded to feel so vigorous until she remembered Julo's body had taken no part in last night's exertions. She stretched languidly, then went rigid when she noticed Kara's bed was empty. It was still slightly rumpled from the old woman's nap the previous afternoon.

She jumped out of bed, heart pounding, to search the guesthouse. She found Lute's sister-in-law Nirena in the kitchen slicing ham.

"What's happened to Kara?" Ria cried without greeting.

"Worn out, that's all," said the *femfur* gently. "She's resting in the *koho* sickroom. Can see her 'n Dasher soon as you eat."

"How's the cub?" Ria had nearly forgotten him in her anxiety over Kara.

"Should recover says Doc. No dancing for awhile. You made the difference, Lady Ria." She gazed at her with a mother's eyes and smiled. "Best thanks is to feed you."

While Ria dressed, Nirena prepared a huge brunch of ham, scrambled eggs, cornbread, honey, and fresh blackberries. She nibbled scraps of meat while Ria ate.

"Have you known this ham's from cousin Rakam's private stock. Sent it over this morning as a gift for you and Kara."

"It's delicious."

Nirena cut herself another piece. "Rakam claims he's changed his coat, yes indeed." Her whiskers twitched. "Enjoy it while we can. Soon be his old stuffy self. Get you something else?"

"Thanks, no. There's more good food here than I can finish."

"You aren't as hungry as the other soul artists? They came to limp as dead fish. Those of us without the talent're scurrying around feeding those of you with it. Got to get your strength up for tonight's feast."

Ria felt obliged to help Nirena with the dishes before leaving.

Food was already being set out in the main hall of the *koho*. Ria dodged throngs of noisy *perfur* carrying bowls, trays, and baskets. Their efforts to thank her for saving Dasher added to the confusion. She did manage to find the sickroom chamber down in the basement. She heard Lute and Doc outside the door.

"Wouldn't let her do it again for my own grandchild," said the doctor.

"Throw a block on her myself before—" Lute waved at Ria.

"Is Kara really all right?"

The caution in Doc's answer was itself an answer. "She's resting peacefully. You can look in on her if you like."

"That isn't quite what I asked."

"She's not in immediate danger but the prognosis. . . ."
He shook his head.

They took Ria inside. The clinic was thoroughly sound-proofed and surprisingly cozy. Curtains divided it into small, den-like compartments. They let her see for herself that Kara was indeed asleep and breathing normally. A young *solexam*, one of Ellesiya's apprentices, kept a careful watch over her.

Ellesiya herself was in the adjoining section attending Dasher. Assisting her were Amris and the cub's mother, a skinny *femfur* named Lekera. The cub looked pitifully small in his heavy cast. Shame more than pain showed in his half-closed eyes.

"How're you feeling, Dasher?" asked Ria, a touch too heartily.

"Not Dasher any more," said Amris. "Gave'm a new name: Still There."

"Take a lot on yourself, Amris, changing m'son's name. But if it makes him quiet. . . ." Lekera's voice was as thin as her body.

"Don't hurt now, Lady Ria."

"Thank the *solexa*. Was she saved your skin," said Lekera.

"There were scores of us," said Ria firmly. "The others in this room deserve equal thanks." Lekera's ungenerous nature made her a fit helpmate for Rakam.

"Didn't mean to cause that trouble, didn't!" The cub's eyes went so wide Ria could see their white rims. "Promised mother no more jokes."

Lekera snorted but Ellesiya gave a wistful sigh. "No jokes at all, Still There? Rest of us need that bit of laughter. Even more, need you." She brushed his eyes closed and sent him to sleep.

The visitors took this as a sign of dismissal. Amris left with them. Once the door was closed, she said, "Take him months to heal right but he'll be a ranger yet."

Lute and Doc began talking at once, stumbling over each other's words as they climbed the stairs. The *perfur* in the hall were making too much noise for Ria and Amris to hear them. They hustled outside where it was quieter.

"Know what this means, Ria?" cried Lute. His speech blurred into chittering.

Doc said, "We'll call it ni Prizing's method. It's a whole new way of doing surgery by *solarti*." Excitement brought a flush to his leathery face. "Lute and I were fit to burst our skins waiting to explain it to you." He flashed a rueful smile. "See, when I'm among *perfur*, I start acting like them. Point is, access to an off-branch *solex* like you gets around the time limit. We'll be able to do complicated operations we couldn't do before. Think of the lives we can save because that fool cub broke his neck."

Ria shivered. "Surely you don't expect me to sit in on every emergency?"

"'Course not, Ria," said Lute. "Anyone strong in the art will do, long as they're from some other timeline."

"It's a relief to know I'm not the only fish in the sea."

"God only knows how many *solexes* there are on the whole Cosmic Tree. The more we reach, the more we can do without putting too much strain on any one person," said the doctor.

Ria imagined service quotas, like House duties back home, but this world didn't impale persons on schedules.

Doc continued. "We've only found a couple of other branches close enough to ours to use for probability checks. But that may change." He looked closely at Ria. "You just might start some new twig sprouting all by yourself."

"Why so few branches?" asked Ria. "The Great Death must've been a major nexus point."

"Made for some sharp bends all right, but we *perfur* didn't survive on every branch. Or else we didn't make friends with humans." His lips curled back from his fangs. "Could show you timelines where your people wear the fur skinned from mine. Could but won't."

Doc looked anxious to change the subject. "These visiting *solexes* don't have to be physicians. You've proved that, Ria. They can even come from savage cultures that don't understand the theory of *solarti*."

"And," said Ria triumphantly, "you can return the favor. You can help tribal shamans elsewhere cure their patients, too." She glowed at the first stirrings of healthy professional pride. Maybe she could actually fulfill the potential her colleagues claimed to see in her.

"Let's get our thoughts in order while Kara's resting," said Doc. "We can talk this through until the feasting starts."

"You three do the talking," said Amris. "I'm too hungry to last that long."

"There's ham in the guesthouse kitchen—Rakam's own. Help yourself," said Ria, smiling at the other's glee. *Perfur were absurdly easy to please.*

Amris dashed away. The others followed at a slower pace. The guesthouse proved to be a refuge from the surging commotion of the village. Doc's enthusiasm did not prevent him from laying out his theories in an orderly fashion, accompanied by various esoteric diagrams. Ria couldn't follow all the technical points he argued with Lute but she gained new respect for the caliber of their minds. Previous experience had led her to associate brilliance with arrogance.

They were able to work undisturbed for several hours until the arrival of Mayor Oren Henderlund and his party from Lafayette. Henderlund was a trim, dapper man of perhaps forty with the amiable face of a beagle. He shook Ria's hand as if campaigning for her vote. He seemed indecently glad that ni Prizing's Method had been discovered in his own district and had to be restrained from calling on Kara in her sickbed.

Ria, Lute, and Doc joined the visitors for the rest of the afternoon which was given over to swimming and boating contests on the lake. She applauded when Lute did, sharing his pleasure in his young nephew's canoe victory and in his niece's performance in the water-dancing. Afterwards, Doc and the Lafayette people withdrew to banquet with Twin Stars' leaders while Ria and Lute went to eat with his family.

The feast itself surpassed all her expectations. Hitherto Ria had loathed fish as a bland but obligatory protein source. She hadn't known there were so many ways to prepare it. Not merely content to broil, fry, smoke, pickle, stew, and bake fish, the *perfur* glazed it with aspic, wrapped it in crust, poached it in liquor, sauced it with fruits, nut paste, or flowers. They nested sets of individually stuffed fish inside one another for layer on layer of contrasting tastes. They were equally inventive with eggs, pork, duck, frogs, eels, snails, chicken, turtle, and crayfish. (Ria was not always sure what a given dish was made of.) Beer, wine, ice punch, and vast expanses of tinted meringues, berries, puddings, torten, and achingly sweet egg candies filled out the menu. The eclectic extravagance of it all reminded Ria of a medieval banquet—she half expected to see a castle of pastry and gilt paper as the centerpiece. Such thoughts were perhaps better left unvoiced lest the *perfur* act upon them.

The buffet line moved along with loud good humor and reasonable dispatch. Doc was right: *perfur* could organize when they chose to. Today the clamor and the mingled scents of furry bodies didn't bother Ria. They matched the insistent aromas of the food. If she visited here often enough, she might start wearing perfume herself.

Right now, she wanted to taste everything. Although she regretted a few choices like the anise-flavored eel, she marveled at the bounty of delicious food. What a splendid way to rebel against the sober dietetic strictures of her own world. Existence here had a richness she'd been hungry for all her life without recognizing it.

By the time she reached the end of the board, she realized

that the meal was as much a cooking contest as a feast. Each elaborately garnished dish bore the name marks of the family, work team, or social circle that produced it. Her friends explained that good cooks earned prestige, a commodity no *perfur* ever had enough of. But given its awesome logistics, the festival forced the clan to cooperate as well as compete. Did their government have much use aside from coordinating the four seasonal festivals? She was told that a new clan gained full acceptance the first year it celebrated the complete cycle from its own resources with suitable pomp. She wondered how long it would take Manita and Tahar's foundation to attain that status. No name for it had yet been chosen. They said they were waiting for one to manifest itself. They didn't anticipate this would happen until after they were actually settled in their new home.

They ate out-of-doors, picnic style. Nirena had had the forethought to spread a blanket in a pleasant spot. Trips back through the line continued for the rest of the afternoon until bottomless *perfur* appetites were sated. Individuals were responsible for cleaning up after themselves. By the time this was accomplished, with much merry chaos, night had fallen. The Midsummer ritual was at hand.

The clan gathered before the lakeside platform which had been soaked with water, spread with sand, and heaped with a mound of brush upstage. A pair of huge, three-pronged flambeaux provided light. Ria and Lute were given places in the center front of the assembly. To their delight, Kara was brought out in a chair to sit between them. Although still weak, the old *solexa* was in fine spirits. Lute chittered a greeting but the sight of her tightened Ria's throat so badly she couldn't speak. She knelt to the left of the chair and lay her head in Kara's lap.

"No need for grieving, child, on my account or any other. Fix your attention where it belongs this night—on the ceremony." Kara's face was unreadable in the dimness.

Lute cried: "Look who's coming!"

Ria stood up for a better view. Two *perfur*, who proved to be Amris and the young apprentice *solexam*, were carrying Still There on a pallet. The cub was perfectly quiet in what a brief touch of his mind confirmed was an induced slumber. Amris and the *masfur* set him down on Lute's right and sat down behind him. Rakam and Lekera took places on the other side of their son.

The ritual began with the ringing of the clan bell, the one the mischievous cub had tried to muffle. Torchbearers led a procession from the great doors of the *koho*. Ria scarcely recognized the next marchers in their ceremonial costumes. Doc wore the same kind of iron cap and charm-laden white poncho Kara had worn when Ria first saw her. A drum hung from Doc's belt and he carried an iron-tipped wooden staff. Beside him walked Ellesiya wearing a metallic mesh vest covered with tiny silver bells. A medallion bearing the Twin Stars crest perched on her bell-hung headdress. Behind Doc came Gemai. He bore the clan mark suspended from a garland of flowers. More flowers covered his body harness. Mayor Henderlund beside him was nearly as festive in his beribboned white suit. Behind these four walked silent musicians, a human trumpeter, and a *perfur* band carrying exotic string and percussion instruments. Four *perfur* couples in flower-trimmed harnesses brought up the rear.

The crowd stayed perfectly quiet during the march. Only the tinkling of Ellesiya's bells and the crackle of the flambeaux could be heard as the procession approached. The torchbearers and musicians stayed below while the others mounted the platform. The four dignitaries stood on pedestals to the rear of the dais with the couples ranged in front of them.

The trumpeter stepped forward and climbed halfway up the stairs. He turned to face the audience and blew a fanfare. A flicker of motion on her left drew Ria's eye. She turned to see the Lafayette people getting to their feet. On her right, Kara stirred and struggled to stand. The old woman did not ask for support, she took it, levering herself upright on Ria's shoulder.

"Get up, Ria," came the whispered command. "We humans rise for our anthem."

Ria scrambled to obey, careful to put a protective arm around Kara. The trumpet solo had a blood-stirring majesty that was ever so slightly familiar. But Ria couldn't recall where she might have heard the tune before. Then Kara and the other humans began to sing. Their voices were few and small beneath the starry sky:

> Mine eyes have seen the glory
> Of the coming of the Lord. . . .

Ria joined in the later choruses with a baritone so strong and true she amazed herself. "Glory, glory hallelujah" kept ringing in her mind after the music has ceased. Kara sinking back into her chair nearly threw her off balance. She resumed her seat as the *perfur* musicians readied their instruments.

Now it was the furred people's turn to stand. Their melody shimmered and rippled. A river of sound rose from five hundred throats:

> Brightwater children:
> Sunray and moonbeam
> On sleek fur gleaming.
>
> Seed-time to leaf-fall,
> Starlight to fireglow
> Living is dancing.

The singing ended. The *perfur* sat down. The music flowed on to accompany the dancing of the four young couples. They swirled and glided across the platform like converging currents. They swept up Doc and Ellesiya, set them at the eddy's heart and spun away.

The two *solexes* confronted each other. The quick, lithe body of the *femfur* opposing the slow, thick body of the man. Her bells spoke to his drum. Their hands touched. Their bodies entwined in a formal embrace. They turned halfway round their common axis and parted. But now the man moved with fluid sureness while the *femfur* lagged. No one had to tell Ria that the two *solexes* had exchanged souls.

"By sunlight, starlight, firelight, reflections of the Light Eternal," they intoned to renew the ancient oath of friendship between their peoples.

Ellesiya spoke through Doc's lips: "We persons of fur,"

He answered through hers: "We persons of skin,"

They said together: "Are children of the same Earth. We pledge ourselves comrades: no hate or harm between us, only fellowship and faithfulness."

"As it was in the days of Rue and Lis," said she.

"As it was in the days of Never Smiles and Sees Inside," said he.

"So may it ever be," said they. "Till every tree is ashes and raindrops turn to dust."

Again the embrace and the half turn. The *solexes* were themselves again. They led the dancers down the stairs.

Gemai and Henderlund stepped forward and touched the palms of their hands together. They crossed to opposite corners of the dais and cautiously lifted the huge flambeaux from their holders. These torches' triple flames reminded Ria of the tridents medieval men used to hunt otters. Given enough time, perhaps every cruelty could be redeemed.

The *perfur* musicians and the trumpeter struck a fanfare together. Gemai and Henderlund cried, "Out of multitude, oneness!"

They plunged their torches into the cone of brush at the rear edge of the platform. A pillar of fire erupted to the cheers of the crowd. The flames reflected far out on the lake, a spear of light challenging the darkness.

Lute was beside Ria, pulling her up and spinning her around like a leaf in a whirlpool. Through the exploding tumult she heard Still There squeaking:

"It's bright! Oh, it's bright!"

Ria was back in her own body curled up on the seat of the stranded bus. Her coworkers were huddled in shivering clumps exactly as they'd been a moment before. She could smell the stink of their fear. Nothing had changed and everything had changed.

# XVII

It was full dark by the time Ria returned to her apartment from the ill-fated expedition.

After a concentrate bar had dulled her hunger, she'd endured the hours of waiting for rescue in tolerable comfort. The other passengers, equally provisioned, kept shivering and cursing the cold. She tried to touch and calm the minds of the worst sufferers—not the easiest task with people she disliked—but she lacked Lute's gift for easing pain. Perhaps she flattered herself thinking that she'd helped any of them. She scolded herself for neglecting to comfort Hannah. Heroic altruism was still beyond her grasp.

Ria turned on the lights and stared at her quarters with something approaching affection. After a day in that reeking bus, she appreciated it as a clean, warm place where the air was fit to breathe. While hanging up her coat, she thought to making a potpourri to sweeten her closet. What had the old scent mixer suggested, coriander?

She ate quickly, then unpacked leisurely. After her adventures in the Twin Stars village, she didn't regret missing the trip to Chicago. But her coworkers were aggrieved at the loss of their treat. She started to punch Carey's phone number but hung up without finishing it. Her constant solicitude wasn't good for him, any more than Ali's was good for Hannah. Let him ask for cheering if he needed it.

Ria flipped on her computer to check for announcements and personal messages. Headlines, schedules, and safety directives for the blizzard droned on. She heard the description of a new learning program in neurochemistry and placed an order for it.

Suddenly, the machine began to buzz like an angry hornet. Ria froze in a silent scream as the dreaded words materialized on the screen. She had been summoned to report for examination by PSI. Once activated, the pitiless white symbols locked her terminal against other use. She couldn't even turn it off to escape the horrid buzzing. She'd have to call the number listed and acknowledge receipt of the message before PSI would encode a release signal. If she ignored the order for more than twenty-four hours, her negligence would be broadcast publicly, making her subject to immediate arrest. There was nowhere to hide.

Ria had the wit to rage quietly. The system might be operating in two-way mode, transmitting the sights and sounds before it. Critical statements or gestures might be held against her. Her inward wrath turned incandescent. She was ablaze to consume every traitorous circuit with avenging fire, all the way to PSI's world headquarters in Sydney. And as for the informant who'd betrayed her—it could only be Hannah—she could cook that skinny bitch's carcass from the inside out.

She spun around abruptly, strode to the window, and mentally hurled her anger from her. Let the storm's white stallions trample it and blind drifts hide it until it sputtered out to ash. Not fire but ice must serve her now. She called for an appointment in a semblance of calm.

On a Friday afternoon two weeks later, Ria sat in PSI's waiting room preparing for judgment. From childhood experience with a diferent arm of PSI, she knew a bit of what to expect and had set up certain defenses. A defiant pedant to the last, she silently recited as much of the *Dies Irae* as she could remember. She breathed in time to its iron-shod meter. Let Thomas of Celano worry "What patron's aid can I secure?" She would have Lute. He'd promised to be with her during the crucial interview but she couldn't feel his warm presence yet.

Her I.D. number flashed on the wall screen. She went to the office indicated.

The therapist who sat inside did not bother to rise when she entered. She stared briefly through Ria as if through grimy glass before deigning to acknowledge her.

"I am Vonh Blanca," she said in a yogurt-smooth voice.

Her features were mannish and her hair an indefinite brown. Although she was small, her body seemed abnormally dense, as though her bones were too massive for their size. She made a needlessly elaborate show of checking Ria's identity card against the display screen inset in her desk before permitting her to be seated.

The delay allowed Ria time to redouble her inner fortifications against what looked to be a formidable foe. Since poise would invite suspicion, she took care to project an air of innocent confusion. She let Blanca direct her to place her wrist on the sensors in the cradlelike arm of the examining chair. There was no strap—questioning under restraint was done elsewhere. One was forced to give continual consent to the monitoring. Ria counted on somatic discipline to generate signals that were normal, but not excessively normal.

"Relax," purred the therapist. "What's there to be afraid of? You and I are simply here for a chat about certain *problems*—" she made the last word a euphemism—"you appear to be having."

Ria smiled weakly.

Blanca continued. "We'll want a record of what we say, just in case it's necessary for us to meet again. This button starts the taping and this board enters my notes."

Ria obediently stared where she was pointing.

"Of course you can't read the symbols." Smugness crept into her tone. "They're a special professional code." Blanca's hand stroked the keys like a noiseless patient spider. The painted nails on that hand looked too perfect to be real: was the therapist a biter? To open the record, Blanca took Ria's case history. She belabored trivial points as if trying to provoke unguarded words.

"How many weeks did you spend in fifth grade before you were advanced?"

"Not long, about a month."

" 'About a month.' Is that three weeks or four or perhaps five?"

"I can't remember," answered Ria, holding her temper firmly. "Don't you have that information on file in front of you?"

"Yes, but I prefer to hear it from you."

"I've already told you I can't remember exactly."

Blanca scrutinized the display screen and purred again. "Your test scores indicate you have a remarkable memory. Your mind appears to exceptionally keen. Otherwise you wouldn't have been chosen for acceleration, would you?" The Eurasian tilt to Blanca's blue eyes helped her pretensions of sagacity. Ria found it expedient to lower her gaze to the other's cheek, which bore the marks of inept dermabrasion.

The tedious quiz continued. The therapist probed Ria's family tree looking for diseased limbs to exploit. Blanca forced her to relive the ugly details of her parents' deaths: her father's fall from a sleet-encrusted tree, her mother's leap from a residence hall roof. Facts did not suffice. She pressed for interpretations and reactions. Why had her mother's mother really defected from the Soviet Union while studying at the University? Surely it must have been more than romantic infatuation with a local man? Ria pled ignorance since the principals had died years before she was born. She likewise denied knowledge of her paternal grandmother's involvement in the Native American movement of the previous century. Her Ojibway grandmother had been too wise to burden her with subversive information.

Round and round the thread of query went as Blanca spun her meandering web. At length she reached the crucial pass.

"Aren't you curious to learn why you were summoned here?"

"Yes," answered Ria. "To see if the reasons confirm my assumptions." At this point candor might confuse Blanca.

No surprise marred the therapist's creamy voice. "Would you like to share these theories with me?"

Ria tried for the right touch of naive self-depreciation. "It was a rocky autumn for me. Nearly got electrocuted in September. Didn't feel quite right for months afterwards. The doctors *said* I was healthy so I didn't want to bother them with trifling problems. Kept putting off making an appointment for a follow-up. You know how it is." She flicked a nervous laugh.

"What were these trifling symptoms?"

"Moodiness, trouble sleeping, lapses in concentration, outbursts of temperament. It's over now. I feel fit and stable again but I'd be the first to admit I wasn't myself a while back. I suppose some overzealous observer must've thought I was about to . . . go noncomp and turned in my name. Isn't that what happened?"

"We discourage the use of the term 'noncomp' here. However the complaint lodged does fit the pattern of abberations you describe. Aren't you glad that citizen acted responsibly?" Her concern dripped in clots.

Ria agreed. "One can't be too careful these days."

"When we give you an official clearance, you can be sure

you're a healthy unit of society."

"That certainly will put my mind at ease," murmured Ria.

"You almost said 'at ease *again*,' didn't you? The way you handle yourself indicates you've seen us before." Blanca was entirely too perceptive.

"I had the mandatory counselling session after my mother died. Isn't that on my record?"

"What about the previous episode?"

"A full trauma report must be on file."

"Your faith in our omniscience is touching." Blanca favored Ria with a Buddha-like smile. "The facts and dates are before me of course but I'd rather have it in your own words."

"You refer to my kidnapping. I was ten years old at the time, in early October, I believe."

"October fifth."

"Thank you. A noncomp—sorry—a deranged middle-aged woman snatched me off the playground after school. She held me captive in a condemned house for a couple of days."

Blanca studied the display screen intently. "Witnesses said the kidnapper cried: 'This one, I've got to have this one,' as she dragged you into a stolen van. Why do you think she said that?"

"I've no idea." Ria made a particular effort to keep her response bland. She'd agonized over that very question for a decade, yet was no nearer to an answer. The kidnapper's choice of her remained a mysterious election that still marked her off from other people.

"So she took you to a condemned house."

"It was one of those Victorian mansions that'd been chopped into student apartments fifty years ago. It had a turret sticking up in the middle, I remember." She also remembered the stench and the cockroaches scuttling through trash.

"The whole neighborhood was going to be leveled for a new housing project. Nobody heard me when I screamed."

"How did she keep you in?" Blanca wanted all the details.

"She watched me every waking minute and tied me up at night." Ria had lain bound hand and foot to her captor like a puppet on strings.

Blanca kept on probing. "Can you explain the woman's motives for taking you?"

Ria shrugged. "She was insane. Isn't that enough explanation? She also drank a lot. She said she wanted me to be her sweet little girl and live happily ever after with her in her beautiful home—she saw that boarded-up wreck as it used to be, with lacy curtains and crystal chandeliers. When she got really stinking drunk, she talked about 'sampling my charms.'"

"What do you suppose she meant by that?"

"I'd rather not know."

"Not know?" Blanca raised an eyebrow. "Everyone benefits when light is shed on dark corners. I must caution you that your earlier remark might be construed as homophobic." She pretended to step outside her professional role to exchange a confidence. "I've always been more male than female myself and feel perfectly comfortable that way. Any reason why I shouldn't?"

"We're taught not to be judgmental," said Ria coolly.

Blanca studied her display again and smiled. "I sense a certain tension in you about sex. Perhaps it's your inexperience. Not many women your age are still virgins."

"I haven't had the occasion to change that status."

"No? There are licensed partners available in Chambana, the same as other cities."

"I can't afford such services." Ria grew wary.

"A course of therapy prescribed by PSI would be free. In fact, that's my clinical specialty when I'm not doing evaluations. Keep that in mind when you decide you want help."

She was fairly avid to be of assistance.

Ria forbade her flesh to crawl and jumped back to the original topic. "Too bad nobody helped the kidnapper when she lost her daughter. I think that's what drove her mad."

"Obviously no one bothered to report her to the proper authorities."

Ria continued. "I don't know where it would've ended—with me dead, I suppose—except that it was a dry October and a grass fire happened to break out in the yard behind the house. I smashed the glass in an upstairs window, crawled out on the roof, and yelled for the firefighters to save me. So I got away.with nothing worse than a bad cut on my thumb. See the scar?" She held up her right hand.

"You must keep your arm on the sensors at all times," Blanca reminded her. "Were there adverse social effects after the experience?"

"After I came home, people treated me as tainted, as if I'd asked to be kidnapped. Other children wouldn't play with me. So counsellors recommended a transfer to the University's laboratory school. I'd been eligible for it all along, but my parents had refused to enroll me—my intelligence disturbed them. I was glad PSI persuaded them otherwise." Ria's gratitude was sincere. "With accelerated progress, I finished my education two years early. But I never had time for anything besides studying."

"So much for the reactions of others." Blanca circled her prey again. "What about your own feelings afterwards?" Her notemaking hand was poised to strike.

Ria chose the example with maximum therapeutic appeal. "I guess the nightmare was the worst of it. I had the same one over and over from the first night I was held captive. This ghastly song the woman kept singing put it into my mind. I couldn't get rid of it for weeks."

"What was it like?"

"Easier to sing it than explain it."

"You still remember the tune?"

"How could I forget? Besides, I've got an uncommon memory for music." Ria wishes she had the use of Julo's voice now to do the macabre waltz justice. But she'd perform it better than its composer, whose contralto had wandered as much as her mind.

> *A carousel laden*
> *With corpses of children*
> *Spins round in the night.*

> Libera me,
> Domine,
> Libera me.

> *The muzak reels onward;*
> *The steeds never falter;*
> *Their burden's so light.*

"That's what I kept dreaming about," said Ria, "a black merry-go-round hung with crepe streamers. The animals the dead children rode were alive. All of them were monsters." Ria permitted herself a noticable shudder.

"It must've been utterly terrifying for an impressionable child." Her sympathy dripped lethal stickiness.

Ria accepted it without flinching. Impressionability was a flaw Blanca would try to exploit. Let the therapist be secure in the arrogance of her trade. Ria wanted her strength undervalued so her enemy would be content to fashion a weaker web than otherwise.

Ria widened her eyes a calculated trifle. "As I said, I stayed terrified even after the rescue. The repeated nightmares wore out what little patience my mother had with me. My father thought an outing might help. So we went to Indianapolis to see their famous Children's Museum. I really was enjoying myself there—can still recall gawking at their mastodon skeleton—until we reached the top floor. Nobody'd warned me that the prime attraction was a fully restored antique carousel. One look at it whirling around and I ran shrieking down four flights of ramps and out the door before my parents caught me. They were so mortified, I think they wished I'd kept running into the busy street and under the wheels of some convenient truck.''

"Then professional care dispelled your nightmare," said Blanca smugly.

"It stopped." Ria doubted that PSI's child psychiatrist had brought her relief. The dream vanished like a videotape switched off the night the imprisoned kidnapper hanged herself. But the after-image of fear still lingered in Ria's brain.

"Now tell me how you interpret—" A buzzer signaled the hour was up. "We seem to have run out of time before we've begun to address your present difficulties. I see that we'll require a series of interviews to resolve the issue."

"I want the chance to prove I'm healthy now." Ria laughed with feeble bravado.

Blanca smiled back, languid and confident. "We'll make the appointments now." She punched a command. The printer in her desk disgorged a hard copy which she gave Ria. "Your schedule. I'm looking forward to our next meeting. You should, too."

Ria bobbed her head. For a fleeting moment, she stood in front of the desk, fixing Blanca's smallness in her mind. She turned and walked out of the PSI Center with measured steps. She did not relax control until she was out on the sidewalk, safely insulated by indifferent crowds.

Long shadows marched across the snow. At least it was too late to return to work. She couldn't face anyone she knew just now. The long walk home would ease the tension. It was good to move her arms and legs again, good to brush against human beings instead of sensors. Vile memories poured out of her like sweat.

She remembered far more of the madwoman than she dared admit to Blanca: a gaunt giantess with huge bony hands that clutched and petted, wasted flesh that reeked of liquor and mildew, dark eyes that were never still.

The captor who ignored her captive's fright had nevertheless wept hysterically over a dead bird. The cardinal must've flown in through a broken window and perished before he could find his way out. The woman fondled the bird and tried to speak to him in his own chirping language. After she gave up trying to revive him, she plucked his wings and stuck the flame-red feathers in her graying frizz.

The odor of frying peppers from a campustown restaurant reminded Ria how hungry she was. She'd been hungry during her confinement, too. The food the kidnapper offered her was rancid and after she spied rat droppings among the sunflower seeds, no amount of coaxing could convince her to eat anything.

Ria turned the corner onto Green Street. The force of the wind funnelled down the thoroughfare tempted her to take a bus the rest of the way. But the wind was at her back now. She'd get home under her own power—and sneer at *Alma Mater* en route.

Her account of the charnel carousel was meant to appease Blanca: psytechs were fond of analyzing dreams. With luck it might distract the therapist from aspects of her behavior that could not bear close examination. She resisted the impulse to describe the nightmare to its last morbid detail. Why dwell on the way the children's corpses grinned or enumerate each monstrous steed? From mirror-pelted manticores to lamias with bloodstone eyes, the named and nameless horrors out of myth were there. And most unwise to mention the carousel's master, the skeleton of ice that kept control. She knew it for a *windigo*, the devouring demon her Ojibway ancestors feared above all else. Only a powerful shaman could defeat this fleshless foe.

Cunning as Blanca was, she would never unravel the nightmare's true meaning, or at least the meaning the kidnapper had claimed for her song. She'd expounded her exegesis at dismal length: having a captive audience unloosed her tongue. The Unmerry-go-round was their world. The chill breath of Federation rule had frozen the children who signified humanity's future. In this environment, only preening monsters could survive.

Ria did not care to repeat such treasonous sentiments to PSI, especially now that she was coming to share them. Initiation had opened her eyes to the profound wrongness of her society. She saw more of it each time she returned from Kara and Lute's world. When would she move from observer to actor? She was terrified by her friends' expectations of mighty deeds from her. Was she the only shaman available to challenge the *windigo*—whoever or whatever that was. How could she lead anyone off the Unmerry-go-round when she didn't know how to free herself from one psytech's web?

Her hunger pangs bit harder. She'd have to eat supper before seeking Kara and Lute for counsel. Why hadn't Lute kept his word to help her during the interrogation? Were his promises written on the rushing wave?

Summer sun filtered through gaps in the shades drawn across the atrium skylight. It traced paths of brightness on the shadowed floor.

Ria was kneeling on a pad beside the fish pond. She was up to her elbows in water and on the point of removing a beslimed rock from the decorative arrangement around the rim. Julo's face stared blurrily back at her. From what she could distinguish, it was an unremarkable face—flatter, narrower, and fairer than her own. Yet it moved and responded in perfect obedience to her will. The sense of being a transient guest in someone else's home overwhelmed her. The burden of responsibility this entailed was almost too much to bear. Kara and Lute had been wise—

She remembered why she'd come. Leaving the rock precariously balanced, she sprang up, nearly tripping over a pan filled with aquatic plants in her haste. She shook the water off her arms and wiped them dry on her pantlegs.

"Where is everybody?" she yelled.

Lute appeared at the west door. He was carrying a tray of dirty dishes.

"Here already, Ria? Should've been watching for you but Julo wanted to start fixing the pond today." His voice was edgy.

"What kind of greeting is that?" She followed him into the kitchen. "You act as if you're sorry to see me."

"You're putting thoughts in m'head, Ria." He set the tray down on the table. The food had scarcely been touched. "You've got worries. So've I." Lute was clearly not himself. Even his whiskers drooped.

"Well, mine happen to be critical. I come here for help and you're too distracted to give it. Some friend! Where were you during the interview? Don't you understand, Lute," she shrieked, "that creature could have me raped or brain scoured or killed with one tap of a false fingernail!"

"Woman," his voice rose in a humming snarl, "shut your brother-loving mouth! Or at least talk quieter." The humming ebbed. "Noise bothers Kara. I'm trying to keep her comfortable but she's weaker every day."

Ria blushed. "I didn't think . . ."

"Start thinking. Stop diving to conclusions. Said I'd be with you and I was. Every minute, except for a few in that PSI woman's mind—squalid!" He shook imaginary filth off his fur. "No wonder your world's so sick, with your healing arts in hands like hers."

"But I didn't feel your presence." She reproached him.

"Didn't mean you to. You were handling the current perfectly well without me. Didn't want to spoil your concentration, risk messing up your control. There were more sensors on you than you thought, like the camera focussed on your eyes to record changes in pupil size."

"I'm sorry, Lute." She touched his cheek. "I'm just that scared."

"I'm scared and sorry, too. Let's talk it out with Kara. But mind how you put your questions."

Kara sat in bed propped up by lace-trimmed pillows. Her face was nearly as pale as the white gown she wore and her flesh hung loosely on her broad frame. She was knotting fringe on her Tree of Life tapestry while a half-grown calico cat attacked her ball of thread. Ria hesitated in the doorway, reluctant to disturb her mentor. Kara's fragileness made her too precious to approach.

"Are you here to stare or speak, child?" said the old woman. "Come in and sit beside me."

"She's not staying long," said Lute firmly.

Kara chuckled. "You would keep me wrapped in cotton batting if you could, Lute. We know the end is coming soon. Do you fear I may drop dead while your back is turned and cheat you of the chance to exercise your art on me?"

"What surgeon likes to treat a loved one, Kara?"

"Would it be any easier for my niece Dorel, if she were here and not away in Springfield addressing the Senate? You young folk fall easy prey to gloom. Whose deathbed is this, yours or mine?" She paused to stroke the cat. "Open the window, Lute. We need fresh air."

He obeyed. The warm west wind bore scents of roses and freshly cut grass. As she sat down in the chair indicated, Ria noticed more roses in a vase on Kara's tall chiffonier. The breeze stirred their petals. Some fell from their blooms like drops of blood.

Lute snorted. "See your strategy, Kara. You're acting nonchalant so we'll think you're a saint."

"Perhaps I am." Her blue eyes twinkled. "On the other hand, perhaps my soul is riddled with wickedness like so much dry rot. You will know which is the case soon

216

enough.'' Kara measured thread along her arm. ''The suspense is getting the better of you, dear *perfur*. You may start shedding at any moment.''

Ria listened in bewilderment. Their banter seemed better suited for a maternity ward than a hospice. ''I don't understand,'' she stammered. ''You act as if you're waiting for a birth instead of . . .''

''Quite right,'' said Lute with something of his usual vigor.

Kara said gently, ''I am waiting to give birth to my completed self. Only by dying are we born into everlasting life. I do not regret my passing, nor should you.''

''Hasn't happened yet, Kara. Could be reading the signs wrong. Don't be in such a hurry to leave us. Ria's problem needs looking at.''

''Lute has told me of your plight, child. The threat is indeed grave. Nevertheless, it can be met and turned aside.''

''How? No one gets away from PSI. I try to be brave and unbending like you but I'm afraid I'll break if they push me too hard. See?'' she sobbed, ''I can't even keep this body from shaking.''

''Nonsense!'' said Kara sharply enough to make the cat jump. ''By strong self-mastery you held the interrogator at bay.''

''Once. Next time or the time after she'll get through. I can't hold off PSI forever.'' Ria's sobs dwindled to a ragged sigh.

''You brood overmuch on resistance. Storms fell stiff trees while those that bend survive.''

''Stop being afraid of being afraid,'' said Lute. ''There's more'n one model of courage. Rigid's not my people's style.'' His supple body looped around Ria's chair.

Against her will he made her smile, imagining rows of *perfur* stiff as fence posts. She ran her hand down his curved back.

Kara said, "Once aroused, your enemy's suspicions will be difficult to quell. Do not try to pretend health. Let them discover some illness, then meekly allow them to cure you of it."

"Illness? Or a physical defect that could account for my symptoms, some sort of brain damage." Ria's confidence surged back. "What about epilepsy? In a few cultures, the shamans were epileptics who'd learned to control their seizures."

"Might work, might work," chirupped Lute. "Make them think that's what's wrong with you."

"They'll be hard to convince," said Ria, cautious again. "How can I do the necessary research in secret?" But once formless worry had begun to assume a recognizable shape, her researcher's instincts rose to battle it. She gazed ruefully at Kara and Lute. "And the demonstration is left as an exercise for the student."

"You are equal to this task, Ria, and to far greater ones yet to come," said Kara in a voice turned slow and sad. "Not every *solex* born can stand the climb. Some fall to their dooms never knowing they had a vocation. Such a one was the woman who kidnapped you."

"What?"

"She could've easily been you, Ria. From the bit we saw of her, she'd have made a great *solexa*. Had the gift but not the training. Or putting it another way, you could've easily been her."

Ria squirmed with disgust, unwilling to accept the comparison. Yet there was no escaping the truth of Lute's statement. It confronted her each way she turned, like her own reflection in a hall of mirrors. The words choked out of her:

"You saved me from turning into *that*? So she snatched me instead of another child because she saw herself in me." The kinship made Ria feel unclean.

"Yet see what came of your ordeal," said Kara. "Fear,

218

sleeplessness, and hunger stirred your latent powers. The *solari* you used to kindle that grass fire led us to you. As my own master used to say, 'By winding roads we reach the mountain's summit.' "

Ria was still following the logical path she'd begun. "If the kidnapper was a potential *solexa*, then I must've been picking up the nightmare directly from her mind. That's why it stopped as soon as she died."

"Wasn't just a private horror, either," said Lute.

"We now believe the madwoman's talent shaped that dream. Your world's future is to become a carousel filled with dead children borne up and down and round and round at a demon's bidding." Kara's voice slipped halfway into a chant.

"Good grounds for that belief, from what we've seen happen on some branches close to yours. Been looking at the question closer since Festival." He stared at Ria with terrible earnestness. "That merry-go-round's got to be stopped."

"By me?" She sat transfixed by his unstated conclusion. They had moved her to a place far beyond her prior fears. Her eyes pleaded for another moment's freedom from the burden they were about to lay upon her. Her glance wobbled about the room searching from some refuge. No tapestry, no cabinet door, no rose could shield her from her fate. She envied Kara's sleeping cat its animal nature.

Kara spoke again. "This is the task for which you were made, my daughter. I am certain of it now for I am seeing all things more clearly in the twilight of my life."

Kara eased herself forward from the pillows and sat proudly erect. She rolled her needlework to one side, a gesture that woke the cat and drove it off the bed. Kara stretched out her right hand to Ria who clasped it without being told. The wrinkled skin felt abnormally cool. Lute stood behind Ria keening a wordless *perfur* melody that soared beyond the range of human ears.

"You must find the *windigo* and destroy it," the old *solexa* commanded. Her words fell like drumbeats. "Yours is the fire that will conquer its ice."

"What is the *windigo*? Where do I seek it?" Ria matched her mentor's tempo.

"The frozen mountains of your earliest childhood dream, the mountains you could not spur your steed to climb were blasted by its touch. You alone—"

Kara gasped in agony and fell forward. Lute sprang to her bedside. He pressed comforting hands against her heart and laid her back against her pillows. "Heart! Can't hold her on this side of the Door long."

Ria cried: "What can I—"

"Nothing!" He snarled.

Lute slammed her into a world of gray, distorted forms glimpsed from a corner. The Old One was hurting. The Furry One and the Young One made sounds. The Old One opened her eyes and made sounds. She and the Young One touched faces. They all smelled sad.

Another splash of power and color vision returned. Ria was no longer crouched on the floor bristling and mewing. . . . The shudder passed. She had hands again instead of spotted paws. She realized she had watched Julo and Kara say farewell through the eyes of a panicked cat.

"Sorry," whispered Lute. "Had to get you out of Julo's way a minute."

"Understood." Ria whispered back. She knelt beside the bed opposite Lute, unsure of what to do next.

Kara must have sensed her confusion. She spoke in a faint voice that was almost matter-of-fact. "You have never witnessed anyone die before. Lute knows the way of it well. He has a gift for bringing peace to smooth the going hence. Give me a kiss for the journey, beloved daughter."

Ria clung to her for a moment. She dragged a sob that should have been "Mother" from a throat too tight to speak.

Then she resumed her place to watch through silent tears.

Lute took Kara's hands in his for a dialogue without words. Joy softened the old woman's tense face. He intoned:

"The Shadow of the Door
Now falls across your path.
Kara ni Prizing, do you choose to pass?"

"I do."

And it was done.

"Sunlight, starlight, firelight fade.
Enter into Light Eternal,
Brightness never failing."

Lute closed her unseeing eyes. "Who created us all in the beginning, receive us all at the end."

# XVIII

The brightness hurt Ria's eyes. Its pitiless glare bounced from one slick, hard plastic surface to the next. The dazzle left no deep shadows to mourn in. Her apartment was snug as a well-lit tomb. She stared a while through welling tears, then hid her face in her pillow and wept.

How few hours out of her life had she spent with Kara; how priceless was each of them now. Despite repeated hints, despite the warning signs she'd seen herself, she hadn't actually believed Kara would die that soon. ''She seemed a thing that could not feel the touch of earthly years.'' Now earth would lie upon her, as it would one year on Ria herself.

And what of Lute? His loss was far greater than her own. Seeing him struck down by grief was the first after-shock of Kara's death. Ria expected unfailing good cheer and limitless strength from him as if he were some angel in fur and not a mortal creature.

Although she'd done all she could for him afterwards, she knew it wasn't enough. He'd nearly fainted from the strain of

prolonging the stricken woman's life those extra minutes—
leading a soul into eternity must be the most taxing form of
*solarti*. She'd fed him honey and raw eggs until he stopped
trembling. Ignoring the reek of his distress, she'd held him in
her arms until the first local friends arrived to offer condo-
lences and it was safe to leave him.

Lute had his comforters—where were hers? Craving the
embraces she could not have, Ria hugged herself, squeezing
her flesh hard enough to hurt.

The worst of it was, she dared not give any public sign of
her sorrow, not with the all-seeing eyes of PSI upon her.
Even if she were free of that hazard, she'd still have no one to
confide in. She couldn't even tell Carey. She laughed hol-
lowly, imagining his bewilderment if she tried to explain her
dilemma: how does one mourn a woman who won't be born
for centuries yet?

Yes, whatever Lute was suffering he was luckier than she.
He had his primitive faith in immortality, didn't he? Wasn't
that a handy anodyne? Right or wrong, it had to be better than
the feeble posturings her world made in the face of mystery.

Time for her to attempt some customary gestures. Ria
lurched up. She reeled over to the shelves and ransacked her
store of tapes for suitably melancholy music. *Death and
Transfiguration* was the only appropriate piece she found.
She dropped it in the player while she refueled her body with
food she could barely taste.

Although she let the tape repeat three times, Strauss failed
to pierce her apathetic gloom. Where were the transcendent
insights it was supposed to ignite? The prairie wind could
wail a finer dirge for Kara.

There was always literature. With a simple command, she
could summon the texts of all the great poems on death ever
written, from Gilgamesh's lament for Enkindu onward. She
could smother herself in a blizzard of printouts if she chose.

Or would it help to contemplate art? Ria leafed fitfully
through a few books. What did she hope to find, models for a

projected *Apotheosis of Kara ni Prizing?* Try as she might, she couldn't picture the *solexa* poised on the snowy clouds of any traditional heaven. Memory dredged up one set of images that might solace her. She needed to return to *The Mountains of the Mind*.

She called Carey to borrow his precious book again but his number didn't answer. She managed a faint shrug. At this point, what did one more disappointment matter? She was too benumbed to care.

There were still other alternatives. She had all the necessary resources within herself. Slight neurochemical adjustments could restore energy or induce euphoria. Yet Ria hesitated, recalling her brush with addiction. Masking pain solved nothing, but neither did bleak endurance. It was folly to reject relief for fear of abusing it.

Whooping and cheering erupted under Ria's window. She looked down to see the sidewalk packed with people. It took Ria a moment to remember why they were there. They must be lined up for admittance to the winter carnival being held on House grounds this weekend. The queue had just begun moving. For the rest of the night the complex would be swarming with noisy revellers indoors and out. She'd never get to sleep without resorting to *solarti*.

But the sleep that came brought troubling dreams.

The pathway curved between high banks of thorny hedge whose leafless boughs were pale as weathered bone. Foggy drizzle drenched the scene like tears. However swiftly she ran, her footfalls made no sound on the crushed shell pavement nor could she even hear her own labored breathing. The hand she held before her face melted into mist. The guiding skein of homespun thread she used to have was gone. Devious turnings of the maze mocked her desperation. Never finding, never found, she fled alone down spiral ways that had no end.

Ria awoke shivering. She warmed and calmed herself with care, running her fingers over her body to reassure herself she still had flesh. It was the hour before dawn. The dimness oppressed her. She turned on a small lamp above her bed, just enough light to make the steel in her ring sparkle. With a sigh, she slipped into deep familiar waters. . . .

She dipped her scrub brush in the bucket again, then dropped it with a splash. Julo had been washing the atrium floor. Furnishings and rugs were piled haphazardly to one side of the room. She hoped he wouldn't mind a slight interruption in his work.

"Lute, where are you?" she cried.

There was no answer.

She called again without reply. Through its open door, she could see that the kitchen was empty. Perhaps he was outside. She lifted one shade, but couldn't spy him from the kitchen window. Stifling July heat slapped her in the face when she ventured out the rear exit. There was still no sign of Lute. Why wasn't he home? He had to be here, he had to be here whenever she wanted him. She ran back into the house screaming his name.

Ria stopped short in the atrium at the sight of Kara's door. There hung the *solexa*'s shattered drum and broken staff, tied up with bows of white ribbon. Ria backed away as if she'd encountered the old woman's corpse. She nearly skidded on a patch of wet tile.

Giving the decorated door a wide berth, she opened the one next to it. This revealed a bathroom equipped with quaint fixtures including a huge, half-sunken tub. The bath's other door led to the workroom, which was now in a state of wild disorder. Kara's loom was empty, her spinning wheel still. Ria hesitated to enter what must be Lute's chamber, then took a quick, guilty peek. With the curtains drawn, it was too dim to see much but she noted that rugs covered the walls as well as the floor. His bed was a nest of curving cushions. The last bedroom in the square was Julo's. Here in this bright, tidy room she'd first met Kara and Lute. Was it only a season ago?

Ria leaned her forehead against the cool door frame and closed her eyes. Then she walked back to the spot where Julo had been working when she arrived. She knelt beside the bucket and left him to his chore.

Ria tried to rest after returning but shame over her lack of judgment and courtesy kept her wakeful. Why hadn't she switched to another moment of time once she realized Lute was absent? She probably would've tried Lute's bed on for size if she'd thought of it. What a poor performance from one who clung fiercely to every scrap of privacy society let her have. It was natural to crave Lute's company more now that Kara was gone, but she must not let this rule her life. She needed all her wits about her to preserve that life from PSI.

Finally, hunger overpowered recriminations and she got up to eat. Unfortunately, her larder was totally bare. She still underestimated the needs of a *solexa*'s appetite. Eating breakfast in the House cafeteria would be penance for her sins.

Institutional food was truly an instrument of mortification. Ria glared balefully at the cholesterol-free scrambled eggs and the soy patties that passed for sausage. Both preparations were served in squares that exactly fit compartments in the plastic eating tray. No doubt dimensions were standardized Federation-wide. Her stomach protested from the first bite she ate. She wondered what the *perfur* served at their other seasonal festivals.

Ria surveyed the sparsely populated room. The cafeteria drew little trade this early on a Saturday morning. (One group of diners nearby looked as though they hadn't gone to bed the previous night.) Every face she could see simulated a contentment that was artificial as the food. But then, one never knew what monitor devices might be watching. There were even credible rumors of transmitters implanted in body tissues without the carrier's knowledge. Anyone and everyone could be a spy. Random, undetectable observation curbed behavior as effectively as total surveillance—and at much lower cost.

Only a few tables over, Carey walked past on his way out. He must've been sitting behind her all the while. Ria waved but he didn't return the greeting. He was scratching his neck irritably. What new stress had raised his eczema again?

After breakfast, Ria phoned Carey for an explanation. None was forthcoming. He claimed he was to busy to talk but promised to meet her as usual for their weekly cinema outing. She resisted the temptation to sate her curiosity by an incursion into his mind.

Ria spent the rest of the morning—and entirely too much money—buying groceries at a private market.

After lunch, she resumed her search for Lute. She was prepared to dive as many times as necessary to reach him. . . .

She found Lute sitting in the workroom tying fringe on Kara's tapestry by lamplight. A bottle of whiskey and a half-filled glass stood on the bed beside him. She dropped the feather-duster Julo had been wielding, walked around behind him, and placed her hands on his narrow shoulders. He quivered a little at her touch.

"Vexed her to leave this half-done, Ria," he said. "She liked to see everything through. Not a splashabout mind, not like a . . . *perfur*." He clutched the edge of the tapestry. "Going to finish it for her, show I can do something right."

"What do you think you did wrong, Lute?" Ria asked gently, trying to sound calmer than she felt.

"Lost count of all the people I've led through the Door—guiding's my gift. Proud of myself for having it." He took a sip of whiskey. "Then why'd I fail Kara?"

His remorse clawed at Ria's heart. She drew his bowed

head against her body, forgetting she now lacked woman's breasts for him to nestle against.

The melancholy *perfur* rambled on. "Rite depends on total nearness—*solex* and patient're closer'n partners in any dance, closer'n lovers."

Ria jumped to conclusions. "Do you mean you were disillusioned?" She was uncertain how far to probe. *Solexes* presumably kept professional confidences secret. "I can't believe you uncovered any hidden flaws in Kara."

"Nothing like that!" He showed a spark of his old spirit. "We've been inside each other time and again these seven years. But at the last she held parts of herself back from me—from me!" His voice rose to a wail. "Didn't she trust me?"

Ria had no answer. She knelt beside him and clasped his hand. *Perfur* lived at extremes. Let their usual buoyant optimism falter and they plunged deeper into despair than the average human ever reached. Knowing depression as well as she did, she couldn't bear to see Lute sunk in it.

"But Kara did die well—free of pain and full of peace, thanks to you."

"Thanks for what?" he snarled. "She didn't need me."

"I still need you, Lute. I flew into a panic the other day when I couldn't find you here."

His response was sulky. "Had to make arrangements for burying her."

"May I come to the funeral?"

"Not in Julo's body. He's got a right to be there as himself to mourn her."

Ria blushed at her selfishness. She'd already deprived Julo of his chance for a proper farewell at Kara's deathbed. "I need to mourn her as much as he does," she pleaded.

"Didn't say you couldn't come. Doc's agreed to host you. But you're to ride strictly passive 'less you work it out with him."

"Why can't I watch through your eyes?"

"No!"

The rejection stung. "You come into my mind freely as you please—so why can't I enter you this one time?"

"Not yet."

"But we've already shared dreams." Ria was getting angry. "You promised to let me into your mind someday."

"Day of my choosing. Hasn't come yet." He chewed dismally on his fingers. "Too haunted by Kara to deal with you now."

"Can't I be of any comfort to you?" She brushed his drooping whiskers with her fingertips.

Lute burst into irate humming and batted her hand away. Throwing tapestry, thread, and scissors aside, he jumped up to confront her. "Ria, for once, for once, keep your hands to yourself!"

She cowered as he circled her. His fangs looked enormous.

"Think I'm a man in a fur suit?" He ground his massive jaws together. "Let me swim alone a while."

Ria stood up slowly. Her arms hung limply at her sides. "If that's what you prefer, I won't offer help—or ask for it—until you're willing."

She gave him a long sad look and left.

The once-bright waters seethed wrathfully gray. They cast her upon a storm-lashed shore. Ria lay like one half drowned. Then she shook herself alert. The stubborn core of her still held. She already had to do without Kara. If need be, she'd do without Lute as well. She'd find her own way to escape PSI.

Bold resolution did nothing to ease the pain of Lute's rebuff. Snarl at her, would he? She pounded her fists on her pillow. She ought to have snarled right back. He could hardly have upset her more if he'd bitten her. Ria shuddered, thinking how easy it would be for a *perfur* to rip a human's throat out.

Of course he'd be under less strain after the funeral was over. She wondered what the ritual would be like—more impressive, surely, than the hasty dispatchings her parents received. Could the ceremony cauterize their wounds and start them healing? She devoutly hoped so. Her life has become so entwined with Lute's, any estrangement from him was anguish.

Ria noticed a smudge on the center of her ring. She breathed on it and polished the steel with the edge of the sheet.

That evening, a strangely silent Carey met her at the theater entrance. Ria was surprised that he didn't favor her with his customary lecture on the finer points of cinematic art. He tugged his moustache and muttered each time she tried to talk to him. Waiting in line frayed his patience although the delay was no longer than usual.

Speculating on what was amiss with Carey in addition to her other anxieties did not dispose Ria to enjoy the preposterous swordplay of *Scaramouche*. Watching a fool climb the ladder of expertise seemed singularly irrelevant. But as the naive hero searched for the man who taught the man who taught his fencing master, Carey pressed a tiny wad of paper into her hand. It could only be a note.

Ria held it for a few minutes then slid it carefully into her tunic pocket and pressed the flap closed. She considered leaving her seat to try reading the message in the rest room but that area was likely to be heavily monitored. Reining in her curiosity, she forced herself to pay attention to the film.

By now Sacramouche had learned to perform mime. Ah, there were more ways to communicate than Security could scrutinize. She spelled letters firmly in Carey's palm.

W-H-A-T W-A-S T-H-A-T?

W-A-R-N-I-N-G

O-F W-H-A-T?

D-A-N-G-E-R T-H-E-Y A-R-E W-A-T-C-H-I-N-G U-S

L-E-T U-S T-A-L-K T-O-M-O-R-R-O-W A-T T-H-E
P-A-R-T-Y
N-O-T S-A-F-E
I W-I-L-L M-A-K-E I-T S-A-F-E
H-O-W?
T-R-U-S-T M-E

Ria patted his hand reassuringly although she didn't really
expect him to put his faith in her. They sat very still while the
climactic duel flashed on the screen. Ria wished Lute were
with her. He'd relish shows like this. She must invite him to
come along when things were—her train of thought braked.
She was assuming a happy ending to her own adventures.
The novelty of optimism quite stunned her.

The hero triumphed. The film ended. The audience clapped as the lights came on.

Despite the flush of positive feelings, the walk home was
tense. Carey still wouldn't talk or even smile. Ria began to
worry irrationally that they would commit some infraction of
traffic rules and draw a Security officer's attention. She
didn't care to be searched with that compromising note in her
possession.

Back in her apartment, Ria made a clumsy production of
undressing and stowing her clothes. She managed to reach
the note while appearing to rummage through dirty laundry.
Carey's message said:

> It's my fault they pulled you in for questioning.
> That time I let you use my terminal and I.D.,
> my place was under surveillance. They spot check
> people with high government connections and I'm
> an extra risk because I was under PSI's care a
> few years back. I think they may have had an
> implant put in me during minor surgery. Assume
> they've turned the transmitter on and can hear
> everything I say. Assume our phones and
> apartments are bugged, too. I've got to watch
> every step. Can't risk any more black marks

after this reprimand. One dose of PSI was
enough. I wish I could help you but can't see
how. All I can do is sound the warning.

Poor Carey was blaming himself needlessly for her summons. She knew where the real fault lay. But she decided to check his suspicions of an implant before attempting further contact.

A mere glide past the shining barrier brought her to Carey's sleeping body. She sensed cold metal within warm flesh. A spy device did lair behind a small scar under his jaw. Disarranging a few atoms destroyed its microcircuitry. Any subsequent examination would suggest that a manufacturing flaw had made it fail. As a further favor, she also touched the effector cells in Carey's body that governed allergenic cascades. Eczema should trouble him no more.

Having struck two puny blows for decency, Ria felt ready to try another foray into Lute's world. Doc Lerrow's mind awaited her there past radiant, beckoning waters. . . .

A real blazer of a sunset. Kara deserved that. Would set the stage for a Light Watch to remember. He vowed to stay the full course till dawn, make a merry night of it for her sake. God send them all so good a death. There'd be a hard reckoning if he had to stoke his carcass with stimulants but it was the least he could do to show respect. Until then, a soft seat under a shady tree felt good to his creaking bones.

And it gave him a prime vantage point to watch the other guests mill about eating green cakes and working up a sweat in their best white funeral clothes. The way folks were swarming boded well for the festivities to come. There were carriages and steamers all up and down the street. The paper lanterns were already up in the trees and Julo was hammering in the last of the flambeaux. His loose young face scowled in concentration.

The sight of so many visiting *perfur* would set Chamba

tongues flapping for weeks. Gemai had done Kara's family a
kindness by persuading his clanmates to stay home and hold
their own Light Watch. If all Kara's friends from Twin Stars
had come, who could've fed them? Gemai and Ellesiya stood
in for everybody else—except Amris, of course. She insisted
on attending and, like most times, the ranger got her way. But
she'd come in straight off the trail, mad as hell at herself for
nearly falling into a macrat ambush. (He'd have to check
those dressings on her ears sometime.) Her being here ought
to steady Lute down. That one was taking his loss harder than
he ought.

It was a proof of Kara's fame that Rolling Shores clans
more distant than Twin Stars sent official mourners, too. The
Quail Cloud *solexam* (what was his name? getting harder to
remember everybody these days) had brought a keg of prime
bourbon as a gift. Not quite sure if that was largesse or
boosterism. Well, he'd toast Kara in it cheerfully just the
same. He could do with a cold glass of something right now
but was too lazy to get up and fetch one.

Look at Kara's old comrade Birka, who used to be *solexa*
of Burning Hills. She hobbled along with her canes through
the crowd, moving slowly only because there were so many
people she wanted to chat with. Might be awhile yet before
they held her Light Watch. She was good for years to come,
bent as she was. Sounder of sense, surely than Keramon, that
bumptious wondercub from Blossom Rain. If he didn't stop
flirting with Ellesiya, he might get some cuffs that weren't
love blows.

He shrugged. It was all part of the cycle. Life-wheel turned
the same whether you were *perfur* or human.

Dorel's two grandchildren scampered by, squealing like
*perfur* cubs. They were dragging a length of yarn for Kara's
cat to chase. Dorel herself had a string of locals in tow. She
was a right fine sight in her full regalia as presiding *solexa*.
The hair under her iron cap was mostly still black though it

had been awhile since she and he were Kara's apprentices together. The Chamba title of Wise Woman had a proud ring that fit her. But he was glad the Lafayette *solex* wasn't called "Wise." A plain fellow like him couldn't carry off the part.

Ah, the sun was officially down. Time to get moving. Dorel led them inside. With all those bodies pressing together, the twilit atrium was stuffy but the odors of potted plants, fish pond, and the sharp leafy mourning scents the *perfur* wore made it bearable. He found a place next to Lute in front of the mass. The guests ranged themselves like tree rings facing Kara's bedroom door where the broken emblems of her office hung. A great thick beeswax candle stood on a tall stand in front of the decorated door.

Dorel signalled for quiet and the company joined hands. After the invocation she intoned:

"Let memory be kindled!"

The candle burst into flame. The watchers raised the tribute hymn whose tune was more than a thousand years old:

> *Her toil is over, labor done;*
> *To light Eternal she has won;*
> *Now sing her praises everyone.*
> *Allelulia!*

Chanting spread outward through the circle, like ripples on a pool. One by one, Kara's friends acclaimed her. Sweet, rough, shrill, deep, their voices lapped like waves.

"Highest climber," Dorel sang.

"Our beacon in darkness," Gemai sang.

"Good lady," Julo sang.

"She hunted wisdom," Amris sang.

"Weaver of lives," Lute sang.

"Healer of all things broken," he sang and yielded his body briefly to Ria's control. His lips formed her words:

"Mother of my spirit."

# XIX

Ria awoke Sunday morning intent on the struggle ahead. Determination burned in her like a steady flame, as if she'd carried something of the memory candle's glow back with her. Calling Kara "Mother" had melted certain inner constraints, leaving her that much freer to concentrate on her duel with PSI.

Had the ritual also lightened Lute's dark mood? Surely it must have. But she preferred not to contact him until he gave some sign he wanted her company.

After a prudent scan of University announcements, Ria flipped on the news channel while she showered and dressed. Science head Jon Detmold was defending his controversial earthquake prevention program at a news conference. Detmold's lashless, hairless face was repulsive, yet compelling, like the snout of an exotic reptile. Her research on tectonic catastrophes had left Ria with just enough knowledge to appreciate the problem but not enough to evaluate the proposed solution.

She shrugged and changed to the music channel.

The eerie trills and thumps of Katsusai's *Earth Spider Concerto* provided background for her thoughts. Convincing PSI she was epileptic rather than insane required far greater familiarity with the condition than she presently had. Purchases of medical texts could be traced. She dared not use her own terminal or anyone else's to remedy her ignorance. The public Medivise was not to be considered. She couldn't even risk searching in the library stacks because the ubiquitous Security cameras would record whatever volumes she inspected.

Was an indirect attack possible? Although it might be a trifle obvious to order Dostoevsky novels, what would seem suspicious about obtaining a biography of King Louis XI of France? He was the most prominent medieval epileptic she could recall. Her knowledge of recent eras was too sketchy to suggest the names of other victims to study.

Ria turned to her well-thumbed copy of Eliade's *Shamanism*. (Odd that Kara and Lute had confined themselves to oral instruction. They hadn't permitted her to read any of the scholarly treatises on *solarti* in their collection on the grounds that she lacked the requisite formal preparation.) Eliade's discussion of epilepsy among primitive shamans was amply footnoted. Some of his references must contain enough medical data to get her started. PSI wouldn't have the wit to spy danger in anything called *Primitive Religion*. But she'd have to order the works cited in the works cited in *Shamanism*—the whole root-system of information. At that rate, she might overrun her monthly quota of computer time. Well, if she failed to convince PSI, debt would be the least of her worries. If she succeeded, she'd solve the money problem when she came to it.

One other possibility was to do the necessary studying in Lute's world. No. She wouldn't beg him for favors. She'd stitch up her own patchwork solution first. It was vital that she win the victory herself.

Ria entered her commands and read output until the characters in the display swam before her eyes. She tried to clear her head with a brief visit to the winter carnival outside. She sipped bargain-priced hot chocolate and admired the entries in the snow creature contest. But a glimpse of Hannah skating on the improvised rink annulled whatever benefits she might have derived from the event.

Unfortunately, the anthropology references proved only marginally useful. She mined out the vein by nightfall. Rather than fret, Ria decided to attend the dance that was to close the carnival. It was a small pretence at normalcy that might camouflage another thrust at her objective.

The House gymnasium essayed a seasonal sparkle for the occasion. Counterfeit aurora borealis flickered on plastic snowflakes and foil ice. What the scene lacked in originality, it made up for in noise. After a patient search, Ria found Carey huddled in the shadow of a cardboard sleigh. Over his protests, she dragged him onto the dance floor—brute strength did have its advantages.

Neither she nor Carey were familiar with the figure being danced, but she stumbled through an approximation of the proper motions as the rows formed. The difference in their stature made it unfeasible for her to whisper in his ear during the pairwise steps. So Ria counted on the music and other people's chatter to mask their conversation. PSI wouldn't have bothered mobilizing the most sophisticated listening devices against them—yet.

"Quit the silent act," she told Carey as they clapped hands. "Say whatever you like."

The suggestion froze him in place. "I told you why I can't."

She yanked him out of another dancer's path. "You're worried about nothing."

"How do you know?"

"I have ways of finding out."

He frowned instead of answering. The pattern carried them

to opposite ends of their lines. She framed another approach as they worked their way back together. He might think an irrelevant question safe enough to answer.

"By the way," she asked, "does anyone you know have epilepsy?"

"If they do, they're keeping it mighty quiet."

"No suspicions?"

"None."

"Think harder." They swung round in a star formation.

"Wait. That time I took Leigh Franz to the Saturday film instead of you, he said something or other about epilepsy in his family."

"What?" She tried not to look too eager.

"I don't remember."

The dance ended. Ria lingered in the crowd, reluctant to surrender its cover.

"Could you talk to Leigh for me, find out who has the condition?"

"I will not," he snapped. "That's too personal."

"Of course it is. I'm being perfectly outrageous. But I need that information." She touched his arm. "Please, as a favor to me."

"You ask the damndest things." He shuffled his feet and glanced around furtively. "Besides, he's not here. At least I haven't seen him around this evening."

"Would you be so good as to call and check whether he's in his apartment? If he is, invite him down."

"All right," he agreed sullenly. "But you're getting awfully pushy."

"Pushy, am I?" She drew herself up to her full height and placed her palms against his thin chest. "Why, I could push you into the Grope Room this minute. Who knows what I might force you to do in there?"

He backed away as if burned. "Enough is enough! I'll make your call."

"Only joking, Carey. I do appreciate your help." Her smile was not returned.

She stood beside him as he placed the call from a public telephone. Leigh was indeed at home but uninterested in the dance. Carey's tepid invitation failed to communicate enthusiasm. Ria thanked Carey and let him go his own way. She hesitated to phone Leigh herself in case his quarters were bugged. *Solarti* might offer a more subtle means of persuasion but she didn't feel like walking all the way back to her apartment to practice it. She strode purposefully toward the Grope Room, a place she'd never investigated before. She nearly collided with Hannah at the entrance.

"I didn't know orgies were your style, Ria." The little blonde smirked. "So . . . unaesthetic."

"Do you find the Prospect Avenue establishments more to your liking?"

Implying that she had to pay for sex threw Hannah into a fury. She stomped away so angrily, she neglected to be graceful.

Ria scolded herself for stooping to cattiness. Hannah couldn't possibly afford the rates charged on Prospect Avenue. Also, it was demeaning to take revenge in such small bites. (Kara might have said it was demeaning to take revenge at all.) She sighed remorsefully and approached the door.

The Grope Room offered none of the amenities to be found in commercial pleasure centers, only darkness and mattresses. This lounge was made availble on weekends for residents who preferred anonymous group sex activities. It seemed a safe enough place to enter a trance.

Once inside, Ria nearly gagged on the stench of human rut. Subsonics throbbed beneath the moans and giggles. Dim red lights on writhing bodies made it a scene out of Dante for her. A prompt retreat might have saved her but she hesitated a moment too long. Several pairs of hands pulled her down and started mauling her. She kicked her assailants and scrambled free. Screams chased her out the door.

That much noise in any other place would've attracted precisely the attention she was hoping to avoid. Misled by an excess of innocence, she'd been guilty of *hubris* again. She was lucky to have escaped with nothing worse than a scare.

Ria straightened her dress and humbly climbed the stairs. She invaded Leigh's mind from the security of her own bed. Hasty probes of his memory failed to reveal the data she sought. A thorough search would take more time and skill than she possessed. She'd have to question him in person, but preferred to try it amidst the safe clamor downstairs.

Could mental stimuli persuade him to attend the dance? When delicate flickers of suggestion drew no response, she attempted to conjure up the prospect of a desirable woman waiting to dance with him. Unfortunately, Leigh's brain assembled her signals into an image of the ex-lover he was anxious to avoid. Patiently, Ria tickled an even lower appetite—an insatiable thirst for hot, spiced punch. She set the remembered pungence of cloves and cinnamon aglow within him and raised a slight persistent chill that had him shivering for a warm drink. The dance was the only place he could satisfy this craving immediately.

Ria returned to herself and listened for the sounds of hasty grooming in the bathroom. She waited for a few minutes after Leigh departed, then followed him downstairs. She permitted herself a small victorious smile when she found him sipping punch near the refreshment table. She let him finish his cup before approaching him. Once she'd steered him into the crowd at the edge of the dance floor, she began her inquiry:

"A while back, Leigh, you offered me a favor."

He nodded uneasily.

"I'm going to claim it by asking you a question I hope you'll be willing to answer." Even in the dim light she could see him shiver. "Do you know any epileptics?"

Relief flooded his face. "Yes. It so happens, my mother's had psychomotor epilepsy for years. But it's under control now." He moved closer to Ria and lowered his voice. "I've been worried about going the same way myself."

"Why so?"

"I got a concussion in that . . . fall last month—still have headaches from it. A tendency to epilepsy runs in our family, which means we can develop it after head injuries other people might shrug off. That's how it was with my Mom."

"What happened to her?"

"She had an accident, about ten years ago while I was in college; an elevator she was riding in fell. The seizures started after her skull fracture healed."

"That's too bad." Ria was dutifully sympathetic. "Does the condition interfere with her working?"

"No, indeed. She's the administrator in charge of Kickapoo Park and has her own house in Danville. A nice house—I should get over there more often than I do."

Ria drew him out at length about his mother, an easy task since he was proud of her executive achievements in the Park Service. Privately, Ria judged these somewhat overstated. Kickapoo was only a minor facility. But one had to claim whatever status one could.

They stood up for a few dances together, a mildly enjoyable activity because Leigh was a skillful partner. He seemed pleased with his snap decision to attend the dance. Perhaps he was more sociable by nature than he'd first appeared. This relieved Ria's misgivings over the tactics she'd employed to coax him down and was about to employ again. She maneuvered him into the cozy seating area behind the sleigh where Carey'd hidden earlier. Sliding her left arm around Leigh, she carefully tilted her ring to catch the shimmer of the fake northern lights.

"You've been so kind, let me show my gratitude," she murmured and clasped him in a light embrace while her soul made a final swift inspection of his mind. As she intended, he mistook her limpness for ardor and was embarrassed by the gesture. Ria pretended to look sheepish, apologized, and withdrew to her apartment.

The clumsiness of the operation disappointed Ria. She knew it wouldn't have met her mentors' standards. (Curious that she felt guiltier about peeping into Lute's room than intruding into two men's minds.) But at least she'd won the information that should arm her against PSI. Between her questions and the unspoken thoughts those questions had raised to the surface of Leigh's mind, she now had a sufficiently detailed portrait—and a thread of affinity—to locate Shelia Franz's mind by *solarti*. Inexperienced as she was, Ria needed directions to find a specific target. She commenced the search at once. She had only three more days to prepare for her next appointment with Blanca.

On the first clean plunge, she found her quarry sitting at a well-equipped home desk, wearily evaluating performance reports on subordinates. Ria made repeated forays to refocus her image of Shelia Franz, compensating for a son's idealization of his mother. There were shadows as well as highlights in the busy woman's life. At the cellular level, Ria explored the scar where shattered bone had knit and senses the blood-borne drug that now prevented seizures. Then she withdrew to seek an alternate version of Shelia whom she could observe free of the restrictions governing soul-flight on one's own branch of time.

Another plunge scarcely different from the first brought her to her goal. This Shelia sat behind a desk of different design reading a microfilmed journal for managers. The ease of finding what she sought astounded Ria. The other branch was so perfectly parallel, it had scarcely budded out from hers. Unless some momentous event altered many lives, this new growth on the Cosmic Tree would soon wither and snap off into nothingness. Then bark would creep over the stump to cover the spot where the ill-fated twig had been. Ria wondered why it had come into existence and what must happen for it to continue existing. She wished she could stop and locate the original nexus. What an exciting research problem that would make for Lute and her to study together.

But for the present, survival came before scholarship. Ria put her speculations aside and set to work. However, when she skipped back a decade seeking the moment of Shelia's accident, she arrived nowhere. The budding branch must still lie so close to hers at that point, travel there would, in effect, be travel into her own actual past. She beat her wings in vain against the wall of paradox.

She prudently retreated forward in time. Then, using the scar on Shelia's skull as a marker, she hopped back week by week until she was as close to the target event as possible without violating the laws of *solarti*. Luckily, it was near enough for her purpose: the regrown bone was still fresh and the victim had not yet suffered her first fit.

Now Ria settled in to witness the progress of the disease. Clinically detached observations recorded by her excellent memory should equip her to simulate epilepsy. Success lay within her grasp since she could spend as much time as she needed on this alternate branch and still meet her deadline. She was proud of herself for coming this far alone.

The unfamiliar technology of electroencephalography and brain scans enthralled her. Procedures which intimidated Shelia intrigued Ria. She listened attentively with Shelia's ears as doctors explained the diagnosis; she read through Shelia's eyes as the patient educated herself about her condition. Her host was a teaching machine which happened to be alive.

But this strategy was inherently flawed. Ria had grossly underestimated the amount of data she had to learn, especially when she had no control over the learning process. Since Shelia was indifferent to charts, Ria never got a close enough look at ECG tracings to understand them, much less memorize them. Text descriptions of "six per second rounded waves" and "flat-topped four per second waves" did not suffice for mimicry. She'd planned on manipulating the recorder by *solarti* an ECG tracing characteristic of psychomotor epilepsy. But if she misplaced waves and spikes—as she was certain to do—PSI's interest in her would be fatally sealed. There had to be another way—one that didn't depend on Lute's intervention.

Ria slept poorly and dreamlessly Sunday night. She was so desperate for fresh input, she'd have welcomed a nightmare for the stimulus of novel images. She walked through her workday like a robot and returned to her apartment no nearer to inspiration.

She abandoned the treadmill of worry for dinner. This evening Ria cooked with ceremonious care, turning the meal into an act of defiance against all that was false and regimental around her. January's alcohol allowance permitted her a bottle of adequate white burgundy. She used part of it for simmering herbed chicken which she garnished with fresh mushrooms that she'd carved into pretty pinwheels. The result was delicious. Even Lute might've liked it. Drinking the rest of the wine relaxed her enough to rethink her predicament.

Ria had to admit she's taken the wrong route. Machinelike objectivity couldn't save her. She and her host were persons, not linked computers. Therefore the personal element was the key to victory. She'd learn more from sharing Shelia's attacks than makeshift study could teach her. *Solarti* would allow her to experience the physiology of a seizure more completely than its semi-conscious victim could.

She turned from wine to waters deep as thought. . . .

Something terrible was going to happen. She knew it deep in her bones. But what could hurt her here in her own park? It was that heavy lunch. Hadn't set quite right. And maybe one of her headaches was coming on. She gingerly touched the hair hiding the fracture site. A walk around the Visitors' Center might do her good. Too nice a day to be fretting.

The burning bush planted outside the main door had gone full scarlet overnight and the woods showed the first touches of frost under a hard blue sky. A sugar maple growing at the swamp's edge waved one bright orange bough like a torch while the rest of its leaves remained green. Fallen acorns crunched under her feet and squirrels chattered overhead. Three huge raucous crows flapped by. Their wings cast shadows across her path.

What was that stink? Some camper's garbage on fire? She'd have the careless bastard brought in. But after she finished her walk. A fine day for walking. Yes, indeed. Lake Vermillion looked so glittery beyond the trees. Too glittery. Everything was too bright. Where was she? She'd never seen this place before—

Shelia fell forward with a cry. The gravel cut her face. Her body tensed rigid as a log. Her limbs jerked spasmodically for a few moments, then grew still. A wet stain spread under her body.

Pity as well as shame overwhelmed Ria. It was one thing to read a textbook account of clonic shocks, another to inhabit a human body tormented by convulsions. Ria determined to help Shelia. Although she had no power to eliminate seizures that had already occurred, she might be able to free the other woman from dependence on medication by healing the inoperable epileptogenic cortex. The cure would seem like a spontaneous remission. And if she enlisted Doc Lerrow's aid, he could also treat the Shelia who lived on this timeline. It was a way to make amends for exploiting their misfortune.

Ria devoted Tuesday evening to locating each seizure episode Shelia had experienced before the right preventive drug and dosage was found. Then she lept from one moment to the next sharing these attacks. Neurons sparked in wild discharge. Metabolites peaked and troughed. Aberrant rhythms made flesh quake. It was as if she stood unsheltered on a headland above a storm-wracked sea and let the lightning crash about her. Would Lute praise her boldness if he were here?

The next step was to apply her firsthand knowledge and induce the same neurochemical reactions in herself. She had to practice it at least once before the command performance. But what if she damaged her brain in the process? What if she had latent epileptic tendencies waiting to manifest themselves? Shelia's symptoms bore a terrifying resemblence to those Ria had displayed during her initiation ordeal. No wonder epilepsy and shamanism had been entwined throughout history.

Ria cringed at the risk she had to take. The odds against her were far longer than she'd let herself believe. She trembled so hard she began laughing at herself—hoarse barks of gallows humor. If she didn't take control, her fear alone would precipitate what she feared. But she decided to postpone the experiment until the next day when she would be better rested. And her dress rehearsal would be pointless without a properly appreciative audience.

Ria waited until she heard Leigh return to his apartment Wednesday night. Her first knock on his bathroom door was answered. He must've been working late since he still wore lab coveralls and the cheesy scent of fermentation clung to him.

"What can I do for you, Ria?" he asked.

"I don't quite know," she mumbled. "I need . . . something. I'm looking for something I can't seem to find. So I keep walking round and round the room trying to remember what it is. Oh, please come talk to me, I'm horribly confused." She gave a weak sigh, then groaned as a wave of nausea hit her.

Leigh frowned sympathetically. "Are you sick? You're so pale, you look like you're ready to keel over." He followed her into her apartment.

She stumbled around squinting and blinking. "Why's the place so dark? Didn't I turn on the lights?"

"Ria, come sit down before you faint," he cried.

She complied. Leigh perched like a stork beside her on the sofa bed. Ria clenched her fists and willed a violent surge of voltage through the left temporal lobe of her brain. . . .

She tumbled into a dream where silent thunderbolts struck a frozen sea.

She nodded awake and stared drowsily at Leigh. His arm was around her shoulder.

"I don't know how to say this, Ria." His words were nervously gentle. "But it seems to me that you've just had a fit—an epileptic fit. At least it was like what I remember my Mom having. You'd better get over to Health Service."

"As it happens, I have an appointment with . . . a health professional tomorrow. You think it might be epilepsy? I'll tell you," she licked her lips, "I've been worrying about that possibility for months, ever since I nearly electrocuted myself at work—you did hear about that, didn't you? I was too afraid to see a doctor since and find out for sure."

"So that's why you were asking those questions the other night. You were afraid of the same thing I was." Irony wrinkled his shaggy brows, then he burbled: "This isn't the end of the world, Ria. They've got good medicines now to control seizures. My Mom does just fine."

"That's good to know. Thank you for being here, Leigh. I needed you. Really, I did. Now let me get some sleep. I'm exhausted." She waved him up.

"Sure you'll be all right? If not, you call me, hear?"

"Don't worry. Goodnight."

She grinned broadly as soon as the door closed behind him. Her performance must've looked convincing. But could she fool trained eyes—and sensors? Tomorrow's review was the only one that counted.

Ria stayed home from work Thursday to save all her energies for confronting PSI. The timing of her appointment might work to her advantage. By late afternoon the staff would be restless to finish up and start the long King Day weekend. Could she perhaps slip through a gap in vigilance?

She began inducing epileptic auras in the waiting room. By the time the call board summoned her, she was sweating profusely. Dizziness hindered her trek to Blanca's office.

Once there, she observed that the therapist was as languidly watchful as ever. She mustn't be the sort to respond to holidays.

"And how are you feeling today?" Blanca purred.

"Not well. My stomach's in an uproar." Ria kneaded her abdomen.

"But not sick enough to cancel your appointment. It's very dutiful of you to come despite this . . . illness." The merest quirk in her smile spoke disbelief.

"Pardon me," asked Ria. "Is something on fire? Don't you smell it?"

"No. Do you?" Blanca sniffed and glanced around. "There's no alarm on, either."

"I know I'm being paranoid," she said with a self-deprecating chuckle, "but could you check in the hall? Please? Just to put my mind at ease."

Blanca gave her an indulgent stare. She rose, went to the door, felt it, and peeked out.

"There's nothing there."

"What?" cried Ria. "I can't quite hear you. The chimes—"

Brightness blazed behind her eyes.

When Ria regained consciousness, she was sprawled halfway out of her chair. Blanca was leaning over her, looking as dismayed as a spider who'd leaped and missed. In her crispest professional voice she said:

"You appear to have had some species of seizure. Don't move until the Emergency team gets here."

"I wouldn't even think of moving an eyelash," answered Ria dreamily.

*"The snare is broken. The prey flies free."* Lute's triumphant voice rang in her mind.

# XX

March was warm that year. Shrunken patches of snow still lingered in shadowy places but the first blades of new grass sprouted on the graves in Mount Hope cemetery. Amorous sparrows swooped and twittered among the boughs of budding trees. A single white crocus, survivor of some planting long ago, bloomed beneath a weathered memorial star.

Carey opened his jacket a little to bask in the spring sun.

"Thanks for the fabulous dinner last night, Ria. I haven't dined that well since I left my parents' house."

"What's the use of having money unless you use it?" Ria hugged herself with glee. "I'm going to savor, relish, utterly wallow in being rich." She stretched like a playful cat and arched her back against the trunk of a battered oak tree. "It's fun doing things for people I couldn't afford to do before—such as taking you for dinner at the Evergreen."

Carey still looked embarrassed by her generosity. "And the view was even better than the food—all that glass. Amazing how beautiful Chambana looks at night."

Ria chuckled. "If you're up high enough, anything looks good."

The right vantage point could turn even their drab city into kilometers and kilometers of sparkle.

Carey shifted position on his tree stump. He turned boyish blue eyes up to Ria. "The bit I can't get over is you sending your entree back. I wouldn't have had the nerve to complain."

"They tried to pass off mutton for lamb." She shrugged. "Maybe they were saving the spring lamb for more important customers—they found some fast enough when I yelled. It shows you what passes for a fine restaurant these days."

"Well, I admire you for doing it. It's the same kind of daring that made you your fortune. If I ever draw a winning lottery ticket, I'll stop right there. But you went on pressing your luck with all those horse race parlays. Incredible."

"Carey, I wasn't risking as much as you think. I had a foolproof system."

"Lots of people claim to. Yours worked."

Ria said nothing. She gazed off into the distance as if expecting the Assembly Hall to finally slip its moorings and fly away. She couldn't possibly explain that every bet she placed had been a sure thing. She'd picked her winners according to those recorded on the parallel branch of time where she'd studied epilepsy. Gaming results appeared to be identical in both worlds. This knowledge could make gambling a steady source of income for her until the authorities found some excuse to bar her from play. No, she couldn't begin to explain, lest she draw new accusations of madness.

Carey shyly picked up the thread of conversation. "All in all, you're a different person these days, Ria. It's as if an ice dam broke and let you flow free."

"Of course I feel freer since they diagnosed my trouble as epilepsy. I no longer worry about losing my mind. And it's almost a social advantage to have the handicap. Everyone feels obliged to be nice to me—Ali's been absurdly considerate, especially since my promotion came through."

"Do you think pity influenced her recommendation?"

"No. The promotion had been in the works for some while—I don't have to tell you how slow bureaucrats are. My work on Professor Clyde's disaster project did the trick. I didn't get preferential treatment."

"I didn't mean to imply. . . ." Carey flushed. "But something more has changed about you besides your health and your work grade."

He was more persistent in his questions than expected. Ria was delighted. Perhaps he would be receptive to her message after all.

Carey continued. "You've got a sense of purpose now you didn't have when we met last year. Why?"

"Oh, you might say I've read a fiery gospel writ in burnished disks of steel." She admired the way her ring flashed in the sun.

Carey looked at her quizzically, as if he almost recalled the source of her quotation. He said in a small voice: "Could you show me how to read it, too? I'd like my life to have some point beyond mere existence. I spend most of my energy just trying to defend myself. I think it's the same for a lot of us nowadays. So if you've found some alternative, would you please let me in on the secret?"

Ria knew what that speech had cost him. She decided to take a chance. "Carey, we've talked a lot over these past two months. I've finally gotten you over the fear that you're carrying a hidden transmitter which will have Security pounding on you any moment. Did you trust me because you thought I'd stumbled onto some secret data?"

"There are ways to access any program."

"The important thing is, you came to trust my judgment—otherwise we wouldn't be talking this freely now."

He nodded hesitantly.

She continued. "You say I seem stronger now. It comes of learning to be myself, even when hard data's lacking. The accident last fall was a watershed event in my life. Since then, I've come to rely increasingly on intuitions and perceptions our society doesn't recognize. I want to lead others to make the same discovery. It's time for the pendulum to start swinging back in the direction of mystery. The purpose of my life is to bring dreams to the dreamless."

"How much difference can one person make?" asked Carey bitterly.

Ria squared her shoulders. "Although I'm only one person, perhaps I can start a chain reaction to warm up this world with myth and magic. Otherwise, it'll freeze to death in its own bare rationality."

"That sounds superstitious, occult even." He turned away from her.

Ria moved to face him again. "Yes, my program is occult in some respects. Don't worry, I'm not going to offer a demonstration of my paranormal powers at this point. My special gifts will only make themselves felt after I've bought my way into some position that shapes public attitudes."

"Do you really think you can get away with that?" Carey guffawed.

"If I'm careful. Do you know that Soviet Russia tolerated seers and psychics while condemning political dissidents to prison? I plan to set myself up as a kind of sibyl in Washington. Given the right promotion, the government classes will come to me for counsel just like the *apparatchiki*'s children flocked to fortune tellers."

"Ria, you can't be serious about moving to Washington."

"Serious enough to give notice at the library. I'm leaving next week to begin my mission. You say you want your life to have purpose. Then come share mine. Come help me cast fire on the earth."

"Me?" Carey tensed to take flight.

"I'm offering you a job. I'll need a secretary I can trust. Your bureaucrat-watching hobby would make you especially useful in my plans."

"In their own way, top officials are more interesting than media stars."

"Then you accept? I'll send for you as soon as I'm established."

"Not so fast. You're overlooking something. Money can't buy you a residence permit in Columbia, much less Washington. They're ultra-strict about whom they let live there."

"I intend to find employment—for cover—before my tourist visa expires."

"If you manage that, you, an unknown without connections, then maybe I will believe you have mystic powers." He laughed. "In which case, I'd be happy to come work for you."

"It's a bargain."

They shook hands.

"Did you notice, Carey, I didn't have to persuade you that our society needs changing. You take that proposition as much for granted as I do. Let's go by the barns on our way home. The horses are sure to be out today."

A breeze sprang up. A cardinal alighted in the oak tree and began singing his claim to territory weeks ahead of schedule.

Ria's last week of work sped by. She was too busy being happy to bait Hannah or bristle at Ali's smothering attentions. Come Sunday's flight, she'd be well rid of them. Federation Day this year would find her in Columbia.

By Friday night she could scarcely sleep for the excitement. Joy emboldened her to try another ride over the enchanted mountains she longed to cross. Her troubling childhood Dream hadn't returned since the accident because Lute had stopped sending it to her. But she could induce it for herself now if she chose. She longed to pit her *solarti* against that old frustration. Kara had spoken of the Dream just before she died. Did those words predict eventual victory or was she reading a meaning she wanted into the message? Ria set her course and lay down to dream. . . .

High above plowed fields and greening prairie, she rode a horse the color of golden wood. The mountain rampart reared up as before. And as before the barrier grew to block their progress howsoever high they flew. The road of air was closed nor could mere wishing win them through. She reined her steed to seek a trail on solid earth. They lit upon the largest mountain's barren flank.

Dismounted now, she wandered through an avenue of looted tombs whose brazen doors gaped wide to show gnawed bones. A serpent made of ice glided forth to strike her heel but she crushed its head to glassy shards. A screaming whirlwind struck. Horse and rider, skeletons and marble slabs, were spun away and shattered to fall in bits like bloody snow.

Terror did not vanish upon waking. Ria still could almost feel the flaying wind assault her flesh. Lines from an ancient ballad unreeled in a closed loop through her mind:

> *O'er his white banes when they are bare,*
> *The wind shall blaw for evermair.*

The raven jeered at the slaughtered knight; events mocked her ambitions. Yet she knew she would prevail someday. No mountain could bar her way forever.

The feeling of dread persisted even after she'd eaten and dressed. Perhaps the dismal weather was to blame. Dirty gray clouds had gathered overnight to spoil their taste of spring and she could sense a cold front moving down on them from the north. Turning on the weather announcements while she packed, she heard:

. . . POSSIBILITY OF THUNDERSTORMS THIS
AFTERNOON WITH LOCALLY DAMAGING WINDS.

The forecast was threatening but not alarming. Ordinarily,
Ria enjoyed watching storms—seeing energy unleashed
exhilarated her.

Yet no previous nightmare had left such a residue of
depression behind. Was it a premonition of disaster? Lute
would know. At least now she was secure enough in her art to
ask him for advice without resentment. Their minds were
finally learning to partner each other.

She sought the remedy of soothing waters. . . .

Her hand was full of fish guts. Lute stood beside her
cheerfully boning carp. The sink was stacked with other fish
awaiting attention. She flinched at the smell.

"Glad you're here, Ria." Lute chirruped and kissed her
nose. "Must stay till evening and see Amris. Takes a lot to
feed m'sister." He waved his knife at the food. "Even got a
watermelon for her chilling in the cold box."

"Sounds delicious." She dropped the offal in the slop
bucket and washed her hands. "Mind if I just watch? I don't
know how to clean fish."

"And tomorrow, tomorrow, know what? She'n I are going
to visit Manita and Tahar. They're scouting Lake Vermillion
this week as a possible aquaculture site. Then—"

"Lute!" She tapped his shoulders. She hated to interrupt
his chitters but she hadn't come to socialize. "Last night's
dream frightened me badly. Can you help me discover
why?"

He apologetically offered her a chair and sat down to listen
to her tale.

"Your instinct's right, m'lady. That nightmare was a
warning. *Solexes* can't see the true future but events on other
timelines can seep into dreams triggered by *solarti*."

"As if nearby branches were casting shadows on mine?"

"Quite right. But the shadows flicker and you don't know what's casting them."

"How do I find out?"

"For a start, I'd scan your twin branch's future the way you did for the race results," he replied. "Shouldn't need me to tell you that."

She blushed for overlooking the obvious. "But I knew what I was searching for then. Am I supposed to jump blindly?"

"If some disaster's pending, the bloodshed will draw you. Moments of multiple death bend branches."

She nodded with understanding. "I'll try it. But don't let me keep you from your work. Those fish shouldn't stand longer than necessary."

He bounded up. "Keep talking. This'll take a while. Make yourself some tea if you like. There's egg candy on that covered plate."

Ria declined, politely hiding her shudder. Lute resumed preparing his catch.

"Tonight's a double celebration, Ria. Besides Amris coming, I got the better of Wilamine Hork today." He snuffled happily.

"Who? Oh, the Buzzard Lady, the one who hates *perfur*."

"Her. She's been circling me like a waiting vulture ever since Kara died." He kissed his fingers to the old *solexa*'s memory. "Trying to stir up trouble over Kara's will. You see, Kara left me this house and half her estate. So Hork went to Dorel with whispers of undue influence, even—" he snarled, "hints of foul play."

"That rotten bitch!" Ria cried.

"What do you expect of a woman who'd marry her own first cousin?" He snorted. "Never occurred to her Dorel was on my side, knew about the will since it was drawn up, and wasn't looking to break it."

"Such creatures assume everybody thinks like them."

"The mourning month's up today and Dorel's made it

known she's letting me keep the Memory Candle stub. Proves to the town she holds me in regard."

"That's a lovely gesture, but will it stop Hork from trying something else? I wouldn't expect her to give up that easily."

"I'll out-swim her the next time, too. Not to worry, m'lady."

Lute went on cleaning fish but Ria brooded on dead knights and carrion birds.

A delightful evening with Lute and Amris made her forget her anxieties temporarily. But as soon as she returned, Ria prepared to probe the adjacent timeline. She decided to begin with today's local events and work forward.

Wan waters roiled about her. . . .

Another ambulance yowled by.

For once, he was glad to be a rookie. Better to be stuck on traffic detail than be up there mucking around for bodies. Without thinking, he moved a few steps backwards as if to put a bit more distance between him and the sodden ruins. He shivered despite the warm sun.

His long shadow raked shattered display windows. A solar panel from the building behind him had blown into the dress shop opposite. Curly strips of roofing draped across racks of cloths. Flying debris had pockmarked plastic storefronts. Sign boards were plastered with soggy wrapping paper and smashed Easter eggs. A big plush toy, shapeless from the rain, dangled from a bent lamp post. A mannequin's head lay in a lavatory sink on the sidewalk. Filthy torrents raced in the gutters.

The red smear that had once been a bird raised a taste of vomit in his throat. It looked too much like the sights along Neil Street. And if he got sick before the day was over, well, earlier he'd watched a veteran Emergency worker drop a body bag to puke her guts out. He almost wished a few sonofabitching gawkers would get through the Security cordon. Would serve them right to see what glass splinters did to human flesh.

Ria fought down nausea of her own to make repeated plunges into minds at the disaster scene. She saw for herself the sleet of glass and the rain of blood clotted together on familiar streets. She pieced the story out of scraps drawn from many witnesses. During a thunderstorm, a funnel cloud had materialized without warning above Athletic Park and plowed a short but grisly furrow across downtown Chambana. Casualties ran into three figures, with major fatalities in and around the Evergreen restaurant. Most of the victims had been guests at an official Federation Day luncheon when the glass walls of the luxurious penthouse exploded around them.

She had less than three hours to prevent the same tragedy from occurring on her own branch of time. Even now, the area's leading citizens would be preparing to attend the opening event of the holiday weekend. Unless she found a way to intervene, most of them would die at 1305 this afternoon.

Ria gulped a second breakfast while planning countermeasures. Why hadn't the tornado sirens sounded an alert? Weather Service was generally reliable. People were well-drilled to obey announced watches and warnings—one could be fined for ignoring the signal to take cover.

Using her computer, she hastily surveyed Weather Service operating procedures in the Prairie Region. Warnings of dangerous weather originated at the North American Severe Storm Forecast Center in Kansas City. These were relayed to Chambana by the Federation Weather Service Office in Springfield which also had the responsibility for issuing specific local storm warnings. What had broken the normal chain of command? She could find out by searching the parallel branch again at a time prior to the storm. Ria armed herself with all the biographical information she could find on Ellie Corto, the meteorologist in charge of the Springfield office.

She reached through murky waters. . . .

"If I get one more funnel cloud report from District 10, I am going to go noncomp myself. I may garrote Samuels with a telephone cord. Sighted near Ivesdale this time, was it? No independent confirmations. How very convenient. Maybe there's a whole nest of pranksters out there inventing tornadoes every time a Cumulonimbus system rolls in. Wilson, how do I know those calls are really coming from Pesotum? Maybe some noncomp's found a way to access the system. All the more suspicious when the Marseilles radar's down, thanks to noncomp sabotage. It's not your random craziness like they claim, Wilson, it's a goddamn conspiracy. If Samuels makes one more whimper about 'hunches,' I really will strangle him. You can't send people scurrying for shelter on a whim. We'll go by the book or not at all."

At last she knew. Without the Marseilles radar, tornado tracks couldn't be plotted. Perhaps the Ivesdale funnel had dissipated before other witnesses could corroborate its existence. The killer tornado had apparently dropped out of the clouds directly over the heart of Chambana.

Ria checked the latest local forecast. While she'd been occupied with *solarti*, "possibility of thunderstorms" had been upgraded to an official Severe Thunderstorm Watch. The Marseilles problem did not affect that announcement since it originated in Kansas City. She glanced outside to verify the danger. The sky was darker than before. A wall of black clouds reared across the horizon and gusty winds whipped trees. She saw a flash of far-off lightning.

Could she impell her own world's Ellie Corto to issue a tornado warning before lives blew away? Again and again Ria battered at the meteorologist's paranoid mind without avail. This woman was every bit as rigid as her alternate.

Bending a bureaucrat's will was a task that would baffle even Lute. Ria's attempt to work through the assistant meteorologist Langley Samuels only provoked a quarrel between him and Corto that left the latter less receptive than before.

Ria still refused to admit defeat. As a last resort she could attack the local warning system itself via *solarti*. Her computer gave the address of Chambana's Emergency Operating Center on Elm Street as well as the names of those who worked there. Details of the siren activation mechanisms were classified for security reasons. However, Ria was able to pluck them out of an employee's mind—her memory-scanning technique was improving with practice.

The hardest thing of all was the waiting. She must sound the alarm early enough to give people adequate notice but not so early that they would leave shelter prematurely. While she waited, she ate, as much to relieve anxiety as to replenish energy. Time that had flown so fast now crept. Thunder rolled, Ria fretted. On the click of 1245 she sprang. Her fury raged at the siren controls. Her ardor seethed along the open switch.

Nothing happened.

Ria cursed her inexperience, then regrouped. It required more concentrated effort to melt a copper contact than ignite a dry milkweed pod. At several kilometers' distance, the deed was beyond her present ability. But if she moved nearer and drew on a host's reserves as well as her own, she might yet prevail.

While lightning cracked outside, she found the mind of an Emergency Center clerk. He was napping his lunch hour away at a desk near the control panel. She willed warmth into the target and sensed it gradually envelop the minuet of energies that was the metal. Temperature rose and with it, tempo. Atoms danced a mad gavotte, faster, ever faster. Contact closed, electrons flowed. The steady blare of sirens sounded Ria's triumph.

Footsteps clattered in the hall outside as other residents scampered for the basement. Ria made no move to follow. A rebellious spark kindled in her heart. The day's exertions demanded some dramatic gesture of release. Huddling below would not suffice. She opened the door and ran—for the roof.

Ria stayed inside the rooftop enclosure covering the exit. Protected by reinforced glass, she could watch the storm for its spectacle value. With her own eyes she wanted to see the killer's blow fall harmlessly. And she wanted Lute to see it with her.

No sooner did she call than he came hither. She instantly knew his dear touch in her mind, but they held their silence while the tempest raved. Two selves behind a single pair of eyes, they gazed westward into chaos.

The wind drove churning clouds before another lightning riven squall line. The sky was one vast bruise, purple above, livid below. Layers of different darkness slipped past each other and twisted back upon themselves to form a vortex coiled within the lowest ragged band.

Invisibly, it struck. Bursts of debris rose from the skyline of Chambana. The top of the tallest tower erupted into gouts of glass and matchwood. Outlined by dust, the snaky shape wavered another moment, then disappeared as quickly as it had come.

The rest of the storm passed over them with rain that lashed so hard, their refuge might have been a diving bell at the bottom of a lake. They watched until the last thunder faded and the sky shone brightly once more.

Ria came out on the wet roof and danced a few splashing pirouettes among the solar panels. Only then did Lute speak:

"*Magnificent!*" he called within her mind.

"*It does make a splendid show—provided it doesn't hurt anyone,*" she replied in the same silent way.

"*Why didn't those people you saw killed take cover? Danger couldn't be plainer.*"

"*Like us, they depended more on official warnings than on their common sense. Well, complacency didn't cost them their lives this time.*"

"*Your doing entirely, m'lady. Kara'd be as proud of you as I am.*"

She might have wept but his delight would not let her. "*It's to your credit, for teaching me.*"

"*Teaching's another sort of learning, climbing, growing. We do what we're put here for, what's there to fear?*"

For an instant Ria felt that the two of them were alone—invincible and content—on the summit of a very high mountain. Joy caroled in her. "*Then shall we see 'no enemy but winter and rough weather?'*"

She whirled one last time and skipped downstairs.

# XXI

On the way back, Ria met Hannah and Ali at the stairwell leading to her floor. The younger woman looked pale and clung to the older one's arm.

"Why are you walking down now, Ria, instead of up?" asked Ali. Surprise sharpened her bland features.

"Your clothes are wet," said Hannah accusingly. "You didn't take shelter, did you?"

"Go ahead, Hannah, why don't you report me? Your tattling caused me enough trouble last time."

Hannah cringed behind Ali. "I don't know what you're talking about," she whimpered. "You can't talk to me like that. Tell her she can't, Ali."

Lute's voice spoke in Ria's mind: *"Hannah didn't betray you. Ali did. I saw that in the therapist's memory."*

Ria stood transfixed. The world had turned upside down. For the first time, she saw Hannah as a victim instead of a villain, a victim she herself had helped to injure. She cleared her throat and stammered:

"I seem to have done you an injustice, Hannah. I was convinced you were the one who denounced me to PSI because I didn't think I had any other enemies. But I was wrong. There was one other, wasn't there, Ali?"

Ali blustered. "What do you mean, 'enemy'? I only did it for your own good. I'd do the same again for any sick misguided person."

Ria's reply was icily correct. "Don't worry, Ali. I'm not going to make a scene. I've got better things to do with my life than waste time on revenge. Besides, breaking free of you and everything you stand for is the best possible vengeance. Hannah, you might try making the same move. It's astonishing how well one can stand on one's own feet."

Ria descended the stairs, leaving the two women speechless behind her.

Once she was alone in her own quarters, Lute spoke again. *"Glad you did that m'lady. Hate's uncreative. Here's something pleasanter to think of instead. Let me host you when Amris'n I visit Mania and Tahar."*

"You really mean that? You're going to let me into your mind?" Ria was ecstatic.

*"Better than that. I'll give you control of my body for part of the trip so you can see what it's like to be a perfur."*

"Lute, you're too generous. What a wonderful holiday we'll have. How I wish you were here in the fur so I could hug you!"

Ria couldn't stop petting her beautiful fur. Stubby *perfur* fingers were as sensitive as human ones and the sleekness of Lute's pelt proved irresistible. (Fortunately, he seemed more amused than outraged by the liberties she was taking with his body.) But if fur was extravagantly sensuous, a tail was merely comical. It interfered with sitting and never seemed to be quite where she thought it was.

Adjusting to a radically different—and phenomenally fluid—body language was more difficult than she'd anticipated. The forward-sloping head-bobbing gait of the *perfur* felt disturbingly alien despite practice at Lute's home prior to departure. She also wanted to try swimming in the outdoor fish pond but was asked to postpone the experiment until they reached Lake Vermillion.

She noticed that colors were generally muted and the visible spectrum was shifted to longer wavelengths. Although roses showed flamingly red, the irises and clematis vine growing near the house looked black. Other senses were heightened. She could detect a giddy profusion of scents and heard higher notes in bird songs than before. *Perfur* vocal cords allowed her to sing a whole octave higher than she was used to. She startled herself the first time she snuffled.

Ria loved the train ride to Danville. The gaudily painted steam locomotive, the wood paneled cars with their lace curtains and antimacassars had the quaintness of another age. It was wholly unlike the swift but drab diesel engine that had taken her to Indianapolis as a child over approximately the same route. The conductor obligingly adjusted their seats to accomodate *perfur* anatomy. However, she noticed one sour-faced man change his place when she and Amris sat down.

The tracks ran due east from Chamba past tidy farms whose buildings were inevitably paired or clustered with those of neighbors. Amris explained that this arrangement had been adopted centuries earlier as a defense against macrats. People on adjoining homesteads often owned heavy equipment in common or marketed their harvests together. Ria saw a horse-drawn mower haying. Horses and other farm animals were much in evidence. Corn was still the main crop, as in her world, but fields here were smaller and more wheat was grown alongside the corn.

Amris had arranged for them to be met at the depot by a friendly farmer named Webber Riksun who would drive them part way to their destination north of town. Riksun was a fuzzy-haired bear of a man who looked strong enough to carry Lute under one arm and Amris under the other. The two *perfur* hunched on sacks of flour and bolts of cloth in the back of the farmer's wagon. Ria concentrated on keeping her seat during the jolting ten kilometer ride but Amris chatted with her friend.

"Keeping your rat-watch keen?" she asked him.

"Keen as ever. You won't catch me letting shrubbery grow around my house like some folks do now. My fences 're stout and I check my property for rat-sign regularly."

"More humans did the same, m'job would be easier." Amris sighed. "Any sightings here lately?"

"I heard tell someone south of town lost a calf. A tree tiger—or even two of 'em—couldn't do that. And poachers wouldn't have been so messy."

Amris bared her fangs. "Not good. Rats 're getting bad on the lower Wabash. Be raiding up here before you know it. Talk to your sheriff after I've seen m'kin."

"Say, what's that young *perfur* couple up to at the lake?"

"Looking for land to settle. Twin Stars is about to bud off a new clan. As founders, they've got to scout the country themselves."

Riksun frowned. "That lake's too small to support a whole village and the Vermillion system's just a bunch of big creeks."

"Wabash Valley south of here's too deep, flood plain's too wide to suit us. Trying something new: a clan of scattered settlements matched to human ones where we can earn cash. It works, be a big thing for our people."

Riksun grunted. "If you say so. Maybe in a few years I can hire me some stock handlers. Your kind's naturally good with beasts."

Ria's bones thought the ride would never end. How could Amris endure this with such good cheer? There she sat, talking nonchalantly about the current drought and the possibility that today's overcast would yield rain. Ria pretended to doze so she wouldn't be required to participate.

Eventually, Riksun let them off at the waist of the five-kilometer-long oval lake. This was the point nearest to the dirt road. Now they would circle north to Manita and Tahar's camp on the opposite shore. Since she was still a bit uneasy in the presence of firearms, Ria offered to take the pack if Amris would carry her own weapons. The ranger was fully equipped with a Bowie knife and light shotgun in addition to her Colson rifle. She planned to return to patrol immediately after the visit.

Before beginning the trek, Amris took an odd-looking strip of accordion-pleated leather out of her pack. She laced it around her neck as a gorget, taking care to leave the throwing knife that hung between her shoulder blades free.

"What's that for?" asked Ria.

"Trail armor. Gives rat teeth something to bite 'sides m'skin."

"Are you expecting trouble?" Her brows creased.

"No more'n any other time."

At last Ria grasped how alone they would be in this cut-over woods once the sound of Riksun's team and wagon dwindled away. The wind felt cool for August. She refrained from speaking while they walked because Amris seemed intent on studying their surroundings. They had come about a kilometer along the lake shore when the ranger signaled a halt.

She whispered hoarsely in Ria's ear. "Total quiet from here on. Mind where you step. Been watching buzzards light ahead of us. Want to see what's dead." She unlimbered her rifle and carried it loaded in the crook of her arm.

Although unable to match the wood-wise ranger's gliding movements, Ria obeyed as well as she could. Amris stopped occasionally to listen and sniff the wind. Another buzzard spiraled down. In a blackberry thicket north of the lake they found the kill.

It was Tahar. He lay like some empty, ruined seed pod. His belly was a gory hollow, its viscera devoured by macrats.

The bones of his upper arms and legs showed where flesh had been stripped away. His throat was bitten through and his tail was chewed to shreds. Vultures has already gotten his eyes and were loath to abandon the rest. Amris drove the last one off with her rifle butt.

Tahar's shotgun still hung from its strap, unfired, but he'd managed to kill one attacker with his teeth. A second dog-sized gray form lay at some distance from his, possibly slain by its fellows. The greedy rats'd even finished the black-berries the *masfur* had been picking when ambushed. Crushed berries stained his empty collecting bag black.

Ria stared blindly, refusing to acknowledge the gruesome sight but the slaughterhouse smell mingled with rodent mus-tiness attested what her eyes denied. She was too paralyzed with horror to retch.

"Lute, get back here!" commanded Amris in a rasping growl.

He instantly seized control from Ria and tried to thrust her out.

*"Go home!"* He screamed silently.

*"I'm staying with you, come what may."*

Their wills grappled but she held fast. The stubbornness that surprised her angered him.

*"Passive then,"* he said. *"Don't want to know you're there."*

"Agreed."

The scent of blood and rat-filth fed his frenzy. He hummed and snarled and clashed his heavy jaws together.

Amris loomed over him, tall in the power of her office. "Under orders! Save rage for killing rats. Warn Manita. Warn Riksun."

Obedience owed a ranger curbed instinct. He sought the *femfur*'s mind. The brain he touched was close to death. His frenzy flared anew.

Amris cuffed him. "Too late for her? Warn Riksun. Hu-

mans have to know in case we die. Protect first, then
avenge.''

He hummed in anger but obeyed. Hard to find the human's
mind. Hard to fit inside. Hard to care when kindred had been
killed.

During his brief trance, Amris buckled on her ammunition
belt. She handed him the Bowie knife, shotgun, and pouch of
shells. They abandoned the pack and rushed to aid Manita.
Rat-sign and *perfur*-scent marked the path clearly. They
followed Tahar's footsteps along the lake to reach his dying
wife.

The rats had ripped Manita's belly open and torn living
flesh out of her haunches, only to vomit up the half-chewed
gobbets beside her body. She was not entirely dead.

"Done for spite," growled Amris. "She'd gotten two of
them." She pointed at the slain rats lying between Manita
and the water.

He lay down beside the bleeding *femfur* and joined his
soul to hers. He drew her aside from the Door she was
scratching to enter. Holding her being against his own, he
made the twisting straight and the roughness smooth. Ambi-
tion, giddiness, and pride faded out like mildew bleaching in
the sun. He took consent and led her into brightness.

"Who created us all in the beginning, receive us all at the
end," he whispered.

Amris pried him away from the corpse. Manita's blood ran
in rivulets down his drenched fur. He sat dumbly and
watched it drip. His sister forced trail ration into his mouth.
She ought to know he hated the stuff. It stuck to his teeth.
Would that bother macrats? How did they pick their teeth
after they ate *perfur?*

Amris was shaking him. "Get your strength back. Need
you lively. Wind's carrying them our scent. They'll scatter.''

He ate the gluey cake and washed himself off in the lake.
Amris showed him Manita's shotgun, gnawed and gouged by

angry rats. They had also torn the *perfur* couple's bough shelter down and fouled their belongings. Within minutes he was recovered enough to follow Amris in the chase.

Rage welling back within him lent him stamina for the ten kilometer run. He trotted after her tirelessly through crackling-dry woods and meadows towards the tree-lined river. The wind was behind him, the killers before him, all else a blur. He almost failed to notice when Amris called a halt, then squatted gasping as she scratched a map in the dirt.

She said: "This fork of the Vermillion's got swampy banks. Rats hit the river, they'll spread out. Can't circle behind us 'cause we'd smell 'em. Want you to set fires on this side, north and south, closer'n closer together each time. Drive 'em against the water they hate. Given the chance, they'll charge rather'n swim and we'll pick 'em off. Tonight's rain'll douse the fire."

She gave him directions and distances for his *solarti* attack. He let his hatred of rats blaze up to kindle grass. Bands of smoke rose in response. He let it burn awhile, then struck again, repeating the process until Amris judged its work was done.

Advancing cautiously, they finally spied their quarry from a rise overlooking scrubby land that flooded in other years. Amris climbed the low crotch of an oak while he braced himself against the trunk below her. She was to have the first volley when the last fires drove the rats to charge. She estimated that they faced no more than a dozen of the creatures.

He struck two more sparks with his mind. Vengeful flames leaped up. Half a score of squealing rats erupted from the brush.

"Steady," the ranger cried. She felled four and wounded another. "Now, Lute!"

He blasted the nearest rat. The rest of the pack was almost upon him.

"Relax trigger, squeeze again."

He caught a second rat in the chest as the others closed. He heard Amris shoot once more and jump. Grasping the shotgun barrel in his left hand, he clubbed a rat aside while he drew the Bowie knife. It nearly took off one assailant's head but another ran under his guard to assault his throat. He stabbed clumsily at the rat's back but it held on and raked his belly with its claws.

Suddenly Ria hurled her consciousness into the rat. She had a fleeting glimpse of Lute's bloodsoaked fur through its eyes before her wrath cooked its spinal cord.

He sliced the suddenly paralyzed rat under the foreleg as it died. Meanwhile, the rat stunned earlier scrabbled at his legs. Falling on it, he bit out the back of its head and gorged himself on its warm, salty brains.

Afterwards, he sprawled on a sandbar in the river coaxing his wounds to stop bleeding and hurting. They threatened to reopen each time the smoky wind made him cough. Amris had only a few scratches. She'd knifed the last rats while he was struggling for his life—a life he owed to Ria.

"*Glad you stayed, m'lady,*" was all he could manage to say.

"*I'm stubborn, dear heart, stubborn.*" She fell silent to ease the awkwardness.

Amris appeared carrying a handful of rat tails. "Twelve," she said, shaking them. She tied them up with string and hung the bundle from her belt

"Too bad no spare gorget, little brother."

"I'll mend."

"Won't have to spend the night in the open. Riksun and his folk should be riding in soon."

"They were by the lake last time I looked." He shifted uncomfortably. "Maybe humans'll start worrying again about macrats on their doorstep."

She shrugged. "Worry more when their kind gets killed."

"One way or another, our kind'll come back. The new clan'll flourish."

"And call Manita and Tahar founders." She kissed her fingers to the dead. "I'll have time counted for them here next spring. Tail-bounty'll pay a *solex* for the ceremony."

"Who'd ask payment in this case?"

Amris did not seem to hear him. She stared across the river. A shudder of wind ruffled its surface. Rain was on the way. Beyond the line of trees, the late afternoon clouds glowed red.

"New clan's got a name now," she said.

"What?"

"Bloodwater."

# EPILOGUE

Wind damage at the airport delayed Ria's departure for Washington by one day. She spent Sunday taking a final walk around campus, finishing up at the corner of Wright and Green. As she waited for a bus back to the House, she surveyed the scene for the last time. Twigs and other debris littered the sidewalks but the redbud trees nestled against Altgeld Hall were unharmed. A pinkish tint on their branches said they'd bloom within the week.

*Alma Mater* was splattered with wads of paper. The contents of a trash basket must have blown against her during the storm and dried in place. Ria smirked at the mess. Why has she ever feared that silly statue? She flicked a mental spark at a scrap clinging to the Mater's foot. The paper caught fire as her bus arrived.

Monday morning Carey and Leigh looked almost tearful when she left for the airport. They insisted they'd miss her. She wondered whether she'd miss them. The leave-taking got a bit maudlin.

Ria had shed no tears over leaving. The redness in her eyes came from weeping for the dead *perfur*. She brooded on the tragedy all the way to the airport. At least she'd had the satisfaction of helping to kill a macrat. In so doing, she'd made another break with the values of her society. Contrary to the slogans she'd been taught, there was a time for violence as well as peace. In Lute's world, they knew which was which and were saner for the distinction.

The weekend's events had left her bone-weary but she was determined to enjoy her first plane trip. She endured the tedious check-in procedures with uncommon good grace. It was worth it. How exciting to watch the ground fall away and see the monotonous checkerboard fields of Prairie vanish below the clouds. Already spring must be creeping up the Appalachians. Flowers would be waiting beyond the mountains in Columbia. She sang the old Shaker hymn softly under her breath . . .

*And when we find ourselves in the place just right,* . . .

Lute came into her mind.

*"It's your happy day, m'lady."*

*"One I never thought to see. But how are you feeling now?"*

*"The bites are healed. Took nearly as long to mend my mood as my skin. Had to talk it out with Ellesiya."*

*"The way your people died was hideous."*

*"Hope I never attend an uglier death than Manita's. But that's my work; I can deal with it. What I couldn't deal with was the fighting. I'm a solexam, not a fighter. Done my share of hunting but never killed anything like that hand to hand. Never felt the killing frenzy before."*

*"That makes two of us."*

*"Now because of the raid, there'll be a big macrat drive in the fall,* perfur *and humans together. Going to sweep clear down to the Ohio."*

*"Then maybe they didn't die in vain. But why couldn't they have lived lives as full as Kara's?"*

"Not for me to say. Kara's passing doesn't trouble me now the way it did. Found a letter from her explaining everything. She held me off at the end to keep me out of her memory. She risked going into eternity with soul-flaws unhealed to guard secrets for you."

"For me?"

"She couldn't let me learn what will pass between you two in the future."

"In the future? What are you talking about?"

"Kara foresaw you'd need help fulfilling your destiny as the sibyl of Columbia. She left blocks of private time for you to return and consult her. Each visit will have 'always' been even though none's happened yet from your vantage point."

"In other words, we're making a clever detour around a time paradox. I still seem to be too timid about the ways the Cosmic Tree can be climbed."

"But remember, the number of hours is limited. They have to last a lifetime. Save them for moments of great need, don't run to her every time you feel lonely."

"You can help me decide when needs are greatest. I watched you preside over Kara's death. I was with you when you opened the Door for Manita. Now I understand what your gift is. Will it be 'you who lean over me on my last day?' Say that it will."

"If I can, m'lady, if I can. Enough talk of dying. I'll leave you with a lucky image that'll bring fair dreams."

Ria closed her eyes. She still saw exactly the same outside view the airplane window gave. Then a bank of cloud became a mighty banner which bore in black the imprint of strange letters and the outline of a horse. Its saddle and bridle were splendid. On its back there rode a flaming jewel. The steed neighed and reared. It sprang forth from the cloth alive to gallop lightly on the air. Soaring past mountain-high thunderheads, the Wind Horse of Victorious Fortune raced across the sky. Demons fled before its flashing hooves.

# WHY WASTE YOUR PRECIOUS PENNIES ON GAS OR YOUR VALUABLE TIME ON LINE AT THE BOOKSTORE?

We will send you, FREE, our 28 page catalogue, filled with a wide range of Ace Science Fiction paperback titles—we've got something for every reader's pleasure.

Here's your chance to add to your personal library, with all the convenience of shopping by mail. There's no need to be without a book to enjoy—request your *free* catalogue today.

## ALL TWELVE TITLES AVAILABLE FROM ACE
### $2.25 EACH

- ☐ 11630 **CONAN, #1**
- ☐ 11631 **CONAN OF CIMMERIA, #2**
- ☐ 11632 **CONAN THE FREEBOOTER, #3**
- ☐ 11633 **CONAN THE WANDERER, #4**
- ☐ 11634 **CONAN THE ADVENTURER, #5**
- ☐ 11635 **CONAN THE BUCCANEER, #6**
- ☐ 11636 **CONAN THE WARRIOR, #7**
- ☐ 11637 **CONAN THE USURPER, #8**
- ☐ 11638 **CONAN THE CONQUEROR, #9**
- ☐ 11639 **CONAN THE AVENGER, #10**
- ☐ 11640 **CONAN OF AQUILONIA, #11**
- ☐ 11641 **CONAN OF THE ISLES, #12**

Available wherever paperbacks are sold or use this coupon.

**ACE SCIENCE FICTION**
P.O. Box 400, Kirkwood, N.Y. 13795

Please send me the titles checked above. I enclose $ _____
Include $1.00 per copy for postage and handling. Send check or
money order only. New York State residents please add sales tax.

NAME_____

ADDRESS_____

CITY_____ STATE_____ ZIP_____

A-04

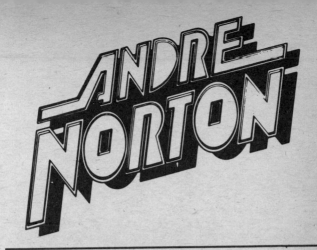

**ANDRE NORTON**

---

## WITCH WORLD SERIES

☐ 89705 **WITCH WORLD** $1.95

☐ 87875 **WEB OF THE WITCH WORLD** $1.95

☐ 80806 **THREE AGAINST THE WITCH WORLD** $1.95

☐ 87323 **WARLOCK OF THE WITCH WORLD** $2.25

☐ 77556 **SORCERESS OF THE WITCH WORLD** $2.50

☐ 94255 **YEAR OF THE UNICORN** $2.50

☐ 82349 **TREY OF SWORDS** $2.25

☐ 95491 **ZARSTHOR'S BANE** (Illustrated) $2.50

---

Available wherever paperbacks are sold or use this coupon.

---